ACCIDENTAL DEATH

Tybalt Kelly choked back a sob as Commander Veck strode toward him from the downed 'Mech. There was blood on his hands. More blood spattered his arms and legs and there was a big smear across his cooling vest. It wasn't his blood. It was Stübel's. Gunter Stübel's. It belonged to the man Kelly had just killed. Veck's voice was cold as ice.

"Did you, at any time, disable or tamper with the umpire in your 'Mech?"

Tybalt said, "I never touched the umpire, sir."

Veck's eyes narrowed. "There will be an inquiry."

Of course there would. "I understand, sir."

"Understand this, Kelly. The *incident* happened on my watch. I don't like it. I don't like it at all, and I *will* see justice done. The person responsible for the death of Subcommander Stübel will be found out and will be brought to justice. And if the Count's courts can't do it . . ."

Veck leaned forward, and whispered.

". . . *I* will."

MECH⚙WARRIOR

INITIATION
TO WAR

Robert N. Charrette

A ROC BOOK

ROC
Published by New American Library, a division of
Penguin Putnam Inc., 375 Hudson Street,
New York, New York 10014, U.S.A.
Penguin Books Ltd, 80 Strand,
London WC2R ORL, England
Penguin Books Australia Ltd, Ringwood,
Victoria, Australia
Penguin Books Canada Ltd, 10 Alcorn Avenue,
Toronto, Ontario, Canada M4V 3B2
Penguin Books (N.Z.) Ltd, 182–190 Wairau Road,
Auckland 10, New Zealand

Penguin Books Ltd, Registered Offices:
Harmondsworth, Middlesex, England

First published by Roc, an imprint of New American Library,
a division of Penguin Putnam Inc.

First Printing, December 2001
10 9 8 7 6 5 4 3 2 1

Series Editor: Donna Ippolito
Cover art: Doug Chaffee

 REGISTERED TRADEMARK—MARCA REGISTRADA

MECHWARRIOR, FASA, and the distinctive MECHWARRIOR and FASA
logos are trademarks of the FASA Corporation, 1100 W. Cermack, Suite
B305, Chicago, IL 60608.

Printed in the United States of America

For FB, in gratitude for
a push at the right time.

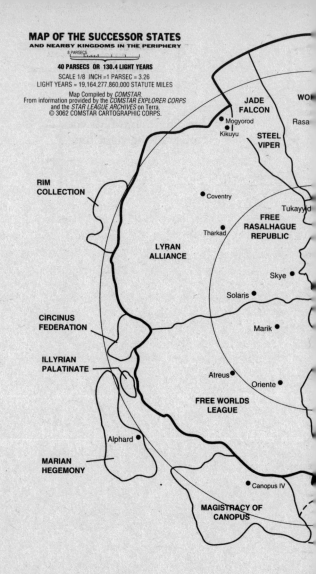

MAP OF THE SUCCESSOR STATES
AND NEARBY KINGDOMS IN THE PERIPHERY

8 PARSECS

40 PARSECS OR 130.4 LIGHT YEARS

SCALE 1/8 INCH =1 PARSEC = 3.26
LIGHT YEARS = 19,164,277,860,000 STATUTE MILES

Map Compiled by *COMSTAR*.
From information provided by the *COMSTAR EXPLORER CORPS*
and the *STAR LEAGUE ARCHIVES* on Terra.
© 3062 COMSTAR CARTOGRAPHIC CORPS.

JADE
FALCON

WO

Rasa

Mogyorod

Kikuyu

STEEL
VIPER

RIM
COLLECTION

Coventry

Tukayyid

FREE
RASALHAGUE
REPUBLIC

Tharkad

LYRAN
ALLIANCE

Skye

Solaris

CIRCINUS
FEDERATION

Marik

ILLYRIAN
PALATINATE

Atreus

Oriente

FREE WORLDS
LEAGUE

Alphard

MARIAN
HEGEMONY

Canopus IV

MAGISTRACY OF
CANOPUS

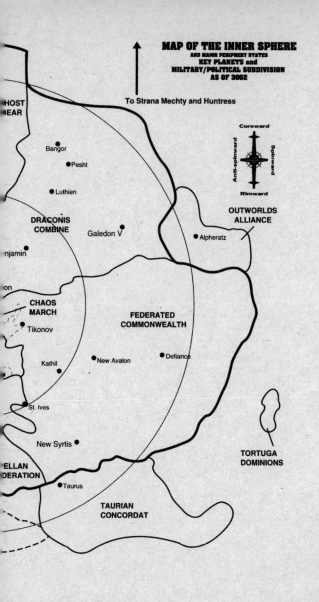

MAP OF THE INNER SPHERE
AND MAJOR PERIPHERY STATES
KEY PLANETS and
MILITARY/POLITICAL SUBDIVISION
AS OF 3062

To Strana Mechty and Huntress

Coreward

Anti-spinward — Spinward

Rimward

HOST
EAR

Bangor

● Pesht

● Luthien

**DRACONIS
COMBINE**

Galedon V ●

**OUTWORLDS
ALLIANCE**

● Alpheratz

njamin ●

on

**CHAOS
MARCH**

Tikonov

**FEDERATED
COMMONWEALTH**

Kathil

● New Avalon

● Defiance

● St. Ives

New Syrtis ●

**TORTUGA
DOMINIONS**

ELLAN
DERATION

● Taurus

**TAURIAN
CONCORDAT**

PART 1

New Dog,
Old Tricks

1

Redvers Badlands
County Shu, Epsilon Eridani
Chaos March
26 November 3061

The particle beam caught Tybalt Kelly as his *Lineholder* emerged from cover among a stand of wind-weathered sandstone columns. Crackling energy clawed at his armor. He fought to retain his balance as red blossomed on the status board. Alarms rang. Leg armor gone! Actuator damage! Structural damage to lower torso!

He snapped off a shot at his tormentor, more to distract the pilot than damage the 'Mech. Kelly didn't take the time to aim, being more concerned about getting his *Lineholder* turned to present his less savaged armor to the enemy as he ducked back into cover. The neurohelmet pressed down into his shoulders, heavier than ever. He wanted to toss it off, but he didn't dare, since its electronics were running a feedback loop, using Kelly's own sense of equilibrium to react to the data from the 'Mech's gyroscope. That feedback system was the necessary edge he needed to keep the machine upright. The helmet's scalp contacts seemed to drill into his skull as he fought to bring his 'Mech around.

Slow. Too slow!

Lasers flashed past him. A particle beam blasted chunks of hard sandstone from the canyon wall. Rocks spanged against the *Lineholder*, but that was all, nothing more lethal chewed into his ravaged armor. He'd gotten the *Lineholder* turned and managed to put some of the canyon's spires between him and the enemy. The tapering rock columns were the only things in the arid landscape big enough to hide a 'Mech. Kelly had taken no hits on that pass for which grace he whispered a prayer of thanks.

He'd done well against the first enemy, a *Vindicator*. No great achievement since his *Lineholder* outmassed the other 'Mech by a good ten tons. But then its two buddies had shown up and turned him from hunter to hunted. If he'd been part of a lance, even if he'd had a partner, things would have gone differently, but that wasn't the case. When he'd fought one-on-three battles in simulations, it hadn't seemed such a big deal, but here, now, it was different. He could smell his own stink in the close confines of the cockpit. Was that what fear smelled like?

Sweat runneled his side in defiance of his cooling vest. He had good reason for fear. According to the status board, there wasn't an area on the *Lineholder* that was intact. When the two *Commando*s had suddenly showed up, he had hesitated, unsure which to target. But they hadn't hesitated. They'd dumped everything they had on him. They weren't great shots, and that was all that had saved him. Even so, they had hurt him badly. His internals remained intact, but at this point his armor was wrecked. He was vulnerable to anything bigger than a medium class laser almost everywhere.

And it was three to one. He squinted through the forest of variegated stone spires that filled the broad canyon. They were out there. His two *Commando* opponents were yet undamaged. The third, his original antagonist, had to be in nearly as bad shape as he was. If only he could be sure. He was sure that the battered *Vindicator* still had an operational particle projector cannon because the *Commando*s didn't carry heavy armament like that. At least he didn't think they did. They were too small. They were only twenty-five-tonners, weren't they?

Cha! He was losing it.

Missiles slammed into the *Lineholder*'s back. Multiple hits. Kelly throttled up, shifting away from what he guessed was his enemy's line of fire. He spared a glance at the scanner. Twin blips showed that the *Commandos* had circled around and gotten behind him.

He swung up the *Lineholder*'s right arm, intending to teach one of the *Commando* MechJocks a very large laser lesson. Only the thickest armor on a *Commando*'s torso could withstand such a shot. It wasn't until he pulled the trigger and nothing happened that he realized the last salvo had taken out the weapon.

What now?

The *Commando*s where dodging among the rock towers, fleeting targets as they moved in to better take advantage of their short-ranged missiles. He couldn't afford to let them.

He launched a spread of his own missiles. They went wide, but they sent one of the *Commando*s diving for cover behind the talus slope of a long-ago demolished spire. The other slowed, but kept coming. Maybe its pilot was surprised that Kelly was still fighting back. Whatever the reason, Kelly intended to capitalize on his opponent's sluggishness.

He spun the *Lineholder* hard, intending to catch the smaller 'Mech with a full bank of laser fire. The Intek lasers in the *Lineholder*'s torso weren't as powerful as the arm-mounted BlazeFire, but there were four of them. More than enough to ruin the *Commando*'s day.

Only three fired, the fourth had been knocked out unnoticed. But three on-target shots—and they were on-target—were enough to discommode the *Commando*. The light 'Mech rocked back. Its missile launch went awry and sent smoky contrails arcing over the *Lineholder*'s cockpit.

Gotcha!

Kelly sent another flight of missiles at the wounded *Commando*, intending to press his advantage. He didn't get to see if he scored because the *Lineholder* shuddered and spun under the impact of a PPC beam. The *Vindicator* was back and had caught him from behind. Alarms screamed as the *Lineholder* toppled, crashing into the sheer wall Kelly had been using to ward his left flank.

The shock jarred him to the core and slammed his teeth together so hard that he was certain he had chipped a tooth or three. He realized that he had bigger problems as the cockpit flooded with heat. The reactor shutdown warning was flashing. He tried punching the over-ride code. The angle was awkward and he struggled against his restraining harness, trying to reach the control boards in the canted cockpit. His fingers were slow, fumbling. Main power failed as the *Lineholder*'s engine went into shutdown.

Kelly lay there, straps cutting into his shoulders. He was hot, battered, and drenched in sweat. Defeated! His hands shook with anger at himself. He'd blown it. His eyes morbidly fixed on the status screen where a sullen red glow covered most of the *Lineholder*'s structure. There was no blue, nothing undamaged. The head alone showed in green; only the cockpit was still carrying any significant armor. He was safe, still alive, but his 'Mech was nearly dead.

"It's over."

The deep voice boomed in Kelly's headset, echoing his own thoughts and dragging him from the dark timeless pit in which he'd sunk. Hydraulics hissing, the cockpit's access hatch unsealed and yawned open. A dark shadow interposed itself between Kelly and the bright sunlight outside, like the dark shape of death's angel coming for him.

But it wasn't death's angel; it was Subcommander Veck.

Shadows masked the force leader's face as his blunt fingered hands started disconnecting Kelly's neurohelmet. Kelly wanted to see what expression that face wore. He imagined disapproval at the least, scorn at the worst.

He tried to help, but had his shaking fingers contemptuously brushed away. Embarrassed, Kelly let the force leader finish his task. With the helmet swung up into its cradle, Veck leaned over and cupped Kelly's chin, turning his head from side to side.

"You okay?"

He gave Veck a sheepish grin. No real damage. Just lost the fight.

The subcommander leaned back just enough that the sun caught his weather-lined face. He wore no expression at all. "I've seen worse."

A wild hope surged up. "Then I'm in?"

"I didn't say you were any good. I just said that I've seen worse."

Veck popped the panel on the umpire, the gray box that had been acting as an interface between Kelly's controls and the *Lineholder*'s systems, and he made some sort of adjustment. The boards came live again. Damage vanished as the computer system forgot all the hits the *Lineholder* had taken during the trial. Veck snapped down the jumpseat and crammed himself into it. "All right, get this hulk on its feet and take her back to the barn. And try not to walk into anything on the way."

2

**Redvers District
County Shu, Epsilon Eridani
Chaos March
26 November 3061**

Kelly re-rigged the neurohelmet, glad of the masking effect the enshrouding headgear offered. He was embarrassed by his performance. Maybe his father was right. Maybe he wasn't meant to be a MechWarrior. He had waited for this his whole life and now he had failed.

He had never done so badly in MechWarrior simulations! He should have been able to take the *Vindicator* out before the two *Commando*s showed up. He shouldn't have let the *Commando*s catch him from behind. He should have been able to take out at least one of the *Commando*s. He shouldn't have forgotten about the still-active *Vindicator*. He should—

Shouldn't—

What did it matter? It was over. Veck's silence told the tale. Kelly had made a mess of his test.

Determined not to make matters worse, he piloted the *Lineholder* with all the care he could muster. The machine's gait was smooth and steady as they left the badlands and moved into greener country around the river valley. Normally the sight of the towering pines and thick bushes with their bright flowers would have been a welcome sight after the sere browns and reds of the badlands. Just now all they meant were that he was on his way to the training center where County Shu's new BattleMech facilities were sited. On his way to judgment.

He strode the 'Mech into the hangar, more careful than ever to "not walk into anything," a task much harder in the confines of the hangar than it had been outside. He turned the *Lineholder* and eased it back into its maintenance cradle. The board confirmed docking, and he started the shut down routine.

Veck was up and unsealing the cockpit before Kelly finished stowing the neurohelmet. On his way out the hatch he said, "Commo. Showers. Barracks call at 1700."

Kelly understood the last two, but the reference to "commo" puzzled him, until he looked down and saw that he had left the communications system live. Stupid! *All* systems were supposed to be shut down when docking in the maintenance cradles. Veck probably thought that he'd wanted to listen in clandestinely on the evaluators' channel to find out how he'd done. Cursing himself, he fixed the omission, then hauled his very tired body out of the 'Mech.

The air in the hanger was a lot colder than that inside the *Lineholder*, and the scanty uniform that served well in the tight confines of the cockpit was inadequate. He shivered in the sudden chill. At least, he wanted to believe that was the reason for his shaking. It couldn't be that he had just blown his chance to become a real MechWarrior. Could it?

No, he tried to console himself as he descended the stairs of the gantry down into the maintenance bay. *You don't know that you screwed up beyond hope. Not for sure. The other candidates might screw up even worse.*

Yeah, right! None of the ones who'd come back before he'd gone out had returned shaking like some kid whose puppy dog had been run over by a groundcar.

You should be a tech, he heard his father's voice. *You*

have the aptitude. Don't waste yourself chasing a Mech-Warrior's dream.

I'm not, he replied, almost aloud. *I can be a MechWarrior!*

The habitual fury subsided as fast as it had blown up. A true MechWarrior would have done better in the test.

He was grateful that at least there weren't crowds to witness his far from triumphal return. From the base of the gantry all he saw was a tech rolling a cart toward the *Lineholder* and Veck striding along the catwalk above with deliberate speed. The subcommander was going to meet the *Vindicator* that was settling into its cradle. Kelly's first opponent and chief evaluator was piloting that machine. Veck's veiled accusation of eavesdropping wasn't far from wrong. Kelly *did* want to know what his evaluators thought, but there was no way to hear what was being said.

With a sigh, he headed out of the bay. He hated not knowing whether he'd passed or failed. He hated even more feeling that it was almost certainly the latter.

"Hey, 'Jock!"

He looked up to see the tech with the cart approaching. Kelly knew she couldn't be addressing him since he wasn't a MechJock. Might never be now. Still, those deep green eyes weren't aimed at anyone but him.

"I'm not a pilot, just testing."

"You look like you pass muster to me." She grinned as she surveyed his scantily clad body.

Kelly was in no mood for bantering. "I don't think I did very well."

"Yeah? Maybe you did better than you think."

Could he have? He wanted to believe so, but Veck had been cold. Surely if Kelly had made the grade, Veck would have been warmer to someone who was about to become a fellow MechWarrior.

"It was you bringing old number two home, wasn't it?"

"Yeah."

"Like I said, maybe you did better than you think." She gave him a wink as she rolled her cart past him and onto the gantry to the *Lineholder.* "Why don't you look me up if you make it? Name's Meryl LaJoy-Bua. I'm the one that keeps these tin men running."

She wore a lance sergeant's rank tabs, which marked her as a senior technician, important but hardly the one in charge. Still, she outranked him, although she wouldn't if he became a MechWarrior. The obvious invitation in her tone prompted him to give her a second look. Her hair, tucked up under her cap and away from her narrow-chinned face, was glossy black. Ah, her green eyes—startling and memorable, those. And she *did* have a figure under those coveralls. She might even be pretty if she was cleaned up. But while his brain was processing that data, his body had already gotten interested and his perking hormones were trying to stir him out of his dispirited funk.

He didn't let them have their way. What was the point? This Meryl was interested in a MechWarrior, something he was not. And now might never be.

With a glum nod, he turned away and started for the showers. Cold water would wash away his physical urges.

And maybe his dreams as well.

Between him and the showers lay the ready room where the other applicants waited their turns to test. There had been twenty of them this morning, including him, all testing for the last few MechWarrior slots available in the County Shu Volunteer Battalion. There'd still be at least five hopefuls waiting.

He squared his shoulders and prepared to face them. Facing them would be easier than facing his father and listening to the old man crow about how right he had been.

There were six wannabes still waiting. And five of them homed in on him like heat-seeking missiles after an overheated 'Mech. The barrage of questions was unintelligible in the aggregate, but the general topic was the test. They were the same questions they'd asked of the other returnees, but that didn't dampen their enthusiasm. They were testing soon, and they wanted to know what to expect. Did they think he'd come back with some secret knowledge to share with them and make their test go easier?

As if he would. A MechWarrior had to earn his slot. By himself. Bayard Sten, arrogant bastard though he was, seemed to understand that and held himself aloof from the mob.

"Hey, Mr. Chill." That was Jorge Jurewicz, or JJ as he insisted on being called by his friends, one of whom Kelly had become without noticing. JJ had dubbed Kelly "Mr. Chill" right after the written examination a few days ago. He'd been impressed by how cool Kelly had seemed at the time. But cool wasn't something that Kelly felt right now, and it certainly wasn't how JJ looked.

"How'd it go?" JJ asked, apparently channeling his own anxiety into concern. "You don't look so good. Did you do okay?"

"Not good."

"Sorry. It's—"

"Just too damned bad, isn't it," sneered Sten. The crowd parted before him as he approached. Sten was tall, well-built, and had the smooth Eurasian features that could have made him a fortune in holovids on Sarna or even Sian itself. They had certainly made him sure of himself. Kelly hadn't liked him from the moment they'd met at the test center, and what Sten said next only strengthened that first impression. "Real talent shows itself though, doesn't it? But don't worry too much, Kelly. You know your place now, and have no worries. No worries at all. Me and my 'Mech will protect you now that you've been born-again as a groundpounder. A gropo."

"Shut up." Kelly snapped angrily. He wanted to put his fist where it would rearrange some of those perfect features. But pointless brawling wasn't something a MechWarrior did.

But Sten wouldn't let it go. "Harmony is only achieved when all is as it should be. When everyone is in their place. Be grateful that you've learned your place."

Kelly would have been grateful if Sten just shut up, but he didn't.

"You'll be looked after, gropo. I've got to look after the little people, you know. It's a MechWarrior's obligation."

"Look after this—"

But somebody grabbed his cocked fist. And JJ was in front of him, pushing him back. "Stow it, stow it, stow it," JJ insisted. "Fighting could get us all marked down."

Sten didn't care. Why should Kelly care?

"Some House warrior you are."

JJ's remark caught Kelly between the eyes, deflating his anger. For years he had espoused the ideals of the Capellan Warrior Houses, tried to live according to those ideals. Even his new acquaintance JJ knew that. JJ knew as well as Kelly that displaying anger wasn't a part of those ideals. Kelly had tried to live up to those ideals before he'd joined the military, before he made his try at being a MechWarrior. Nothing had happened to change the worth of those ideals or the value of trying to live up to them. Years of disparagement by his father hadn't driven Kelly from doing his best to adhere to those ideals. Sten's arrogantly snotty remarks were a raindrop in the ocean compared to the studied, habitual contempt Kelly's father displayed. Sten wasn't the problem here, Kelly was. His anger and temper were what was wrong. Punching Sten, however appealing, wouldn't change Kelly's situation in any way except maybe for the worse.

Even a straight path offers choices, the Warrior House aphorism advised. Kelly made his choice.

Surrendering to the hands hauling on him, he let himself be dragged away from the smirking Sten.

The concerned trainees, having assured themselves that there wouldn't be a fight, drifted away, disassociating themselves from Kelly the Troublemaker. All except JJ. Kelly was pretty sure he didn't deserve such fidelity.

"Forget the ass. He's just blowing air to inflate himself," JJ told him. "He ain't got nothing worth listening to. Leastwise not till he's been out himself. Now you, my friend, have been out there. Tell me how it really went."

"I froze up," he admitted. "Forgot stuff. It's not like doing a sim."

"Shit, if Mr. Chill froze, I'm dead meat!"

Kelly didn't know what to say. He started to offer a rote encouragement, but he was cut off by Subcommander Veck's bellow.

"Jurewicz! Sten! Sung! Front and center!"

JJ started at his name, nostrils flaring.

"Looks like you find out now," Kelly said, slapping his shoulder. The touch rocked JJ out of his shock. He scrambled up, and headed for door.

"Wish me luck," he requested over his shoulder.

Kelly couldn't honestly wish him better than second place, but couldn't bring himself to say it aloud. A MechWarrior of the Capellan Warrior Houses wouldn't be so small minded. "Luck," he called to JJ's rapidly departing back.

3

The Hylant Hotel
Palatine of Duvic, Epsilon Eridani
Chaos March
26 November 3061

Cara Price, Presider of the Palatine of Duvic, hadn't gotten where she was by being stupid. She knew who Roman diMassi was. More importantly she knew *what* he was. Of course, many people thought that they could say that. They were the sort of people who would take one look at diMassi's Word of Blake robes and reach their conclusions. But Price looked beyond the robes. She looked at the man, listened to him. She also listened to what he didn't say. Price knew that diMassi's Word of Blake affiliation was only part of the story, and that knowledge gave authenticity to the smile she put on her face.

"So we are agreed then, Adept diMassi?" She leaned forward and poured herself a glass of water from the pitcher the hotel had set up on the table.

The adept's narrow face stretched slightly with a curling smile. "I believe we have reached agreement, Presider Price. Blessed Blake be praised."

"And you will personally act as go-between?"

A flicker of concern flitted across the man's normally serene face. "I had not thought to do so. These matters are better left in other hands."

"*You* are the one in whom I have placed my trust, Adept diMassi. No other. Can I place the safety of the Palatine of Duvic into the hands of strangers? I think not."

"There are others who—"

"There are no others for me, Adept diMassi. You do understand, don't you?"

DiMassi sat quietly for several moments, clearly considering the situation. Finally he stood and said, "Yes, I believe I do."

She doubted that he did. She knew that he was a servant of more than one master, and she had been very careful to make sure he believed that their interests were aligned. She stood and shook his hand. The deal was made, and he was at least as committed to it as she was.

They left the small conference room separately, as they did the Hylant Hotel. Security reported no untoward interest in the Blakist's departure, or in her return to her office.

The rest of the day was routine, leaving Price to believe that the meeting had been successfully concealed until Negotiator Aaron Waterhouse, puffing from unaccustomed effort, his round face drawn into a scowl of distaste, scurried toward her as she walked down the broad marble steps of Government Palace. He stopped her about halfway down and spoke softly in his best conspiratorial tones.

"I'm told you saw Roman diMassi today."

If Waterhouse's spies were good enough to alert him even to the possibility, she'd best not deny it. "Yes, we talked. He's making the rounds as a goodwill ambassador for Word of Blake."

"That diMassi is nothing but trouble looking for a place to happen. The Word of Blake is more reactionary than ComStar ever was. They are enemies of progress."

"And so they're our enemies."

"Precisely. If we are ever to see our planet's independence assured, it will not be through association with the Word of Blake. Epsilon Eridani does not need *friends* like those fanatics." About five years prior, the Capellans tried to wrest Epsilon Eridani from the Federated Commonwealth. When the invasion stalled, then Duke Benton led the planet to independence from both Successor States. The planet's tenuous hold on autonomy was one of Waterhouse's favorite annoying tirades.

"Aaron, it's been a long day. You didn't go through the trouble to waylay me just to give me a speech, now did you?" She sighed to emphasize her lack of interest in posturing. "What is it?"

He nestled his number one chin in among its fellows. "I wanted to discuss this new report we've gotten on what Shu is doing."

"The County Shu Volunteer Force?"

"Precisely. Our agents confirm that it is an all BattleMech force. Nine *Lineholder*s shipped this morning from the Kressly Warworks on the southern continent. All nine are going to Shu, bringing his total up to eleven."

"Nearly a full battalion. Very patriotic of him." *Lineholder*s were produced on Epsilon E, but the choice was an economic one as well since they were a relatively cheap design, if one could call any BattleMech cheap. And cheapness suited Count Gabriel Shu.

Price gazed at the people in the street, hurrying home from a long day's work. She was anxious to be headed that way herself. "Our reports say that the rest of his 'Mechs are old and tired. Some don't even have all of their parts."

"We should not underestimate this force. It is under the command of Major Essie Ling-Marabie, a veteran of the anti-Clan campaign," he said, stepping in closer for emphasis.

"Ling-Marabie's is a nepotistic appointment." Price waved her hand in dismissal. "The good major is the niece of Count Shu. I believe that if you look into her war record, you will find that it is far from stellar. Supply line defense in quiet sectors, mostly. She is more a Desk-Warrior than a MechWarrior."

"That may be so. But she has command of an entire battalion of BattleMechs! That is a force that even a DeskWarrior can wield with devastating effect. We must do something or Shu's regional power will eclipse our own. And then, with the current instability of the planet, who knows what might happen."

"We are doing something."

"What?" asked Waterhouse with narrowed, flinty eyes.

Price didn't like the stridency in that demand. It was a mode Waterhouse was taking all too often these days, as if he, and not she, was Presider. But the expression of anger had a time and place. Now was a time for concil-iation and coddling. "In due time, in due time," she smiled.

"Cara, I begin to think that you are losing your confi-dence in me."

He sounded hurt, but they'd been in politics together long enough for her to know that his "hurt" was a posi-tion, not an emotion. Still, it needed to be dealt with. "Not at all, old friend, not at all. It's just that negotia-tions are at a delicate stage right now and the fewer who know precisely what is going on, the better for security. I know you understand the necessity. But I can tell you," she leaned in, Waterhouse mirroring her, "that we have successfully negotiated a contract for some mercenaries of our own. Yes, that's what diMassi was doing here. The Blakists do so dream of the old times. They still think they have a central role in brokering contracts, and I see no reason to disabuse them when the situation is in our favor. Do you? Of course not. And what diMassi was hawking, I thought Duvic could use, so I have taken advantage of our robed friends. Now we won't need to rely on President Benton's leftovers any more."

"MechWarriors?"

"Yes, indeed. Elements of the Tooth of Ymir. Since the Sarna Supremacy, nominal employers of the Tooth, has fallen under Capellan sway, some of their most notable MechWarriors found such affiliation unpalatable."

"Warriors with principles, then."

"I don't know whether they really have principles, but they do have BattleMechs, and whatever their politics, we can use them. These are veteran troops, each one a match for two or more of Shu's Volunteers."

He raised a bushy eyebrow. "Then you are thinking of proceeding against Shu in some way?"

"Oh, I'm doing more than thinking, old friend. Much more than thinking." She laughed harshly as she quickly descended the rest of the steps, leaving him to make of it what he would.

The Precentor smoothed his robes under him and sat down in an armchair by the window in his office and read the report once again.

TO: Precentor Blane, Gibson, Free Worlds League
FROM: Adept Roman diMassi
DATE: 27 November 3061
RE: Epsilon Eridani—Status Report

Matters are progressing well here; I have made several useful contacts in the city of Dori, and most have expressed at least guarded interest in our proposals. A few walk away upon learning who we are—some because they prefer not to work with "a gang of fanatics," as one put it, others because they still remember Operation Scorpion and equate us with Primus Myndo Waterly's failed attempt to redeem civilization. Most, however, look first to their purses, where we measure up quite well. Our work here should be finished within two months, at the rate things are going. I have also learned the names of several dealers—some based on Epsilon E, others based elsewhere—whose merchandise makes them suitable for our purposes. Attached are the names and brief descriptions of the most likely candidates; hopefully, this information will be sufficient for

ROM to come up with a fuller profile of each. Extra leverage can be very useful when dealing with these people.

I met President Benton briefly, though I have not yet spoken frankly with him. I thought it best to take the measure of the man before doing so, and ascertain just how deeply his commitment to Epsilon E's independence runs. He is an excellent leader of men, with immense personal integrity and charisma. He would make a persuasive advocate for our cause, provided we can convince him of its justness. Toward the Word of Blake in general, he appears wary, though not hostile. He is among those who distrust "fanatics," and he has little taste for politics outside of his own planet. If he sees our activities as political meddling, he is unlikely to want anything to do with them. At the same time, however, he will not hinder us unless he believes we pose a danger to his world.

Epsilon Eridani's HPG stations may offer us a way to get what we need here, with or without Benton's cooperation. As one of the few safe havens in the Chaos March, Epsilon E is a thriving center of commerce, which depends upon swift and easy communication. The sheer amount of business that takes place on this planet entails heavy HPG use, which is currently enriching the coffers of the ComStar heretics. If we can offer a better deal—to President Benton or to a sufficient number of prominent local businessmen—we can likely engineer ComStar's departure.

I will continue my inquiries and report back in two weeks.

The Precentor set the noteputer on his lap and looked out the window for a long moment. "All is proceeding," he whispered softly, smiling. Then he stood, smoothed his robes again and crossed to his desk to send another message.

4

Redvers District
County Shu, Epsilon Eridani
Chaos March
27 November 3061

The meeting called for the morning after the testing wasn't for an announcement of who had won the coveted slots as everyone expected. Instead Subcommander Veck announced a leave for everyone. No one seemed happy to be left hanging—Kelly certainly wasn't—but almost everyone seemed pleased at the idea of free time. Except Kelly. He didn't have anywhere he wanted to go, and with the military quarters closed to him, he had to go somewhere.

Service with the County Shu Militia might be honorable as all get-out, but it didn't pay. Living on base and eating in mess hall, Kelly had never found that to be much of a problem, but a quick check of rates for local rooms showed him that he couldn't afford to stay anywhere on his own with what little he had saved. Prices in the nearby town of Mirandagol were a lot higher than he remembered, and Mirandagol was a backwater. A lot of people said that prices had risen since President Benton had kicked the butts of the Capellan Reunionists off of the planet. Some blamed rumors of the Steiner-Davion civil war that was brewing or a possible local system grab by House Marik or a threatened offensive by the Capellan Confederation. Whatever the reason, prices had risen and he'd been insulated from it. It was a sudden education in just how high costs could go. Independence, it appeared, had a steep toll.

He had to sleep somewhere, and he didn't intend to make his bed in one of the local parks or alleys. His effective poverty left him nowhere to go but home. Reluctantly he made the transportation arrangements. While he was at it, he dumped half of his credit chips into the family account, just in case his regular deposits weren't generating enough good will. He intended to avoid a scene with his father about any burden to the family's finances. To forestall another set of histrionics, he spent some of the rest on some civilian clothes to wear for his homecoming instead of his paternally unwelcome uniform.

Barrhead
County Shu, Epsilon Eridani
Chaos March
28 November 3061

The homecoming the next day went well enough, especially since his father was still at the Trade Union building when Kelly arrived. His mother was glad to see him, gladder still when he told her about the deposit he'd made. To his surprise, his little sister Cordelia was there, living in his old room. She was home on familial sufferance while she recovered from a messy divorce. The news made it easy for him to accept that he would be berthing on the couch in the basement of the family's bungalow.

At least his grandfather was glad to see him and he started in immediately asking about Kelly's service experiences. His grandfather was the biggest influence on Kelly's military career. From the time he'd been a young boy, the old man had filled his head with stories about the glory days of Capellan rule and tales of the great and honorable Warrior Houses.

But before Kelly could get a word out, his mother cut her father off, citing his promises. Grandfather grumped about the impropriety of the younger generation, meaning Kelly's father, dictating to their elders, but acquiesced. "If he has any honor, a man must acknowledge the ruler of a house," he harrumphed and said no more about anything military.

Things didn't get truly uncomfortable until his father limped through the door at the end of the day.

"What are you doing here?" Augustus Kelly barked.

"I'm on leave, Dad."

"You don't take leaves, Mr. My-Life-Is-The-Military."

"They didn't give me a choice this time."

"Cashiered then," he concluded, sounding somewhat pleased as he slung his coat onto the coat rack behind the door.

"I haven't been cashiered!"

"No? Too bad. Then you might have *no choice* but to get a *real* life."

"Augustus!" his mother warned.

"The boy's better off as a tech."

"I'm not a boy any more," Kelly protested. "I'm a man. And I'm going to be a MechWarrior." The old familiar argument began again.

"You're telling me you want to get yourself dead."

"Grandfather was a MechWarrior. He didn't die."

His father's expression hardened, eyes focused far away. "It was different then."

"What was different?" Kelly asked, not for the first time. He watched as his father limped into the living room and fell gracelessly into an armchair.

For some reason today, instead of walking away when he got the usual stony silence in reply, Kelly persisted and said something that had been in his mind for years. "It's your leg, isn't it? You never talk about how you lost it, but I bet a MechWarrior was involved and now you can't stand them. That's it, isn't it?"

His father continued to stare off into the distance.

Something snapped in Kelly and he hissed, "I bet you lost your leg crouching in the dark while *soldiers* fought to defend you."

The ice in his father's eyes and voice warred with the flush creeping up his thick neck. "You don't understand, *boy*."

"Make me understand. Tell me what was different," he demanded.

"Everything," his father said softly. "There's more to lose than just a leg. *You don't understand*."

That was no answer. "Do you think I'm too stupid to get it?"

His father started to reply, but his mother spoke first. "It's not you, Tybalt. It's never been you."

It seemed to Kelly that it really *was* about him, at least where his father was concerned. When he was a boy, his father had told him to be strong, to not let anyone get in the way of him being what he wanted to be. Yet his old man had stood square in his path since the day he was thirteen and he'd announced that he wanted to be a MechWarrior. At first it was a sort of a game, flaunting the idea and seeking the forbidden. As his suddenly estranged father had grown more abusive about Kelly's dreams, it had become open rebellion fueled by a stubborn determination to prove the old man wrong, specifically about who and what MechWarriors were. And, more importantly, about whether Kelly had what it took to become one.

Before Kelly joined the military he'd looked for, and occasionally found, opportunities to prove his father wrong and had taken joy in it. Once he'd signed up, things had gotten even more distant and he'd pretty much given up on trying to break through the wall, accepting his father's hostility as the way it was going to be. He still nursed a hope that one day his father would see the light. Until then, Kelly was unwilling to give up on the rest of his family. He kept in contact, though not often nor for long.

Coming home had opened the old wounds. Still, after all these years, he thought his father might have learned something about his character.

"I'm not stupid," Kelly insisted.

His father snorted. "Wanting to be a MechWarrior says otherwise."

"Augustus—"

His mother's protest was stifled by a single glare from his father, but he made a concession and changed the subject. "What's for dinner?"

That shut down the argument for the moment, but everyone knew nothing had been settled. Life would go on in the Kelly household as it had been going on for years, which is to say, badly.

The dinner was awkward, with no real conversation. The next one was less so, mostly due to his mother and Cordelia. Kelly women were always peacemakers, even if having peace meant hiding things in the closet. By the next dinner, Kelly and his father had established the latest in their series of cease-fires.

As the week wore on, Kelly settled into a routine. He'd exercise in the morning and take a turn around the neighborhood. For some reason, 'Mech simulator games, once the mainstay of his idle hours, didn't call to him, so he spent most his day flopped in front of the vidscreen. When he couldn't find an entertainment of sufficient interest, he'd call up the Epsilon News Network.

On his eighth day home, Carolyn Genetian, ENN's top military affairs reporter, was commenting on the latest bandit raid.

"With one battalion of the elite Eridani Guard still committed off-planet, General Horatio Sung of the Planetary Defense Office says that forces just were not available to intervene. However, the general has assured this ENN reporter that pursuit of the raiders' DropShip is underway. Eridani spacecraft are on an intercept course and contact is expected within the next thirty hours. What the general did not say was whether the raiders will reach their JumpShip before the intercept and disappear—as have entirely too many other such pirates."

"Do you think they will?" Cordelia came into the room and handed him a bottle of beer: Kai Lung, a Capellan brand and his avowed favorite. He took it, slopping a little of the expensive brew as she slumped onto the couch at his side. "Well, will they?"

"Will they what?"

"Catch the raiders."

"Maybe," he said, though he really didn't think there was a chance. Any really successful seizure had to be made on the ground, or at worse, in orbit. Since only a madman would fire on a JumpShip—those fragile craft were mankind's only links across the depths of space— the raiders were safe once they reached theirs, something they were likely to do given their head start on the EE aerospace forces.

"I hope so."

"Report's not done," he said, hoping to distract her so he wouldn't have to burst her bubble.

Genetian's report went on to explain that the government's position was that the Eridani Guards were required to remain in the central and southern regions. One battalion guarded the heavily populated areas around the capital, while the other defended the strategically and economically vital Kressily Warworks from threat, especially from raids by the increasingly aggressive bandits.

It was those more numerous raids and lack of success in the government's defense policy that had changed the nature of the Epsilon Eridani military. The raiders were no longer confining their depredations to the hinterlands of the northern and southern continents. President Benton had hired mercenary forces to deal with the problem, but the recent raid was just the latest evidence of the failure of that program. In several regions, "Volunteer" units were being raised by certain counts and palatine authorities. Count Shu's BattleMech force was one such unit.

"These Volunteer units are effectively private armies," Genetian concluded. "And many outside the government see in them a sign that Epsilon Eridani stands poised on the brink of feudal anarchy."

"Better loyal household troops than mercenaries," Kelly growled back to the screen.

A rebuttal commentary from some government spokesperson emphasized the legitimate and legal nature of defense forces raised by legitimate and legal heads of political units, making a rational argument to support the position that Kelly knew was right. The commentary was followed by a recruitment commercial for the planetary militia. Not a coincidence, he was sure. There were lots of 'Mechs in the ad. Kelly knew it was hype, but the shots of the mighty battle machines in action revved his engines anyway.

It took him back to his adolescence, when all he could think about was being a MechWarrior. He'd scanned everything he could find on the great Warrior Houses, those bastions of honor. He'd tutored himself in the glory stories of MechWarriors, played all the game-sims, followed the exploits of notable MechWarriors (though not the faked triumphs of the Solaris arena-warriors) and decorated House units. He could cite unit histories and describe battles in minute detail the way most of his schoolmates could babble about professional teams and recount sporting events. He'd known then that he was set apart from his contemporaries.

When his father had objected and he'd made it his goal, he hadn't really had any idea how to make it happen. The only martial connection that offered itself was Honorable Duty Time. He'd taken it not just because it had gotten him out of his father's house, which it had, but because he'd believed it to be an open door for a kid without—Grandfather aside—a MechWarrior family tradition. Despite his objections to his father's characterization of him as stupid, he had to admit he'd been stupid at the time. His two years of HDT had been strictly infantry with no 'Mechs to be seen save in training videos, and when his hitch had come to an end, he had realized that the army of Epsilon Eridani was in sad shape. It was not the planetary force that public relations made it out to be. In fact, each region was almost autonomous, with their branches of the planetary militia under the local authorities' command, and the only true planetary force, and the only BattleMech force, was the elite Eridani Guards, and they never recruited except among veteran MechWarriors. Kelly's lofty dreams had looked like they were going to founder on the rocks of reality, as his father had so often said they would.

Kelly had feared that he was faced with mustering out and returning home with his tail between his legs—something he absolutely did not want to do—or staying on in the militia as a groundpounder, a hardly more appetizing prospect.

Then he had heard that Count Shu was inaugurating a 'Mech force. The timing seemed heaven sent. So when his HDT was over, he'd headed straight for the County Shu recruiting desk and announced his intentions.

He still remembered how the force commander at the desk had looked him up and down. "So you want to be a MechWarrior?" The expression on his weather-beaten face had been suitable for a high-stakes poker game. "It's tough. Not every wannabe makes it."

"I will!" Kelly had said confidently.

"There's tests."

"I'll take em!"

"They're tough."

"I'll pass 'em!"

"The Count can't afford to test any old body. There're only a few slots, and only the best in the army will make it."

"I'll make it!"

"Think so?"

"I do."

"Okay. Sign here."

Kelly had signed. "When do I take the tests?"

"When you're told you can. You're in the army now. The infinite wisdom of the brass now rules your destiny."

He had been so young and stupid to think it would be that easy! After a year of grueling work proving himself, he was finally allowed to test in a live trial for a 'Mech. And he had failed miserably.

"So when do you get your 'Mech?" Cordelia asked.

Apparently when the hells all freeze over. "I'm expecting orders any day now."

"I think you're gonna look great in a Guard uniform."

"Sis, I'm not going to be wearing a Guard uniform any time soon." *Or maybe any time at all.* "They only take veterans. And there aren't any slots anyway."

"What do you mean there are no slots?"

His father's voice shocked him into almost dropping his beer bottle. He should have heard the old man coming down the stairs, but the days of soft living at home had dulled him.

"Tyb says the Guards are full," Cordelia explained.

His father raised an eyebrow. "Really? It was a fool's hope anyway. Get smart, boy. Let it go the way of your pipe dreams about being part of a Capellan Warrior House. Not that those over-rated megalomaniacs saved the Capellan Confederation for all their supposed greatness."

"The Warrior Houses—"

"Are gone! And good riddance, I say. We'd all be better off if all MechWarriors were gone."

Cordelia fled the gathering storm; she knew this wasn't a time for peacemaking. Kelly tried his own avoidance technique. He just stared at the ceiling. He couldn't go down this path again. He knew it led nowhere. *A warrior doesn't fight a battle he cannot win.*

"Nobody told you to join the military," his father went on. "I made no complaint when you did your Honorable Duty Time.

Untrue.

"Then the militia. You had to join the militia. Well, I had to say something then, and I did, but did you listen? Of course not. You had to be a soldier. No, not just a soldier, but a MechWarrior!"

A warrior's warrior.

"Nothing to say, boy?" His father's glower grew stronger with Kelly's silence. "You like to say that you believe in the best that Capellan culture has to offer, that you cleave to their ideals."

I do. His focus on the ceiling was unwavering.

"What about the Capellan ideal of filial piety? What happened to honor thy father? You could have had a good career in something technical. God knows you're good enough at all those things. But no, you had to chase after being a no-damned-good MechWarrior! Why, I'll never understand."

Because you don't want to, Kelly wanted to say. *You don't even want to listen.*

"Give it up, boy. Get out while you can. Before it's too late. Find yourself a real life."

I have a life and sometimes, like today, it's all too real.

"Nothing to say?"

Kelly took a swig of his beer and said levelly, "I'm expecting orders any day now."

His father's nostrils flared, and he stalked from the room. Kelly sat and sipped his beer. The vidscreen droned on.

5

Barrhead
County Shu, Epsilon Eridani
Chaos March
6 December 3061

When Kelly's orders finally did come, all they said was: reassignment. That, and a time and pick-up point in Mirandagol. He got his tickets, packed his bag, and made his good-byes. His father's parting words were, "You've dug your grave, go lie in it."

Despite his secret misgivings, Kelly was determined to keep his mind set on the positive. He decided to take his father's words as a proverb, like the one about making a bed or the one about lemons and lemonade. Yes, he had chosen his path, and so, yes, he was going to take advantage of it, even if it didn't mean a BattleMech assignment. Whatever came his way would be a chance to prove his father wrong. He would make the best of it, no matter what.

The weather didn't cooperate in supporting Kelly's optimism. From his seat aboard the bus, he watched as rain showers swept across the roadway. The day was gray, the lowering clouds shifting between full weeping gloom

and hints of hidden warmth and light. The chancy
weather suited Kelly's shifting mood. Heading back to
duty was a relief, but the vague orders didn't offer a hint
at what his fate was to be. Was he heading back to an
ignominious life as a groundpounder? Or was there sunshine just around the corner?

The bus dumped him at the Mirandagol station. He
shouldered his duffel and hoofed it from there. The orders said he'd be picked up in the parking lot of the city
stadium. Early, he circled the locked and shuttered sports
palace twice before he spotted the hump-shouldered silhouette of another soldier toiling down the road.

Like Kelly, the guy was one of those who had tested
nearly two weeks ago, but beyond that, they didn't know
each other and had little to say. Another soldier showed
up. Kelly didn't recognize her at all, but she knew the
next guy to arrive and they drifted off for a private conversation. When the fifth guy showed, Kelly revisited his
fears that he was doomed to being a groundpounder. He
could see more hunched figures humping their way
toward the stadium. More soldiers on the same orders.
Hadn't he been told that there were only four MechWarrior slots? They couldn't all be going to MechWarrior
school.

The sixth guy to reach the stadium was JJ. His orders
were no clearer, but he had suspicions of the reason behind them. "You hear about the raid at Trophilly?"

How could Kelly not have? Yesterday, Trophilly became the first town in Count Shu's territory to be hit by
raiders since the count had announced his intention to
cease relying on President Benton's troops to defend the
county. A BattleMech had disabled an ore barge, then a
CargoMech had come in and looted the ore, the two
machines lighting out before any response could be organized against them. The count's troops hadn't been positioned to catch the bandits. Neither had Duvic troops
been able to cut off the raiders when they crossed into
Palatine territory, since the Duvic forces were busy reacting to a raid against one of their own mining facilities.
General wisdom held that these brigands had established

a base somewhere out in the hinterlands. The only problem with finding them was that there were a lot of hinterlands on the northern continent.

"I'm guessing that's why we're mobilizing. We're going to go on a hunt," said JJ, stretching his broad shoulders. "Suits me. Benton doesn't seem to know how to do anything, so Count Shu is going to show him."

It made sense, but if Kelly was going hunting BattleMechs, he wanted to do it from inside one. Watching the straggle of soldiers gathering made that seem more and more unlikely. The clouds did the crying for Kelly, opening up and driving the soldiers to huddle in alcoves along the stadium's outer wall. Two of the new arrivals picked the same haven Kelly and JJ had taken. Kelly recognized both: Bayard Sten, with a permanently applied sneer, who seemed to be becoming Kelly's personal affliction; and Harry Trahn, a rangy fellow with a unruly thatch of straw blond hair escaping from his cap, who Kelly recognized as an old schoolmate. He and Trahn had played together for a season on the Barrhead High School soccer team before Trahn had transferred out, but beyond that the quiet, well-off Trahn and the rowdy Trade Union desk jockey's son Kelly hadn't had much in common. Times seemed to have changed.

"Hello, Harry, what you doing in such trashy company?"

Sten didn't give Trahn a chance to respond. "Hello, JJ, have you found yourself a batman?"

"Call me Jorge," JJ replied, smiling coldly up at Sten. "And, no, I haven't got a servant. Could use one, though. You want the position? On second thought, forget it. I don't need the stiff neck. We're here on orders, just like everyone else."

Sten ignored JJ's jibe. He looked at Kelly and quirked up his mouth. "That true, Gropo? *You* have orders to be here?"

"Yeah. It's true," Kelly said flatly.

"I guess the count will have to review his selection process. It's obviously flawed."

Kelly found himself annoyed by Sten's smirking good humor. "What are you talking about?"

"Are you really that clueless? We brave few gathered here are the soon-to-be-fabled pilots of the County Shu BattleMech force."

"Volunteer Battalion," mumbled Trahn, offering the official name for the locally raised forces, whatever their size.

Kelly exchanged glances with JJ. Did that mean what he thought it did? Did he dare believe it? He had to consider the source.

"Yank the other one," Kelly told Sten.

Sten shrugged. "Tell him, Trahn. He is obviously incapable of accepting truth without it being spelled out for him. It's a common failing among gropos."

Trahn showed them his orders, which differed from theirs only in the address block. "The day I got my orders they came and got a family 'Mech. Told me not to worry. Said we were going to the same place."

Kelly didn't quite believe what he was hearing. "You're from a 'Mech family?"

There weren't many of them left. Kelly had heard that they were all but extinct in the major states, having been replaced by governmental near-monopolies on BattleMech ownership.

Trahn shrugged. "I know I never talked about it much, but yeah, my family are owners. Never figured I'd inherit the seat. Dan was the warrior, a real gung-ho guy, but Dan's gone now." Kelly and JJ made polite murmurs of sympathy, but Trahn shrugged them away. "Supposed to have been very honorable, the way Dan wanted it."

An owner family would know. "So it's true?"

"No truer than when a Blowhard says it," Sten said, revealing that he knew the nickname JJ had slapped on him.

"Yeah, it's true," Trahn confirmed.

Kelly's and JJ's cheers caught the attention of the other soldiers. Once they were in on the scoop, they were only a step behind Kelly in pumping Harry. With Trahn's family's connections, he'd picked up some rumors about their new unit.

Yeah, they were all assigned to one of the BattleMech

forces that was being called the County Shu Volunteer Battalion. No, he didn't know why there were more than twelve of them, but there was supposed to be something different about the unit structure. No, he didn't know who was going to be whose lancemates. Yeah, Essie Ling-Marabie was the commander. Whether she was a hard-assed and no-nonsense butt-kicker as was rumored, Harry didn't know. Yeah, he'd met her, but it was a social thing and that didn't tell you a lot about how a commander behaved in her own unit. No, they weren't getting their pick of 'Mechs, not most of them anyway. Harry, of course, would have a family machine, in his case a *Raven*. Yeah, he'd heard that the 'Mechs are mostly old and tired, and that some didn't even have all of their parts, but he'd also heard that there was a battalion's worth of new *Lineholder*s sitting on the docks at Port Tsing. The last started an argument about the relative merits of Epsilon Eridani's own home-grown Battle-Mech.

Kelly dropped out of that discussion. He didn't care about how good a *Lineholder* was right now. He didn't even care if there were any *Lineholder*s or if they were getting retread scrap. Against conventional forces 'Mechs ruled. And Kelly still wanted to be a MechWarrior. And he was going to be one!

The doubt that had gnawed at him since the testing was gone, replaced by pride. He'd done it! He'd made the cut! He was going to be a MechWarrior! The whole world seemed new, reborn to hope.

His gaze fell on the most vocal of the *Lineholder* detractors. She was slim and trim and her uniform fitted her in a way that could only be described as intriguing. Her close-cropped hair made a curly helmet above her eyes, which were of the sort of sea-blue that a man could drown in. Her nameflash read Liu.

"Now that would be all it would take to make life perfect."

JJ, who had also faded on the discussion, saw where Kelly was looking. "She is that."

They were saved the embarrassment of being caught

ogling by the bass growl of two drab-painted trucks rumbling into the parking lot. To all appearances the vehicles chased away the rain for the downpour sputtered out as they pulled up near the gathered troopers. Though the drivers stayed sheltered in the cabs, the passenger in the lead truck splashed down as the soldiers hustled into a ragged order alongside what was obviously their transport.

The figure rounding the fender moved with a slight limp. Seeing that he wore a MechWarrior's undress uniform was almost anticlimactic, but Kelly experienced a start when he recognized the buzz-cut salt-and-pepper hair, the square jaw with its white scar, and the flinty eyes that dominated the man's face. It was Subcommander Veck. No, Kelly saw by the gold tab that had replaced the voided green bar on the man's collar, it was Commander Veck.

"Keep your papers in your pockets," growled Veck as he approached the group. "I know you. To my sorrow, I know each and every one of you. And I sincerely hope that my knowledge of you will not be to my regret. I will do all in my power to see that it is not so. *You* all will likewise do all in your power to see that it is not so. Or you *will* regret it. Not a promise, just a simple statement of fact. I hope I am clear.

"Now before we leave for our new home, I have a few words for you gentlemen and ladies. Yes, I am talking to you! You are all gentlemen and ladies now. Officially anyway. Don't let it go to your head!"

Veck thrust his face down into JJ's. "You are a gentleman because nothing less noble is suitable to pilot a BattleMech in the County Shu Volunteer Battalion."

Another step took him to Liu, the *Lineholder* detractor. "You are a lady because you are a subcommander. Count Shu says so."

Veck's sharp gaze swept the line. "Your commissions say so. You all get shiny new subcommander tabs for your collars. It don't mean nothing!

"Don't believe me? Gentlemen, I am told, do not lie, and Count Shu says *I'm* a gentleman. My commission says so, too. And I've got the shiny rank tabs. A full *commander's* rank tabs. It don't mean nothing! I run a 'Mech for a living. I ain't nothing but a 'Mech monkey. But I outrank each and everyone of you apes. So what does that make you?"

No one answered Veck's question.

"I asked you a question, 'Mech monkeys. What are you?"

This time a ragged chorus answered him. " 'Mech monkeys, sir!"

"Neurohelmet feedback has been known to cause hearing loss. That ain't my problem, but I can *not* HEAR *YOU!* So, I say again, what are you?"

" 'MECH MONKEYS, SIR!"

Veck turned his back to them and marched toward the trucks. Kelly thought he heard the commander mumble something that sounded like "the raw beginnings of wisdom." Veck halted by the cab of the lead truck. Even with his back toward them, his voice was loud and clear.

"All right, you 'Mech monkeys! You've got your pilot's licenses. It don't mean nothing! You've done simulator time. It don't mean nothing! You think you know something about 'Mechs. You don't know nothing!"

Veck turned back to face them and his cold eyes swept across the young MechWarriors.

"But you're going to learn."

6

Port Tsing
County Shu, Epsilon Eridani
Chaos March
7 December 3061

Flashing her famed smile at the five people around the table, Romano Shu breezed into the conference room. Her long raven hair was swept up in a complicated arrangement of coils and glittering pearls more suitable to a gala ball than a business meeting. She wore a slinky dress overtopped with a gold fringed and frogged bolero jacket in the Marik style that would have been suitable only if that gala ball was a masquerade.

Gabriel, Count Shu, frowned, wishing Romano would treat state business with more gravity. What was his sister thinking? Her airy attitudes and flamboyant style often played well with the media, but they were out of place in a council meeting.

"You're late," he reproved.

"I am sorry, Gabriel, but there was an ENN ambush downstairs." She settled in to her place at the table. "You wouldn't have wanted me to snub them, would you?"

"What were the jackals after this time?" That came

from Justin Whitehorse, the head of Amalgamated Eridani Mining Corporation and a member of the count's council by virtue of his corporation's preeminent position in committal economic affairs. "Business, or is the Lady scandalizing society with another fling?"

"Isn't it all business of one sort or another?" Romano countered flippantly. "As it happens, it was the transit tolls again. Cara Price has made another speech. It seems we are being hypocrites, espousing President's Benton's Economic Outreach Initiative while doing our best to prevent any Eridani state other than our own from making that outreach. Our road, canal, and port tolls are strangling—" she dramatically put her hands to her throat and stuck out her tongue—"absolutely strangling poor dear Cara's free trade. The entire Duvic Palatine is withering away."

"The tolls are fair," protested Finance Minister Ismael Shu-Larabie.

"Of course they are, my dear. And don't you think I told the, ah, jackals—" she nodded to Whitehorse— "exactly that?"

"I don't understand what Price's problem is," admitted Gabriel. "She seemed all for the improvements we made to the port facilities. The money has to come from somewhere."

"Edie's probably egging her on," surmised Whitehorse. Edie Vauxhall was the head of Vauxhall Minerals, a rival to his AEM Corporation with significant interests in the Duvic Palatine. "She would rather see me pay than spend any credit on her own account."

"You *are* getting substantial benefit from the new facilities," Claudia Hall pointed out. She was the Governor of Port Tsing, the county's largest and most important city, and the port about which Price was complaining. If anyone knew who benefited from the improvements, she did.

"As is Vauxhall!" Whitehorse's ruddy faced deepened to scarlet as he stabbed a stubby finger at Hall. "And I *am* paying a fat share, too! Right, Ismael?"

"A share." Shu-Larabie's bland, straight-faced, and not exactly complete agreement drew a few snickers.

Major Essie Ling-Marabie cleared her throat, quelling

the good humor. "Did Price make any threats in her speech, Lady Shu?"

"Major, Cara Price and the Duvic Palatine are not the enemy," Gabriel asserted.

"Are you sure, Count Shu? The Palatine has brought in mercs 'for defense' and in the Duvic media certain sources close to the Presider have accused you of planning military aggression."

"We are political opponents certainly; she is an Expansionist after all. But your concerns about military aggression are unwarranted." County Shu and the Duvic Palatine were not sovereign states, to go to war as they would. Though they had great latitude and, indeed, almost independence under the planetwide federation. Such near autonomy had recently begun to show an unwanted downside as President Benton, disinterested in anything short of planetary concerns, started encouraging the provincial heads of state to look to their own local defense, at their own expense. "The media nonsense is just posturing, political wind. The need for defense, however, is very real as you well know, what with the increased bandit activity. Price is just looking to her responsibilities, same as I am."

"And we have the County Shu Volunteer Battalion do we not, Major?" asked Shu-Larabie. "Although I don't understand why you call this unit a battalion. According to the organization chart, it's got enough BattleMechs for a regiment. Surely that is sufficient force to chase bandits and deter phantom aggression."

"If the organization were complete, I might agree with you on the point of sufficiency, Minister. And your answer to the name and organization issues lies in my original proposal for the force structure, which you have obviously not read. However, I do thank you for bringing up the issue of completing the force structure." The major turned to Gabriel. "Count Shu, how long must my MechWarriors continue living on promises? Where are the new 'Mechs I was guaranteed? Where are the parts for the 'Mechs I have?"

Gabriel sat back, shocked by the major's rude temerity.

"If I may, Count," interposed Hall. "The shipment

from Kressily Warworks is scheduled to arrive in port tomorrow. Is that satisfactory?"

Ling-Marabie sniffed. "It will have to do."

Whitehorse leaned into the table. "Major, let us assume for a moment that there might be some need to be concerned here. I've heard that Price has been hiring mercenaries as well as increasing palatine forces. I wouldn't like to think that Price is contemplating a return to anarchy, but such a military build-up cannot be ignored. Just how dangerous to us are the Duvic forces?"

"That, I regret to say, is an open question, Mr. Whitehorse. Our intelligence reports are not as complete as I would like."

"But our own force increase will surely compensate, won't it?" Shu-Larabie wanted to know. "We have certainly spent enough on it."

"Compensate? In matériel, quite possibly. But there is more to a force than machines. 'Mechs without Mech-Warriors are just so much scrap, and we have far too few experienced pilots."

Whitehorse harrumphed. "I asked a question and haven't gotten a satisfactory answer. Major, I want to know about Price's army. A précis, please."

"Very well." The major was clearly eager to seize upon the chance to expound. "In conventional forces, there has been little change. It is in BattleMech forces that the balance of power is shifting. The two standard lances of BattleMechs Duvic recently added to the Palatine Protectors are both rated as medium. Even one would have held a substantial superiority in combat power over the count's old County Guard lance.

"In addition Duvic has been hiring mercenaries. The first force is two lances from the Tooth of Ymir, one heavy and one medium. Though both mercenary lances are under strength, their pilots are veterans with considerable combat experience. Their medium lance should be considered more dangerous than either of the Protector lances, even though handicapped by a 'Mech. The mercenary unit's commander is one Kingston Crawford, originally from the Magistracy of Canopus. He fought against the Clans before joining the Tooth. We have picked up some references that suggest that Crawford's people have separated from the main body of the Tooth of Ymir. If true, it is good news in that we need not fear that more of the Tooth will be joining them."

"But we don't know, do we?" asked Romano.

"No, my lady, we do not. It is knowledge that is our handicap here. For example, we know little about the second force the Duvics have hired: a mercenary unit that styles itself 'the 48th.' Sources on the Mercenary Review and Bonding Commission report that the 48th has brought a reinforced lance of five light 'Mechs to the Duvic Palatine."

"Five 'Mechs? Isn't that what the Clans would call a star? Are we dealing with Clan mercenaries?" Whitehorse sounded almost frightened.

"That is an alarmist assumption," Hall chided.

"And an ignorant one," the major added, her insulting tone adding fuel to her personal feud with the mining magnate. "The 48th's 'Mechs are all Inner Sphere designs. Most likely these mercenaries are simply following the superior Clan method of organization as we ourselves are. Or would be, if we had sufficient BattleMechs."

"I already told you your 'Mechs are coming," said an irritated Hall.

"The *Lineholder*s alone will not complete the force structure." Again the major turned to Gabriel. "Count, I need more 'Mechs."

Gabriel found the major's demands unseemly. The decisions about what and how many BattleMechs there would be had already be made. And the major knew it. Chastisement was in order.

"Major, you yourself said 'Mechs without MechWarriors are scrap, and that we do not have enough trained MechWarriors. What do you need with more 'Mechs, then? Hadn't you better see to making sure we have the MechWarriors we need to pilot the 'Mechs we already have?"

Gabriel's anger washed over the major with no visible effect. "That process is already under way."

7

Morning PT was usually Kelly's time to let his mind go wandering, drifting easily while his body was working through the exercises. This morning was different. This morning his mind was hard at work, as it had been all day yesterday, making counts and trying to figure out what it meant for him.

It didn't take calculus to do the math. There were twenty-six BattleMechs on the tarmac and thirty occupied bunks in the corrugated aluminum huts that were home to the County Shu Volunteer Battalion pilots. Somebody, several somebodies actually, were going to be without machines. It wouldn't be the four old men who had been Count Shu's Honor Guard. It wouldn't be Commander Veck, nor any of the six hard-bitten veterans who had sat around playing poker with the commander last night, and it certainly wouldn't be the three owner-operators. That left twelve 'Mechs for the seventeen newbies, or rather sixteen wannabes since Trahn, though a newbie was an owner-operator. Twelve 'Mechs and sixteen possible pilots meant four extra pilots.

Four.

Was it coincidence that he'd been told he was competing for one of four slots when he tested?

"I make it four of us getting stiffed," JJ panted as they finished their run.

"But which four?"

"If there's any justice, Blowhard will be one of them."

"From your mouth to the ears of the gods."

The gods may not have heard the plea, but Kelly and JJ heard Veck's bellowing voice calling them into formation. When they were lined up at attention, Commander Veck gave them a tight smile. It made his craggy features look grimmer than usual.

"All right, gentlemen and ladies. Today's business is familiarization. I am sure that there isn't a 'Mech on the field that you 'Mech monkeys haven't tried out in a simulator. And what you learned from that fooling around don't mean nothing. Your days of promiscuity are over! Today you get married. You will come to know your 'Mech better than a spouse. This is good. This is vital. If you do not know your 'Mech, if you do not know every little idiosyncrasy, every quirk, you will die. Not a promise, a prediction.

"Momentarily, you will draw your manuals from Force Leader LaJoy-Bua. You will go to your 'Mech. You may sit in the hotseat, but you should know that I will personally cut off any finger that presses a start button or activates any system. I am speaking to you owner-operators as well.

"All of you unfortunates will wait at your 'Mech until I personally tell you otherwise. Am I clear?"

"Sir! Yes, sir!"

"I am so very happy." He indicated the poker circle. "These most gracious people will visit you from time to time. You may ask them questions, but you will not waste their valuable time. I will visit you as well, and you most assuredly will not waste *my* time. Understood?"

"Sir! Yes, sir!"

"As I am sure you have figured out, four of you will

not be assigned 'Mechs. You four lucky souls will be drawing special manuals and will be accompanying the Old Guard to Hall A. Line up on Stübel here. And—" Veck glared at them—"try not to break your new toys."

The "Sir! Yes, sir!" was very enthusiastic.

As he waited in line, Kelly looked over the battalion's 'Mechs, wondering which, if any of them, he would get. The owner-operator machines were easy to spot. Crews were still painting them in CSVB colors. There was Trahn's *Raven*, a battered old *Vulcan* and an apparently new *Strider*. The front rank of four machines, two *Cataphract*s and two *Commando*s, were the 'Mechs that had made up the count's guard; the recognition shield welded to their left chests proclaimed that origin, but Kelly fancied he recognized them from the subtle individuality of their oft-repaired armor plating. Hard by the maintenance hangar, nine *Lineholder*s stood in three ranks of three, and another two were parked on the far side of the field. Further back he spotted the *Vindicator* and the two *Commando*s he'd fought in his test. Scattered around the field were the rest: a *Javelin*, a dilapidated *Blackjack*, a one-armed *Caesar*, a second *Strider,* and a second *Raven* completed the count.

The number of *Lineholder*s best fit the number of trainees, but it wasn't right on. And they were new, most of them. More than likely the newbies would get the older, less desirable machines. Gods, he hoped he wouldn't get the crippled *Caesar*, but better that than no 'Mech at all. On the other hand, most of the old stuff were light 'Mechs, and there was a school of thought that said you put your best pilots in the light machines. Did their commander subscribe to that belief? Of course all his speculation would be bootless if he was one of the four.

"Looks like you made it after all," said the force leader behind the table as he came to the head of the line. It took Kelly a moment but he recognized her as the tech he'd met after his test. She winked at him and held out a manual. "Offer still holds."

He barely heard her as he checked the manual's cover. *Commando-5S* it said. He'd made it! He hadn't gotten one of the "special manuals." Elated, he started across the warming tarmac without a backward glance. He was heading for *his* 'Mech.

JJ came running up behind him. Good. That meant he'd gotten an assignment, too. "What'd you get?" JJ whooped. "I got the *Javelin*. You?"

"*Commando*."

"You sure?"

Kelly didn't need to look at the manual to confirm. He'd been given a *Commando*. "Why do you ask?"

"Look."

JJ was pointing ahead to where two figures in crisp new CSVB uniforms were scrambling around on the *Commando*s Kelly had tested against. Kelly stared in shock. There had to be a mistake.

They had happened to come to a halt near Trahn's *Raven*, their shadows falling on the foot assembly where Trahn had his head stuck in a maintenance panel. He pulled his head out to see who was cutting off his light. "What's up, you guys?"

"Looks like Kelly's assignment is snafued," JJ told him. "He's got a *Commando* manual, but the two *Commando*s are occupied."

Trahn looked downrange at the two pairs of *Commando*s. "You don't have a problem, Kelly. You've got an honor."

Kelly looked at him, confused.

"Bua and Dok Li, the Old Guard *Commando* pilots have moved up to *Lineholder*s. They're probably just clearing out personal stuff."

Kelly looked again. The figures, now climbing down the access ladders, that he had taken for newbies weren't. They were, as Trahn said, the Old Guard pilots, and they were heading toward the paired *Lineholder*s. It was the new uniforms that had made them appear to be newbies.

"Good karma." Trahn went on. "To get one of those machines, you must have impressed someone."

The last vestiges of concern about how he'd been performing burned away in the fierce heat of joy over this proof that he'd done well. The day was getting better and better.

"Flush some coolant, Mr. Chill. You be too hot to pat on the back."

Kelly suppressed his grin. He gave JJ a punch in the shoulder, then was off like a homing missile, not skidding to a stop till he reached the broad, flat feet of the *Commando*. He stood and stared up at it for a few long moments, dumbfounded but happy. It wasn't big as 'Mech's went. In fact, it was quite small, just twenty-five tons. JJ's *Javelin* outmassed it, as did every other BattleMech model on the field. Slab-sided and blocky and lightly armed and armored though it was, this was *his* 'Mech.

He took hold of the dangling access ladder and climbed. The effort seemed negligible. He found the hatch was open, unsurprisingly. Halfway through the hatch, he *did* get a surprise. The cockpit was occupied. The auburn-tressed Liu was sitting in *his* seat. She looked at him, indignant. "What are you doing tracking mud on my 'Mech?"

"Huh. I think you're the one who's out of place."

"Really? You were assigned a *Commando COM-5S*?"

"Yes."

"Serial number 398-01487?"

"Ye—" He hadn't checked the serial number. He looked down at his manual and saw serial number 398-01486.

His face must have shown his embarrassment because she chuckled. "Thought so. You're next door."

"Guess I got a little eager."

"I understand. Could happen to anyone. Name's Samantha Liu. Buddies call me Sam. You'll probably qualify since I'm betting we're going to be lancemates."

"You got some info?"

"No, but I don't think the sentimental old farts in command are gonna break up this pair. Bad enough they're changing the lance's TO&E."

"I thought you didn't have a scoop. How do you know they're breaking up the Old Guard lance?"

"They're separating the 'Mechs, aren't they? Otherwise, we wouldn't have gotten assigned to them."

"How do you know we're not in with the Old Guard?"

"Two of us. Four of them. How many 'Mechs in a lance?"

"Got it. But maybe the Old Guard are splitting up. You know, each one to lead a lance. Harry Trahn says that Bua and Dok Li have gotten *Lineholder*s."

"You don't break up a team without good reason, and new 'Mechs ain't it."

It made sense to him. "I guess we'll find out for sure when they announce the lance assignments."

"I expect we will. Meantime Veck gave me an assignment, and I need to be about it. Nice meeting you, Nameless Kelly."

Her jibe made him realize that he'd never given her his name. "Tybalt Kelly. But my friends call me Kelly."

"Hey, Mr. Chill!" JJ called from his perch on the *Javelin*'s shoulder.

"Mr. Chill?" Liu echoed. "Not a friend, I take it."

"JJ gives everybody a nickname." More loudly he called back, "What do you want, JJ?"

"Brass on approach."

Veck was indeed headed toward their part of the field. Liu hummed a few bars of "Trouble A'coming," an old standard that had become the theme song for the classic holovid *'Mech Combat!* "Maybe you better move on over to your own 'Mech before old Veck decides you don't want it."

That was the last thing Kelly wanted. He backed from the cockpit, nearly slipping in his haste. Veck had dubbed the trainees 'Mech monkeys, but no monkey ever scrambled down a 'Mech faster than Kelly. Once he cleared the *Commando*'s chest, he slid down the ladder like a navy rating. The friction burned his hands, and he knew he'd pay later, but he made it down and over to his own 'Mech before Veck arrived.

"Problem, Mr. Kelly?"

"No, sir!"

"You will find that many 'Mechs look alike, Mr. Kelly. The enemy may be using the same model as we do, and you cannot rely on silhouette alone. How do you tell an enemy 'Mech from a friendly when they look alike, Mr. Kelly?"

That was an easy one. BattleMechs had an Identification: Friend or Foe system. "IFF, sir!"

"You wouldn't consider checking the serial number?"

Mouth dry, Kelly tried swallowing anyway. He made a strangled sort of sound.

"Carry on, Mr. Kelly. We will speak again before you leave the field."

Which they did, and Kelly was able to make a more creditable show of answering Veck's questions that time. Veck answered almost none of Kelly's questions and what responses he made were limited to technical issues. The laconic Veck and the equally uncommunicative veterans were a popular topic during the evening's brief hour of rec time in Hall A.

Kelly nabbed a bottle of brew and retired to where he could catch the evening news. JJ joined him and together they watched Lady Romano Shu defend the count against allegations of profiteering and improper trading actions.

"Lady Shu's making a hash of that ENN interviewer," observed JJ.

"She's got truth on her side. The count's no fool for letting her be his family's public face."

"And a fine face it is." JJ raised his bottle in salute. "Good-looking and rich. Some people are born lucky."

"The lucky one is the guy who lands her."

"Like you could?"

"Why not? I hear she likes MechWarriors."

"You are talking about the unattainable, Mr. Chill. Don't bother setting your sights on something that's out of range. Plenty enough targets nearby. Which, I might add, is where I'd thought you were aiming. And if I'm wrong, say so, 'cause I surely wouldn't mind that target hand-off."

Before Kelly could demand that JJ explain himself, the vid screen blanked and Romano Shu's delicate features were replaced by the concerned visage of the ENN weekend anchor person.

"We interrupt this report to bring you a news bulletin. Though reports are fragmentary and contradictory, ENN has learned that there is trouble in Severagol."

8

Severagol
County Shu, Epsilon Eridani
Chaos March
7 December 3061

"**W**elcome to Severagol," the sign at the outskirts had said. "Home of Superamalgamations, a division of Amalgamated Eridani Mining Company."

The broad flange at the rear of the *Axman*'s foot clipped the post, snapping it at its base. The 'Mech's pilot didn't notice, busy as he was surveying the town and watching for a reaction to his approach. Everything looked quiet. Bringing up his magnification, he spied on the garrison's motor pool tucked away on the west side. Pools of illumination revealed mechanics working on a stripped-down tank. Identifying the vehicle as a *Goblin* Infantry Support Vehicle, he grinned with satisfaction at the twinned good news. The *Goblin*'s scheduled maintenance was going on, which meant that the defenders didn't know he was coming. It also meant that when the alarm went up, he would not have to face their heaviest and best-armed vehicle.

It was good to know that the informers weren't

double-agents. He hated walking into traps, even more than he hated the soggy climate of this forsaken planet. The forecast was for heavy rain. The lowering clouds that hid the moons and the rising wind promised prompt fulfillment of that prediction. Not before he finished his business, he hoped. Afterwards, it could rain; he'd even welcome it since it would do a lot to wipe out his trail. But that was the future. Right now . . .

The *Axman* raised its right arm. The hatchet it had originally carried in its battle fist was long gone, left twisted and unreparable in the wreck of a *Black Knight* on a far away world. It had been replaced with something suitable, the large laser that had been the primary armament of that fallen *Knight*.

Ruby light speared through the night. The visual component of the beam was not necessary to the weapon's destructive or targeting capabilities, but it did give a MechWarrior a satisfactory feeling to see the shaft of carnage he was unleashing. The *Axman*'s pilot grinned in savage glee as the scarlet beam gashed open one of the mining company's fuel storage tanks.

Kilojoules of energy coursing through the contents were enough to ignite the fuel oil. It exploded spectacularly, sending plumes of flame skywards. Jagged shards of the tank walls whizzed away into the night. Some even found the *Axman*, only to ricochet away from the ferrofibrous armor. Some civilian vehicles near him were not as well protected. Small fireballs joined the first.

That ought to keep the local emergency services busy.

As he was considering igniting a second tank to add to the fun, his commo squawked to life with the voice of his nervous comrade in this little venture.

"Slash & Burn, this is Snatch & Grab. You are lit up like a New Year's Celebration. Suggest you move your butt before you get it shot off."

"Ain't nothing likely to do that in this burg."

"They're supposed to have tanks and APCs."

"The big turtle is taking its nap. The little ones ain't got no more than a sting." Even assuming the defenders could mobilize their vehicles before the raid was over, they didn't stand a chance against the sixty-five-ton *Axman*. "Ain't nothing to worry about but your bucket of bolts breaking down before you make the snatch."

"Which I can't do until the path is clear."

Wind-sucking coward.

The *Axman* stalked away from the conflagration it had started. Its pilot took it along a path that put it back on Snatch & Grab's route. There were people on the streets now, drawn out by the explosion. The smart ones disappeared as soon as they caught sight of the *Axman*. The stupid ones stood and gawked or ran about in panic. The stupidest ones were removed from the gene pool by the ponderous tramp of the BattleMech.

Their own fault.

The only opposition he faced was a cop who futilely discharged his weapon at the BattleMech. The pilot obliterated the fool with a single shot from one of the Intek 4 cm lasers on the *Axman*'s right wrist. He reached the railyard without further incident.

This was a place where the main line met with the narrow gauge tracks that ran to the mines in the mountains the way veins ran to a man's heart. Just before sunset a long-haul freight train had pulled in, too late to be unloaded, too late even to have its cars rerouted along the local sidings. Most of what it hauled was bulk goods to supply the town and empty hoppers for Severagol's mining output, but two of the tank cars hauled something special: the coolant that kept BattleMechs operating. The cars carrying that liquid treasure were easy to pick out by the vapor locks and warning signage.

Ripe for the plucking.

"All clear," he signaled, settling in to wait. His scanners picked up the approaching CargoMech well before he laid eyeballs on it. It was an ungainly looking four-legger, all struts and beams and myomer bundles. At speed, it wallowed like a drunken elephant. The control box and crew platform swayed back and forth as the machine paced forward. It was a wonder that none of the no doubt green-faced scavenger crew were tossed overboard, but those doughties were clinging to their positions tighter than they ever hugged their mommas' skirts. The machine slowed as it entered the railyard, the better to negotiate the cramped quarters.

The pilot took his *Axman* away from the prize, to give the CargoMech room to work and to look for a place that would give him the vantage he wanted. He found it next to a pair of grain silos where he could command the most likely approaches to the railyard.

Behind him, the CargoMech sidled up to one of the tank cars. Lifting its port legs in unison like some insectoid sumo wrestler, the CargoMech straddled the train. Snatch & Grab released the grapple clamps and they snaked down, each one ridden down by a pair of scavenger crewmen. They were brisk and efficient as they secured all the clamps then released the connectors on the tanker. The crew stood away as the tanker car was swayed up to nestle against the CargoMech's torso. The 'Mech took a side step then moved forward over the second tanker. Machinery whirred as the grapple clamps shifted into position to haul in the second tanker. The scavenger crew went to work securing the second tank car as the *Axman*'s external mikes picked up the racketing sound of internal combustion engines and clanking treads.

Someone had called out Severagol's meager defense force.

But did they know yet what they were defending?

Zeroing in on the disturbance, he cursed. Three *Vedette* medium tanks were hauling ass down the road from the militia armory. What happened to the old *Galleon*s that were supposed to be making up the rest of the *Goblin*'s lance? The militia's upgrade to the *Vedette*s wasn't supposed to occur until next week. While the pilot pondered whether he was looking at betrayal or mere misinformation, the militia tanks rumbled closer. He cursed again as the *Vedette*s took the turn that could take them to the railyard. There were plenty of other destinations they could be making for, but the pilot couldn't count on them heading elsewhere.

"Loot secured," Snatch & Grab reported. "Recovering my scavenger crew."

"Do it fast and clear your butt out of here."

"What's going on?"

Snatch & Grab sounded panicky. *No surprise there.* The CargoMech didn't have a BattleMech's sensor suite. He wouldn't know about the approaching enemy, but he'd already fretted about the possibility. The *Axman*'s pilot was in no mood to be soothing. "Lock it up and haul butt. I catch you looking back and I'll shoot your eyes out."

"I knew, I knew it! There's troub—"

"I said move! Ain't no trouble I can't handle." Nevertheless he was relieved to see the CargoMech stride away from the rails. He was even more relieved that he didn't get any more whining, which meant he could concentrate on the problem without distraction.

The pilot scoped the *Vedette*s coming in from their isolated vehicle park as making 70 kph, faster than his *Axman* could travel. They'd have to slow once they reached the more congested streets of the town, but they'd still be nimble. Hounds like these could harry him more easily than he cared.

He didn't intend to give them a chance. The approach they were taking would bring them down a narrow street well in his fire arc. He sighted in, waiting till the *Vedette*s were screened before sending a single short laser shot in to confirm the range. It was too far for his autocannon to hit accurately, but a piece of cake for his big lasers.

When the lead *Vedette* nosed down the street, he let the militia tank have it with both barrels. For good measure, he ripped off with his lighter lasers, too. His heat spiked, but it was worth it. Armor exploded from the side of the tank. There weren't any secondary explosions, but the *Vedette* slewed to the side, spewing track links from beneath its skirts. It might not be dead, but it was stopped. More importantly, its hulk blocked the road. Its companions would have to back off and move around if they wanted to close on the *Axman*.

Sweating, he watched as the two survivors reversed. But instead of heading down the crossroads, they used the intersection to turn around and head back the way they had come. Clearly they wanted nothing to do with the BattleMech that had taken down their lancemate.

The *Axman*'s pilot laughed his scorn at the craven militiamen.

And he'd been worried they might harry him back to base. With the defenders on the run, he was free to do what he wanted in Severagol, but what he wanted most was to get this raid over with.

As he moved back through the rail yard, he noted a loaded cargo net suspended from a crane. Whatever was in that net was valuable enough to string it up away from ordinary hijackers. He got a grip on the net with the *Axman*'s left battlefist and used the right to snap the cable. Satisfied that he had the net securely snagged, he locked the fist down and started after his companion. The *Axman* sagged a little to the left, but that was easy enough to compensate for. That extra mass meant he'd gotten himself a little bonus.

Another fine night's work on Epsilon Neversunny.

9

Mirandagol District
County Shu, Epsilon Eridani
Chaos March
8 December 3061

The next day, Veck began their first official day of 'Mech training with his usual abrupt manner. "We have all heard about the raid on Severagol. That is not your concern," he barked.

Veck's stern glare quelled any objections from the trainees, keeping even Kelly's mouth shut, though it didn't prevent him from wondering about Veck's attitude. How could any patriotic soldier not be concerned? The bold raid against one of the count's cities was the very sort of thing that the County Shu Volunteer Battalion had been formed to combat.

"I will tell you what you may be concerned about," Veck continued. "You will be concerned about your training. You are here to become MechWarriors. Once you have achieved an adequate level of expertise, you may be allowed to chase those bandits, but not until then. These raiders have demonstrated a ruthless efficiency, and I will neither send nor lead you against such an enemy until you are something other than hapless.

"You may also have heard rumors about trouble with our neighbors. That is also not your concern.

"Now, I do not object to you keeping yourselves informed. An informed MechWarrior is a *live* MechWarrior. But news, rumors, even letters from home don't mean nothing. Until you 'Mech monkeys evolve, you exist outside of time. When you return to reality depends on *you*. Frankly, I'd rather see it sooner than later. That would make me happy. And you do want to make me happy, don't you?"

"Sir! Yes, sir!"

"That is good. Now, it will also be good if you 'Mech monkeys give your undivided attention to the following recorded message which our beloved commander has sent to us. It will answer many of your questions, not the least of which is what your lance assignments are."

Kelly wondered why Ling-Marabie didn't make the address in person. A Warrior House commander would have done so. But he didn't spend time pondering the issue because the screen lit up and a House MechWarrior would, as Veck had said, give his undivided attention to the message. And so he did.

It turned out the battalion was to be organized in a novel manner, according to the dictates of Major Essie Ling-Marabie. As the commander's recorded briefing explained, the Clan-originated star, a tactical unit of five BattleMechs, was the most efficient and flexible way to organize the smallest 'Mech unit. Also, according to her, Clan organization fell down in units above the star, but no more so than standard Inner Sphere structures. She had a superior model in mind, and fortuitous political accommodations, combined with Count Shu's commendable will, had played into her hand. The County Shu Volunteer Battalion was to consist of five companies, each of two lances, conventional naming for an unconventional structure of five 'Mechs. Thus the CSVB, once complete at fifty 'Mechs, would be nearly half again larger than the standard Inner Sphere battalion and nearly as large as one of the Clans' mid-range clusters, while being more tactically flexible than either and eminently suited to the needs of County Shu and the demands of Epsilon Eridani. Unfortunately, the CSVB was far from complete. The Major assured her troopers that she was fighting to gather more 'Mechs and matériel, but that some obstacles were proving difficult. Nevertheless, she had done all that was humanly possible to balance her force, juggling both machines and pilots into what she expected to be a potent unit, one of which she would be proud.

Kelly hoped she was right. Only First and Second companies had their full complement of BattleMechs. Third Company was understrength. The short-handed Fourth Company was made up of trainee/replacements without 'Mechs—they of the "special manuals." Fifth Company was purely notional. The CSVB was a far cry from the major's dream unit.

Each company was to consist of a Strike Lance of relatively heavy 'Mechs and a Vanguard Lance of relatively lighter 'Mechs. And it was no small source of pride to Kelly that he was assigned to the Franny Lazlo's First Company, already being called the "Old Guard." Liu had been right; the original Old Guard pilots were staying together. Yi Cha-song and "Black Sartaq" O'Reilly in their *Cataphract*s and Bua and Dok Li in their new *Lineholder*s were serving with Lazlo in the company's Strike Lance.

But the pride of belonging to the Old Guard's Vanguard Lance was tempered by the fact that the Vanguard Lance was to be commanded by Jeremy Veck. Kelly foresaw that Veck's School of the MechWarrior was one from which he wouldn't be graduating; he would be stuck with the hard-bitten veteran even after training was finished. At least he expected to be suffering in good company since JJ and Harry Trahn were in his lance. And so was the intriguing Samantha Liu; the Powers That Be had not, as she had predicted, split up the count's *Commando*s.

Kelly was pleased to hear Sten and his one-armed *Caesar* assigned to Third Company, the smallest of the formations. They had ribbed the Blowhard about getting the mutilated 'Mech, but to little effect. The sneering Sten asserted, "Of course, I got the *Caesar*. I asked for it." But Kelly didn't believe the Blowhard's protests about needing to be handicapped to prevent him from showing up the other recruits. Still, he let it drop and urged JJ to do the same; goading Sten wouldn't help intra-unit relations. The sooner, and smoother, they got though Veck's syllabus, the sooner they'd see action.

Kelly made that point again with his lancemates as soon as Ling-Marabie's message was complete and they broke formation. They groused, but agreed to a temporary moratorium on ragging the Blowhard. Liu demanded a caveat before she agreed: "Unless he asks for it."

Sten soon lost his position as the most bothersome person in their universe. Commander Veck usurped that place. Before their first day of training was out, JJ had dubbed him "the Whipmaster."

Training wasn't exactly by the book, or the simulator. Veck disparaged the simple simulators, which were all that were available, as being no more sophisticated than commercial game simulations. Having sat in a real hotseat, Kelly understood. He still burned a little at the memory of his test, remembering how different it had been from simulated 'Mech combat. And *that* hadn't even been a real fight. He could only imagine how different that would be, believing when Veck assured them all that it was.

And he swore he'd be ready when the time came. Vowing that he would live up to Warrior House ideals, and that he would *not* be caught unnerved as he had been for his test, he accepted Veck's grueling regimen with resolute satisfaction.

Every day from dawn to dusk, and often longer, the County Shu Volunteer Battalion trained in their 'Mechs. They ran maneuvering trials and fired on the training ranges and conducted endurance exercises that took them across the badlands in the upper reaches of the Red Elk River region that surrounded the training facility. And when they needed a 'Mech-on-'Mech exercise, they used the same umpires as had been used in the testing. A M-v-M wasn't quite live fire, but it was a lot more intense than a simulation. Unfortunately, it wasn't always real enough, since the computer interfaces were sometimes faulty, failing to register hits properly and even occasionally forgetting that some weapon or system was available. And sometimes they just flat out quit, locking up a 'Mech until the techs could get out to it and reboot the machine's systems from a portable diagnostic console.

Every day, the pilots of the County Shu Volunteer Battalion got better.

And every night, when they weren't on a march or night operations exercise, the pilots of the County Shu Volunteer Battalion retired to Hall A for their mess and their precious free hours. They mostly spent their time slumped in exhaustion, but a few, like Samantha Liu, seemed to be filled with nervous energy that needed to be burned. The lances tended to hang together, save for the officers who had their own circle, and Veck's pet monkeys were no exception. Since "Slug" Trahn, having proclaimed himself "King of the Couch," usually stuck his nose in a tech manual and JJ developed a strained knee ligament that only seemed to act up when he was off-duty, Kelly was Sam's usual playmate and victim. Pushing him past exhaustion though it did, it had an upside: they spent time together.

And *that*, Kelly had come to believe, was a good thing.

Besides being easy on the eyes, Sam was a good pilot. Of course, she had to be good material or she wouldn't have made the cut, and she wasn't just a one trick pony either, like a lot of the trainees who excelled in only one area. Some like JJ were good shots with one or another weapon system, and some were good at certain aspects of 'Mech operation, like the way Slug excelled at moving his machine through terrain. Sam was good at just about every aspect of BattleMech operations. Sort of like Kelly himself. In fact, the two of them tended to trade off top ratings on the lance's scorecard.

It was developing into a rivalry that worried Kelly because he couldn't remember a rivalry that hadn't ended in animosity. That wasn't the road he wanted to take. But there was no doubt about it, Sam liked to win. When she did, she put on a smile that lit up the planet. When she didn't—well, a hike in one of the northern continent's infrequent but spectacular thunder tempests was more inviting.

With each passing day, he found the sunshine of her smile more indispensable. But he wasn't ready to do anything other than his best. If it meant he edged her out on a gunnery or maneuver test, all the better. He liked to win too.

His dilemma didn't keep him from playing hard at the night's exercise, a fast-paced round of ping-pong. It'd been several weeks since they'd begun their official training and he'd sweated less on the firing range that afternoon than he was now. Sam was glistening too, as she slammed a hard cross-table shot. Though he shifted fast, his paddle didn't quite make the intercept. He retrieved the ball and came back to the table to find her smiling.

"That's 20-18," she reminded him, catching the ball. "Good shooting today, Mr. Chill."

Sam's use of JJ's tag for him rankled. He didn't want her thinking him chilly toward her. "Thanks. I didn't think the scores had been posted."

"Haven't. Want to bet you come in second?"

He learned better than to bet against her when she sounded that sure. She chuckled when he shook his head. "You nearly matched my score. Of course, I wasn't trying very hard."

That, he knew, was bluff. She never gave less than her all, which she proved in the next volley. He worked just as hard. He thought he had her when he got a blooper just over the net, but she dove around the table and caught it before it hit the floor. It should have been an easy return for him, a simple tap to the other side of the table which she couldn't possibly reach in time. But she had gotten a spin onto the ball and it bounced unexpectedly to the left of his paddle, giving her the winning point. Sam grinned, sending the wattage up in the room and burning away the sting of defeat. The beer she bought was additional balm. They racked the paddles and ball and headed for the holovid alcove where their lancemates were snugged. Instead of the usual ENN, some action flick was running.

"Hey, where's the news?" complained Kelly.

JJ didn't bother opening his eyes while informing him that, "The Whipmaster has declared a black-out."

"Why would Veck do that?" Sam wondered aloud.

"And how come you know and we haven't heard about it?" Kelly asked.

"As to number two," he said, raising his head off the couch, "it's because I listen at after-action briefings instead of spending my time going over the kill count and comparing myself to Sweet Sammy." JJ ducked away from Sam's swat with practiced ease and continued. "As to number one, I cannot read the Whipmaster's mind. But I'm guessing it's not his idea, after all 'an informed MechWarrior is a live MechWarrior.'" He settled back and closed his eyes again.

"The major?" Veck might have claimed that the raid on Severagol and the trouble brewing with the Duvic Palatine were not the business of MechWarrior trainees, but Kelly was pretty sure that someone—probably their politically focused, absentee major—was anxious to see that they were ready to make it their business. Somebody had to be holding Veck's feet to the fire. "Somebody higher up?"

"Who cares who? What I want to know is why?"

"Why what, Subcommander Jurewicz?"

JJ's eyes popped open at the sound of Veck's snarl. Despite the Hall A rules that suspended normal protocol, he jumped up and snapped to attention. "Why we're not getting the news, sir!"

"At ease, Jurewicz." Kelly almost thought he saw a smile try to crawl onto the Whipmaster's face as he strode into the room. "This is Hall A. Liberty Hall where the cat can be called a bastard."

"So why aren't we getting the news, sir?" Kelly asked.

"Because you don't need to know, Subcommander. The order came down. It's implemented. You got a problem with that? Any of you?"

Their raggedy "No, sir" would have brought down a tempest on the drill field, but here in Hall A, the Whipmaster let it pass unremarked.

"But you know, don't you sir?" Sam asked.

Something flickered behind Veck's eyes. "Apparently, I don't need to know either."

10

Port Tsing
County Shu, Epsilon Eridani
Chaos March
27 December 3061

The shouts and insults cut off as the door to the armored limousine closed. Gabriel Shu sank into the seat, grateful of the silence. The darkened windows, fragrant incense, and the soft strains of *zheng* strings made the compartment a velvety cocoon of serenity, an utter contrast to the turmoil without.

Romano handed him a crystal goblet tinted lavender by the rich plum wine within. He took it with murmured thanks. She waited until he'd had a sip before speaking.

"I'd say you were not successful."

"They do not want to listen."

Gabriel had hoped that his appearance at this rally would have a calming effect, that he could show the people that he was concerned that they understand his policies, that he cared. But the crowd seemed to be more inclined to chant their inflammatory catch phrases than to listen to his facts and explanations of the toll situation.

It saddened him to think about which would make it to the evening news.

Most of the crowd were from the Truckers' Union of the Duvic Palatine, but there were others as well, including a sympathy contingent from the County Shu Truckers' Union, who were far better mannered than the Duvic rowdies. And none of them carried any of those awful signs accusing Gabriel of stealing food from children, of turning out families homeless into the night, and even of complicity in the deaths of unfortunates who could not afford the cost of medical treatment.

It was nonsense, of course.

What hurt him most was that there were some of his own citizens in the crowd, jeering along with the Palatines. The loudest seemed to be all wearing the lapel badge of the Fairness League. It was a new organization, but fast-growing and very vocal. Their latest cause was the supposedly outrageous tolls and taxes that County Shu levied on goods moving through the state. Security was suspicious of them, though thus far Colonel Bua's ferrets had failed to find anything more incriminating than some tentative links to the noxious Word of Blake. Despite those ties, which could be nothing more than personal connections, the Fairness League seemed to be what it claimed to be: simple citizens expressing their opinions, however wrong-headed and ignorant those opinions might be.

"Our grandfather would never have put up with this sort of thing," he observed. "No Liao landholder would. The Davions changed our world."

"You used to speak of their liberating conquest with some pleasure." Romano's voice held mockery. "Are you wishing for the past?"

He sighed. "No. The last thing I want is to be back under the repressionist Liao regime. Life improved when the Davions took our world from Liao. We did even better under the benign neglect of the Steiner-Davion regime. I only wish we'd managed to maintain such prosperity since our true independence. But to be honest, I wouldn't even want the Steiner-Davions back. I just wish . . ."

"That Cara Price would dry up and blow away," she suggested.

It was a delightful thought, but not the one he'd been thinking. "I just wish it wasn't my problem."

"Don't even think of passing the succession on to me."

"If I were to die today, the county would be yours."

"My, we are morbid today."

"Fatalistic."

"Morbid."

"Driver," he said opening the link. "Can we go no faster?"

"I am sorry, my lord. The crowd presses closely."

He cut the link. "The crowd isn't the only thing hemming us in."

Settling back, he sipped his wine and wondered what karma he had earned in past lives to bring him this life's tribulations. It wasn't until Romano spoke that he realized he had made his last remark aloud.

"Well, are you going to enlighten me, Wise One?"

"About?"

"About what it is that you think is hemming us in."

"Ah, yes. I was just thinking that there is one thing that our old Liao family understood better than the Davions or the Steiners, better than anyone—except maybe the Kuritans—and that is duty. Duty is in the blood of the Liao aristocracy. We may not be Liao anymore, but that blood still runs in our veins. We no longer bow before the Chancellor, but we still have our duty."

Romano's response was preempted as something thunked against the car. Rivulets of light dripped down the window as if some bright liquid had splattered the vehicle. The area was warm to the touch.

An improvised incendiary.

He caught a faint whiff of smoke and combustion and something else. It was the something else that brought a tear to his eye. "I'm sorry, my lord. I did not get the car over to internal air in time," the driver said, stating the obvious.

Gabriel didn't reprove him. There were more important things to be concerned about. If the security people were using gas, the protest had become a riot.

11

Carefully placed foot by carefully placed foot, "Slug" Trahn strutted his *Raven* bird-like among the boulders. As he watched, Kelly mused that appearance-wise, it was the oddball in the lance. It wasn't a humanoid machine like the others. Instead it partook of another widespread 'Mech look, which consisted of avian style reverse-jointed legs, a carapace of a torso that was oriented more fore-and-aft than vertically, and a cockpit housed in the nose of the beast rather than in a head-like structure atop the torso. Some of its stylistic kin, like the *Cataphract*s of the Old Guard, had full arm assemblies with weapons in the lower arms rather than battlefists, but the *Raven* had turret-like weapon mounts attached directly to its shoulders. The lack of arms and the hook-fronted carapace enhanced the avian image, making Slug's *Raven* look like a sandpiper searching the waves for tidbits. This bird was searching for tidbits all right—MechWarrior's tidbits: fat, juicy targets.

Those targets were not hidden among the stony debris through which the *Raven* waded, but out among the Red Elk River badlands where MAD-disrupting metallic deposits and widespread radar-scattering mineral layers made the electronic search for the opposition difficult at the best of times. Of all the 'Mechs in Veck's Vigilantes, Slug's *Raven* was the unit's best bet for that job, having the most sophisticated electronic suite.

Of course, Prentis Moy and his *Raven* were out there, too, making things as hard as possible for Slug, but so far Slug seemed to be winning the electronic part of this match-up between their lance and Commander Chun's lance. Already Slug had helped them catch Reese Fu's *Vulcan* isolated from the rest of Chun's Champions. They'd put a lot of hurting on Fu before he rejoined his lancemates. That little encounter had tipped the odds in their favor and set Veck's Vigilantes on what Kelly was sure was the course to victory in the training skirmish.

"Chun's people won't be calling us Veck's Virgins after we hand them their butts, eh?" Kelly commented to the his umpire. The nickname stuck on the lance by Bayard Sten had galled Kelly from the moment he'd heard it, even more than JJ's privately applied Veck's Victims had. The intra-lance tag he could live with, but he wanted to see the other erased. He poked the umpire the way he might a living listener. "Well?"

The gray box ignored him.

Or did it?

Three missile strike registered on the *Commando*'s left leg. Sensors hadn't recorded any incoming and the phantom missiles of the exercise should have showed on sensors. Nevertheless, he was now listed as having damaged armor on his left leg. To add insult to illusory injury, the status monitor of his arm-mounted streak short-range missile launcher started blinking red.

"Streak-2 system off-line," the computer announced.

It might be a human umpire making the game a little harder—they could embed delayed glitches into the program to keep things interesting for the trainees—or it might just be yet another malfunction in the box. Annoyed, he slapped the umpire's casing. The Streak launcher came back on-line.

"You have an appointment with Force Leader Lajoy-Bua, my friend."

Meantime, however, they still had hostiles out there to deal with. Slug reported a new blip.

"Solid contact six hundred meters out, two o'clock my relative," the *Raven*'s pilot reported. "Mass makes it one of their big boys."

Chun's Champions, their opposition of the day, matched their own lance in three out of five 'Mechs, having a pair of *Commando*s as well as the *Raven*. Their remaining machines were the big boys, medium 'Mechs, two to Veck's Vigilantes' one. The Champions had owner-operator Reese Fu's much-patched, energy weapon and machine gun-armed *Vulcan*, which had a ten-ton mass advantage against JJ's missile-armed *Javelin*. The Vigilantes regained half of that tonnage disadvantage in the match-up between Veck's forty-five-ton *Vindicator* against Chun's forty-ton *Strider*. Five tons wasn't much of a disadvantage.

But the mass difference was somewhat misleading, because the *Strider* was an OmniMech. It was "only" an Inner Sphere Omni and far less fearsome than the Clan 'Mechs that had introduced the OmniMech concept to the Inner Sphere, but any Omni tended to have a battlefield advantage over an ordinary BattleMech of the same tonnage. That technological effect lay with the Vigilantes' opponents today.

In their favor was the fact that lance leader Chun's machine was a cast-off, once a near wreck not considered worth repairing by the House Kurita military. It was one of a pair offered on the gray market to buyers less fortunate and less picky than the mighty Draconis Combine. Aaliyah Shu-Bua, acting as Count Shu's buyer, had snapped up the bargain, and County Shu technicians had labored long and hard to get them up and running. They no longer boasted the latest tech and their armor was a patchwork job, but they were still formidable. Of the two *Strider*s that the CSVB boasted, in Kelly's humble opinion, Chun's was more practically armed. Chun's *Strider* had both large and medium class lasers as a complement to its LRM launchers, a better mix than Shu-Bua's purely missile-armed personal machine.

As if Kelly's pondering on the opposition lance leader's machine had been some sort of magical summoning, Slug announced that Chun's *Strider* was the 'Mech he had detected. What might have been bad news turned out to be good, because for some reason, Chun had separated from his lance. It wouldn't take much to get all of the Vigilantes in position to pile onto him.

"Looks like King Chun has goofed," JJ observed.

"Children, today's lesson is: take advantage of the enemy's mistakes," Veck said. "Trahn, keep updating vectors and watch for bogies. I will flank long on the left. Jurewicz, flank short on right. Liu, Kelly, advance down the middle. Double Weave."

Kelly heard Sam acknowledge the order and did the same. He grinned with anticipation. "Double Weave" was the code for a tactic that he had suggested, inspired by his own confusion on the day he'd taken possession of his 'Mech. It was intended to take advantage of the fact that the lance was equipped with two, nearly identical 'Mechs. The two *Commando*s were supposed to advance in alternate rushes, taking full advantage of cover, continually crossing paths, and never letting the enemy see both of them at the same time. In a sensor-spoofing environment like the Red Elk River badlands, an opponent could get confused, possibly terminally so, by a *Commando* appearing where it ought not be, faster than it could possibly move. At the very least it might get an opposition pilot to confuse which of the two 'Mechs he was dealing with at any given moment.

The trick wouldn't have its full effect on Chun's Champions since they all knew the Vigilantes had two *Commando*s. Still, Kelly was more than eager to give it a try.

Sam was the first to get Chun's attention, catching a laser shot and a pair of LRM hits. She snap-fired her Streak-2 in effective retaliation before hugging cover behind a jut of rock. As Kelly advanced out from cover on his turn, he sighted Chun near one of the many outcroppings of boulders directly ahead. Kelly drew fire like Sam, but the OpFor commander only scored with a glance from his big laser. The umpire rated the hit as striping half the armor from the *Commando*'s left torso.

Nothing but armor, Kelly told himself as he took an immediate turn on the rush. He hit his target with a laser shot, a clean strike on the *Strider*'s waist. His Streak-controlled missiles failed to lock on the dodging *Strider* and aborted their launch. His Artemis-guided six-pack wimped with a measily single hit. Chun's missiles didn't use the Streak system and launched whenever he punched the firing stud. Two of King Chun's spread caught Kelly before he was under cover again.

Both he and Sam were taking damage, but the plan appeared to be working. Chun seemed off stride, as it were. Forced to split his attention in unpredictable ways, the OpFor commander was shooting poorly. It got worse when JJ's *Javelin* rushed forward and dumped a full spread of SRMs on him. Chun had three targets to keep him busy now.

Still, a single hit from Chun's big laser was enough to scour armor from the most heavily protected areas of the Vigilantes' light 'Mechs. A hit on any other area, like the one JJ took on his second pass, started the umpires calculating serious damage.

By the time Veck completed his flanking maneuver, there wasn't a trainee 'Mech that Chun hadn't scored on, but the sacrifice proved worth it because the Whipmaster came up on Chun like the lightning that flared from the *Vindicator*'s PPC. The long-range missiles that the computers said Veck had fired scored well too. The *Strider* staggered. Kelly couldn't tell if Chun's umpire had somehow arranged that or if Chun was hamming it up. Either way, Chun didn't manage to get the *Strider* turned around before Veck blasted him with another salvo.

Limping, the *Strider* started to withdraw just as Slug yelped that he'd been jumped. What the Vigilantes had done to Chun was about to happen to Slug. It might even have been what Chun had planned. Kelly turned his *Commando* as Veck barked the order, "Rally on Trahn."

"The *Strider*?" Kelly didn't want even Chun's wounded OmniMech loose in his rear.

"I'll cover," Veck responded. "Go."

Kelly doubled back to help Slug. JJ's *Javelin* paced him, but Sam's *Commando* accelerated past. She was moving faster than him, not having taken leg actuator damage. Thus, she was the one Moy's *Raven* caught when it emerged from hiding.

What happened after that was a bit confused. With both lances' *Raven*s in close combat, neither team had a controller to vector them on the enemy. A hide-and-seek melee ensued.

Looking to sort real 'Mech contacts from among the confusing sensor ghosts, Kelly found himself shifting from hunter to hunted as Fu's *Vulcan* stalked him. He broke contact and then managed his own surprise, jumping one of the Champion *Commando*s—he thought it was Stübel's—and put some hurting on it.

From the sound of his lancemates' chatter it seemed the Vigilantes were getting the better of the encounter. Then Slug howled as he got caught in a cross fire by a *Commando* and the *Strider*. The umpires declared that Slug had safely ejected before his remaining ammo exploded and gutted his 'Mech. The Vigilantes fought back hard. In a series of slashing attacks, Kelly, Sam, and JJ served Moy as Slug had been served, cheering when the umpires noted the Champion *Raven*'s demise.

The Champions got more cautious after that, but it didn't help. Like three furies, Kelly, Sam, and JJ battered any Champion they caught alone in the continuing game of hide-and-seek among the rocks. Veck joined them to finish Stübel's *Commando*, having gotten Wong's *Commando* by himself. Stübel's loss was the end of it for the Champions. Chun's crippled *Strider* withdrew under the covering fire of Fu's *Vulcan*.

All of the Champion light 'Mechs had been declared dead while Slug's *Raven* was the sole total loss among the Vigilantes. Had the fight been real, they would have been limping home, but as all their damage was only in the umpires' electronic brains, they strode their 'Mechs in smartly. Kelly dismounted as fast as he could. A snapped salute was the only acknowledgment he made of turning the *Commando* over to the techs. The trainees had won their first lance-to-lance exercise. They congratulated each other with slapped backs, wide grins, and whoops of joy. Stony faced, Veck strode through their celebratory knot. "After action debrief. Hut 12. Now."

"Crack goes the whip," JJ whispered.

They encountered Commander Chun and his trainees, also on their way to a debrief. Veck paused to confer with Chun, and the Vigilantes took the opportunity to taunt the day's losers. Veck damped the chatter with a barked, "Who told you to stop marching?" Both lances double-timed to their respective debrief huts.

Kelly thought that the Champions took their ribbing well, and said so as soon as they were out of earshot.

"Only the beginning, Mr. Chill." Sam looked radiantly pleased. "Wait till tonight in Hall A."

It didn't take Veck long to join them in the hut. "Damage" reports from the umpires flashed onto the screen as he entered the room. Striding to center stage, he faced the screen, hands behind his back. His head moved back and forth as he scanned the images.

Kelly contemplated the results as well, grinning to see three of the hostiles showing solid black, indicating kills. The other two had lost limbs and were heavily marked with red for serious damage. The Vigilantes were heavily into the red, except for Veck's *Vindicator*, but that didn't keep the trainees from flashing each other the thumbs up.

"I see a lot of black on the OpFor 'Mechs. That is good. Hurting the enemy is good." Veck turned to face his pilots. His jaw was set, but a hint of a smile played on his lips. "And I can see by the grins on your faces that you're pleased with yourselves.

And why not? Kelly thought. *We won and won big.*

"You look like happy little children." Veck's manner

suddenly lost any hint of approval. "Perhaps you 'Mech monkeys would prefer to go back to playing games in cyberspace because that's how you won this engagement, like children playing in dreamland. Well, I have news for you, you aren't children anymore. The 'Mechs you are piloting are real. They are not some virtual shadow. They will not repair themselves after an action. Repairs cost money. Repairs cost time. During a campaign, the need for repairs can cost battles. They *will* cost lives. *Someone* will pay if you have not had the good and necessary sense to preserve your 'Mech from the enemy's fire. Maybe it'll be your best buddy. Maybe it'll be you.

"Think hard about that," Veck glared at them.

"Right now, I have an exercise for you. Each of you will calculate the cost in C bills of repairing the damage suffered by your 'Mech. You will divide that cost by one hundred thousand. The result is the number of 'volunteer' hours of general maintenance you will be performing on base this week. Stifle the groans! I am not an unreasonable man. Anyone who cannot complete the requisite hours and still log four hours of sleep per night may extend his volunteer hours into next week.

"And you *will* forward your calculations to my comp. And I *will* check them. I wouldn't want anyone accidentally overworking himself or herself. Are we clear, 'Mech monkeys?"

"Sir! Yes, sir!"

"Very good." Veck turned smartly and marched for the door. As he opened it, he looked back over his shoulder. "One more thing. We are replaying Commander Chun's lance again tomorrow at 0600. Same field. Same rules. Sleep well, 'Mech monkeys."

Veck shut the door on unstifled groans of pain.

12

Cara Price smiled politely as Major Kingston Crawford entered her office. He was a hulking brute of man, nicknamed "the Claw," a cognomen given because of the gleaming metal prosthetic he wore in place of his lost left hand. When at rest, his artificial hand tended to curl like the half-flexed talons of some monstrous bird of prey. Such a device was a deliberate choice in a day and age when almost unnoticeable replacements could be had on any civilized planet. Why such a choice? The naked metal talon, when set beside his shaven skull and bushy beard, did give him something of the aspect of a mythical pirate. Some might say there was nothing mythical about his piratical nature. Nothing at all. For was he not a mercenary MechWarrior, one of the real pirates of the thirty-first century?

Cara Price could not afford such melodramatic nonsense, at least not when she wasn't making a public speech. Crawford was a hireling, her hireling. He might be also working for others and he certainly had an agenda of his own, but who didn't? The trick in dealing with men like Crawford lay in staying one step ahead of them, and in being prepared for the moment when they tried to take advantage of that positioning by stabbing you in the back. Price always had, and always would, keep a close watch on her back.

Still smiling, she stood and waved her hand at the rynth-hide upholstered chair before her desk. "Good morning, Major. Please have a seat." She said not a word about his appearance. He wore nothing above his belt save an open cooling vest. It showed off his muscular arms, hairy chest, and the slablike muscles of his torso, but it also revealed the smooth expanse of a well-maintained beer gut. Like the oversized twin slug-throwers he habitually wore cross-holstered on his hips, it was all part of the image. Image projection being something Price understood very well, she was willing to allow him his show.

Crawford passed a gimlet eye over the offered seating and snatched a straight-backed antique Windsor chair from the corner. He plopped it near the corner of the desk, checking to make sure he would have a view of both her and the door through which he had entered, and sank onto it, his belly to its back. The over-stressed wood creaked in protest. Crawford folded his beefy arms on the back of the chair.

"Whazzit ya want ta see me about, Ms. Palatine? Returns ain't satisfactory enough?"

It was a challenge, since they both knew he and his were skimming. She ignored it. Such dishonesty she could afford. For the moment.

"To be honest, Major, the returns have not been as expected, but I will say that they have been satisfactory nonetheless."

"Glad ta hear you're satisfied. A nice lady like you oughta be satisfied." He leered. "Always leave 'em satisfied, I say. Ain't never had no complaints."

She gave him an unamused smile. "Officially this meeting is about the anti-raider campaign. I heard the interview you gave ENN. You sounded quite upset that your MechWarriors failed to bring the bandits to bay."

"I did, didn't I?" He gave her a self-satisfied smirk. "That Carol Genetian's a sweet thing. Got a soft spot for soldiers, ya know. Really, she does. I can always tell. It's in the eyes. The way they look at ya, ya know."

He stared straight into her eyes. She returned his gaze, level and steady and cold. "And what way would that be?"

"I don't have ta tell ya," he said, winking. "Now do I?"

Price frowned at him. Stereotypical pirates, save for a very few fictional semi-heroes, were not known for their good manners and polite behavior, and in that, Crawford fit the stereotype. But despite his barbaric look and presentation, Crawford was canny. Price recalled the tough bargaining that had gone into his recruitment and knew the MechWarrior's gruffness and crudity were acts, a façade calculated to gull the unwary. Price was not unwary, but she was uninterested in his boorish advances. "Major, I hired you and your MechWarriors expecting that you would apply your brains as well as your brawn to the problem at hand. We have a business arrangement. That is all. Do I make myself clear?"

Crawford shrugged. "Ya already said ya ain't got no problems with how I'm doing my job."

"Publicly I may have to be somewhat less contented. There will be factions of my government that will remain sympathetic, however. Did you hear Minister Waterhouse's remarks? He was quite explicit in not calling your operations a failure."

"Kind of him."

"As you know kindness had nothing to do with it, nothing at all. The public has heard that the Duvic Palatine has been subject to increasingly bold bandit activities, just like most of the jurisdictions on the Northern Continent. It is important that people hear that we, unlike certain of our neighbors, send our MechWarriors out to try and catch the raiders."

"Even if we don't manage to catch them slippery bandits." Crawford grinned.

"Especially if no bandits are caught. Some jurisdictions suffering from similar raids do not even send out the BattleMechs they supposedly acquired for that purpose. This is an important distinction that I wish brought to the attention of all Epsilon Eridani citizenry."

"That's not what I do."

"But you can make comments about how quickly a 'Mech force can be put into the field against raiders. Your forces can be seen to conduct such operations, however unfortunately lacking in results they will be."

"Ain't never been paid for chasing my own tail before, but I kinda like it. Beats getting your tail shot off."

"I want to see an end to the allegations that the Duvic Palatine is hiring mercenaries for other purposes."

"Stories coming a little close ta home?"

"Close or not, I want the public's attention elsewhere."

Entirely too many people, not the least that insufferable media darling Romano Shu, were harping on Price's public Expansionist position. It was a position that had its uses. It had gotten her into power, hadn't it?

But Expansionist programs were ultimately doomed, and Price had no intention of going down with them. It was all well and good to dream of expanding the Epsilon Eridani sphere of influence, to build the world into a power in the Inner Sphere. Desirable. Seductive. But practical? Hardly. Any efforts at founding a new Successor State with Epsilon Eridani at the heart were hopeless, a child's dream.

In the Chaos March, nothing could be built that would be free from the influence of the great houses. Any freedom planets like Epsilon Eridani experienced was temporary, born of neglect by the great powers who were too busy elsewhere. Such conditions could not be expected to last forever. She intended to be ready when the tide turned. The signs were already showing up. Expansionism swayed President Benton and had gotten Epsilon Eridani involved with the Duchy of Small and its ambitious duke. Nothing good was likely to come of that alliance.

But to survive, she needed a personal power-base before the day Epsilon Eridani's dream of independence and influence evaporated. She wanted to be well positioned to deal with House Liao, or whoever, when the time came. But she could not afford to be open about it. She remembered what happened to the Liao insurgents who had challenged Benton's independence movement, and she was well aware of the strength of belief in the planet's hard-won independence that was so prevalent among those who could not see as clearly as she did. She could not yet be open about her plans, not even to her co-conspirators.

"Looks like it's your attention that's elsewhere, Ms. Palatine."

Crawford's remark drew her back from her musing. She could not afford to let her attention wander if she was to succeed in her plans. Such a lapse in front of someone more significant than this hireling MechWarrior could have dire consequences, and she much preferred that dire consequences befall her opponents.

"A brief contemplation, Major. I was just considering how to put your participation in Palatine affairs into the best light and show those who listen to our detractors just how wrong they are to do so.

"Rumor can be a powerful tool, Major. People hear a rumor repeated and they lose track of the source. They hear more of it and they come to believe it as true."

"Everybody wouldn't be saying it if it weren't true."

"Exactly, Major. It is in this way that the public's conviction is growing regarding my dear neighbor Count Shu. Each day more and more people come to see him as a money-grubbing, exploitive capitalist who is using the turmoil engendered by the bandits to encroach on Duvic Palatinate resources. Rumors, quite true as it happens, are beginning to surface that he has nearly completed training his new BattleMech battalion. Some people are saying that this is a strike force, that soon he will toss away his mask and reveal his true, aggressive nature."

"Then we smash 'em."

"It would be a pleasant outcome, and I am confident

that you will have a notable part in that 'smash.' " Price made a show of glancing at the calendar on her wall screen. "But the game still has several turns to be played before that comes to pass."

Crawford looked even more eager. "More bandit raids?"

"If there are more of those unfortunate events, I will not be surprised. Perhaps they will even occur while you are visibly doing your duty."

"You're drifting on me, Ms. Palatine."

Price savored his confusion. "Let me ask you this. Have you had a chance to meet any of the 48th?"

The new mercenary unit had arrived two weeks previously, a full week ahead of their contracted time. It was a punctuality that their commander Major Namihito dismissed as simple courtesy.

"You mean the Kuritans?"

"The ex-Kuritans. They were most adamant in denying any connection with the Combine."

"Snakes lie," Crawford said, with feeling.

"In this case, the best information suggests that the only Kuritan connection lies in the ethnicity of many of their soldiers. In any case, I wish your opinion on the suitability of these mercenaries. Specifically, I wish to know if you believe that Namihito's people are the sort who can blend seamlessly with your operations."

Crawford leaned back and tucked his thumbs into his belt. "So, ya want my opinion, eh? I gotta tell ya I think they're a little skewed. They call themselves the 48th. I mean, what kind of a name is that, I ask ya, hunh? The 48th what?"

"Major."

"Ya got a number, you're supposed ta have something ta go with it. Like the 2nd Prosepina Hussars, or the 1st Khorsakov's Cossacks. Even using numbers is hokey if ya ain't house military. Mercs need a good name, ya know. Something ta sell ya and impress the marks. It's a—"

"Major." She let her exasperation slip out. "Have you done anything more than take umbrage at their name?"

"Yeah, I met some of 'em. I went round when their DropShip landed. Me and the guys brought 'em a keg, all friendly like. They sat and drank with us, but we might as well been at a wake. That Major Cold Fish Namihito-sama is such an old-fashioned Kurita samurai type that he might as well be fossilized. His guys are halfway to rock like their boss."

"Are you suggesting that I may have made a mistake in hiring them?"

"Depends what ya want 'em ta do. They'll fight sure enough. Probably regular hellions, or at least as much as anybody can be in those weenie tin men they ride. But as ta the more, er, delicate parts of this operation, I'd look ta yer own people first."

It wasn't the answer she wanted. "Very well then. I will proceed with alternatives. A wise player hedges her bets, Major Crawford."

"Ya don't trust me and my guys ta get the job done?"

"No, I am not saying that." *Saying* it would be most unwise. Doing it was dangerous enough. "Let us say that I am pursuing more than one path toward my goal and leave it at that."

A calculating suspicion in Crawford's eye showed that he wasn't sure how to take her remark. To lure him back into more familiar waters, she said, "It is unfortunate that the 48th are not all that they might be. I was rather hoping for a more, shall we say, flexible unit. They are mercenaries after all."

Crawford raised his bushy eyebrows. "And here I thought ya had a high opinion of mercenaries. Now I see it's just me ya like."

"Some mercenaries are worthy of high opinion, Major, but not all mercenaries are created equal."

"Or paid equal."

Price pretended offense. "Are you suggesting that the Duvic Palatine does not provide equal pay for equal work."

"Just giving ya a reminder." He leaned forward conspiratorially. "And I wasn't talking to Duvic, Ms. Palatine. Me and my guys are doing serious work for ya.

Expensive work. *Good* work. We ain't no samurai knights in shining armor, but we get the job done."

"I understand, Major." She opened a drawer in her desk and removed the envelope she had prepared earlier.

He grinned as he took the appreciation. His grin widened when he placed the unmarked chip into his belt-reader. "I do so like an understanding employer."

"And I appreciate an understanding employee. Especially one who does his work without demanding over-much of his employer's time."

"And I do so like being appreciated. But I can't sit around all day basking in it. I got me a job. Why I bet those raiders will be picking out their next target tonight."

"Yes," she agreed as she showed him the door. "I expect they will be doing just that."

13

Mirandagol District
County Shu, Epsilon Eridani
Chaos March
6 January 3062

Grouchy, bleary-eyed, and brain-numb, Kelly stumbled his way through morning PT. He'd gotten less than the four hours of sleep the Whipmaster had promised, though he couldn't blame anyone but himself for that. His brain had been spinning, working over the results of the exercise and looking for ways to improve his performance. He was sure that he was on the edge of a brilliant tactic when he finally fell asleep. Reveille, it seemed, came immediately thereafter, snatching away the solution his fevered brain had been offering. Neither breakfast nor the supposedly invigorating exercise had restored his lost ingenuity.

He was split-legged on the tarmac, head down, working on stretching his lower back when a familiar voice spoke.

"My, but they do look sweet when they get sweaty, like people doing real work."

It was LaJoy-Bua, standing at the head of a gaggle

of techs loaded down with tool satchels and gray-cased umpires. She was senior among the unit's techs, or to be more accurate, the unit's working techs. The technical staff of the CSVB didn't have an absentee landlord like the MechWarriors' Phantom Major, but everyone above LaJoy-Bua in the chain of command spent their time on administration and logistics. LaJoy-Bua, however, spent as much time as possible on the unit's machines.

She did spare a little time for games. At least that's what Kelly thought of her subtle and not so subtle passes at him. She was, as she'd be the first to admit, just a "lowly grease gopher" of a NCO tech and he was an officer MechWarrior. Liaisons between officers and non-coms were seriously frowned upon by the Powers That Be, though no longer forbidden as they had been under the old Liaoist regime. With the Whipmaster encouraging his pilots to have good relationships with their techs, Kelly had played along, flirting right back. It wasn't going anywhere. Not that LaJoy-Bua wasn't attractive, she was, but besides the issue of rank, there was the fact that Kelly had his eye elsewhere.

"What would you know about real work, you old grease gopher?" he asked. "And don't give me that creaky 'I'm not an officer, I work for a living' crap."

"Hey now, Mr. Chill, you ought to watch what you're saying. If you keep calling the living truth 'crap,' the gods are going to strike you down where you stand. Or squat. Or whatever you call that position you've gotten yourself into." Adding in an aside to the techs accompanying her, "Not that I don't mind the free peek at cheeks."

"It's my 'Mech that's supposed to have your attention, not my glutes."

"I got enough talent to cover both," she said, winking.

"Today isn't the day I find out if you're as good with people as with 'Mechs. Speaking of 'Mechs shouldn't you and your people be about seeing that they're ready for today's exercise?"

LaJoy-Bua rolled her eyes. "Whipmaster Junior speaks."

"He speaks truth," said Hayes, JJ's tech, apparently bored with listening to his boss's bantering.

She nodded. "Too right. Off you go, grease gophers. Time to minister to the mighty 'Mechs of our lords and masters." Instead of leaving with her team, she crouched beside Kelly and spoke seriously. "We've been having some pilferage and more techno-glitches than I care to see. Not that I'm calling it sabotage or anything, but still one ought to be careful. Especially about things you care about." She patted the gray-cased umpire, no different in appearance from the ones the other techs carried. "I thought I'd install yours myself. You know, make sure it's done right."

"You take good care of me."

"I could take better care."

She leaned close enough for him to feel her body heat. He caught her scent, a sweet spicy odor not yet drowned in the stink of lubricant, myomeric gel, and cooling fluids. Then a glimpse down the throat of LaJoy-Bua's no doubt intentionally loose coverall set Kelly to considering the offer. But before his hormones took complete control of his brain, a shadow fell on him and the tech. Kelly looked up to see Sam, sweat-soaked tee hugging her curves, and he remembered why he wasn't taking LaJoy-Bua up on her offers.

Sam quirked up one side of her mouth. "Shall I tell the Whipmaster that you've got a better offer?"

Caught in a mental gear shift, all Kelly managed was a confused look.

"Briefing?" Sam cocked her head quizzically at him. "In five?"

The impulse for self-preservation flushed Kelly's system. Five minutes was the usual span it took to double time it from the exercise area to the briefing hall, and Whipmaster Veck waited for no pilot. He scrambled to his feet and lit out after Sam and the rest of the lance.

He made it—barely—sliding into the room reserved for Veck's own lance just before the Whipmaster tapped the button to close the door.

"Now that you're here, Subcommander Kelly," Veck said dryly, "we'll get down to business."

Business was the day's rematch between the Vigilantes and the Champions. It was not going to be exactly the same as the previous day's exercise. This time the Vigilantes were to head out into the field first and set up an ambush for the Champions. Kelly liked that; he figured that by attacking from cover they had a far better chance to avoid damage to their 'Mechs than they'd had in the previous day's engagement. Sam reached the same conclusion.

"A nice hull-down ambush sounds good to me," she whispered. "The less damage we take, the less punishment duty we pull."

"You cover my back, I'll cover yours," Kelly suggested.

"You sure it's your back you want covered?"

Their exchange was cut off as Veck thundered, "Have you had a tactical revelation, Liu? Kelly? No? Then this briefing is over, 'Mech monkeys. I have received word that all umpires are installed and synched. You will proceed to your machines and start them up carefully. Note I said carefully." Veck's eyes fell on Slug who blushed brighter than the heat status bar on a shutdown-level overheat. "We move in thirty."

The rest of the group was spilling from their own unit briefings as the Vigilantes entered the corridor. Boasts and insults were the order of the day. It was friendly camaraderie, the sort of thing that high morale troops did. At least most of it was friendly. Subcommander Sten's shots were pointed, barbed, and regularly poisoned, especially when they were aimed at Kelly. JJ claimed that Sten's animosity was born of Kelly outpointing the Blowhard on just about every exercise and evaluation, but Kelly figured it went deeper than that. Sam usually out-pointed the Blowhard too, but she rarely was the target of his jibes. On short sleep, Kelly found it harder than usual to stick to his unilateral ceasefire, and he struggled to let the Blowhard's shots glance from his armor of indifference. It got easier when they hit the tarmac.

Magnificent in the morning light, the CSVB 'Mechs stood upon the field. When he had risen for PT, the sun had barely touched the chests of the taller 'Mechs. Now it had worked its way down the machines, illuminating them from head to ankle actuators. The tall machines gleamed in the bright light like twin ranks of titanic knights assembled as an honor guard to some ancient king of the giants. It was a sight that never failed to stir Kelly to his soul.

It also was a sight that showed Sten's sarcastic remarks as the petty, worthless things that they were.

Drinking in the grandeur of the armored titans, Kelly became aware that something was . . . different. It took him a moment to pin it down, but it was the light, the glorious raking morning light, that gave it away. Some of the machines had sparkling pin points where yesterday there had only been shadowed and vacant hollows. He halted, not quite sure he could believe what he was seeing.

"Hey, the missile racks are loaded."

Several pilots told him that he was crazy.

"Look for yourselves."

They did, and the questions started.

"What's going on?" Slug scratched his head as he stared at the warheads nestled in his *Raven*'s Harpoon SRM-6 rack. "We're not scheduled for a live-fire today. Maybe the techs screwed up. Anybody doing live-fire today?"

No one was scheduled for it. Everyone wanted to know what was going on, everybody but JJ.

"The Phantom Major's orders," he drawled. JJ was picking up a reputation for knowing the real skinny. Some of the trainees were starting to call him Ferret for the knack he seemed to have of digging out the news. He claimed to dislike the nickname since "ferret" was widespread Epsilon E military slang for security forces and he was a MechWarrior, not a dirt crawling weasel.

But there wasn't any doubt that he basked in the attention his news-scrounging garnered for him. "Starting today, all County Shu military forces are to be armed with combat loads. We, being part of the aforesaid military forces, thus carry our missiles. I expect you guys with MGs and 'cannons are packing, too. Not that we need ammo for what we're doing, but orders are orders."

"Veck didn't say anything about it," Sam noted. Several other trainees confirmed that their lance leaders had also been silent on the point.

"The outside world ain't our concern, remember?" returned JJ.

This seemed to be a case of the outside world impinging on their isolated training world. Kelly didn't like it. "I think we should have been told."

"Don't like being a mushroom, Gropo?" asked Sten. "You too good to be kept in the dark and fed crap like the rest of us?"

"We're going out on an M-v-M!" That came from Gunter Stübel, a Champion *Commando* pilot and a participant in the day's 'Mech vs. 'Mech battle between the Vigilantes and the Champions. "What the hell are we carrying missiles for? Someone could get toasted."

Sten had venom to spare. "Somebody do a data wipe on you, Guns? The umpires disable all projectile systems, remember? Don't matter whether you're carrying ordnance or not. Your twitchy trigger finger ain't tickling your launchers. Just no connection. Kind of like between your brain and your mouth."

Reese Fu stepped between them before anything happened. "Hey, Ferret. How come you know what's going on?"

JJ shrugged. "Just being an informed MechWarrior."

"Come on," Fu coaxed. "You know more. Spill."

"There were shots fired yesterday. And this isn't the first time."

"Bandits?" "Duvic?" The shouts were about evenly divided. "Where?" "What happened?"

"Duvic," JJ confirmed. "Look, I don't have details, but the gist is this. There have been several confrontations over what the Doofvics are calling 'free trade passage.' They've called up their militia, we've called up ours, and so far it's just been everybody staring at everybody else. A few guns have gone off, accidentally of course, but nobody's been hurt. So far."

"Only a matter of time," Sten observed. "You know what happens when you give a loaded gun to a gropo. Sooner or later, he's just got to point it at someone and pull the trigger. Ain't that right, Gropo?" Sten threw at Kelly.

"Wouldn't know." Kelly stared the Blowhard right in the eyes. "I'm a MechWarrior."

"Really? Then why do you answer to Gropo, Gropo?"

"I don't answer to it. I was just taking pity on the ill-informed. Helping the helpless, you might say, like the Warrior House creeds say any true MechWarrior ought."

"True MechWarriors—"

"True MechWarriors?" Veck's voice sliced through the tension and split the knot of trainees. They snapped to attention as he strode into their midst. "I don't see any true MechWarriors anywhere around here. I don't see any MechWarriors at all. All I see is 'Mech monkeys. And you know that makes me curious, because I came out here expecting to find each and every one of you monkeys sitting in a cockpit. It makes me want to know what you 'Mech monkeys are doing standing around on my time. Anyone want to tell me why that is?"

The trainees' answer to Veck's question was a scramble for their 'Mechs.

Kelly tried to put the belligerent Sten out of his mind as he raced towards his 'Mech, but all he had to replace his annoyance with were worries about his performance. All the way up the access ladder all he could do was note the areas that had supposedly been damaged in the previous day's exercise. He would do better today. He would! Routine gave him a little surcease as he went through start-up procedures. He fumbled some codes and had to rekey them. *Tired*, he told himself. *Just tired.* His emotions and intellect had been whipsawed all morning and it wasn't even noon yet, but all his fatigue and worries burned away when the *Commando* fired up beneath him.

Anyone who had ever piloted one of the gargantuan battle machines knew the feeling. Sitting atop a minimum of twenty tons of protective armor, myomer pseudo-muscle, and foamed endosteel, all powered by its own fusion reactor, was heady enough, but having all that power move at one's command was even more so, to say the least. And the neurohelmet's feedback loop that used the pilot's own kinesthetic sense almost subconsciously to keep the machine upright and moving smoothly only added to the illusion that one had become god-like. You didn't need the weapons to foster the intoxicating sense of power, though the array of destructiveness available to BattleMechs certainly added to the sense of ultimate might felt by the person in the hotseat. Most MechWarrior training with its emphasis on making the control of the walking engines of destruction as second nature as using one's own body increased user-machine identification by doing as much as possible to blur the line between the two.

Of course, Kelly reminded himself. *A true MechWarrior became the machine, but never lost his humanity in it.* At least that's what the House warriors believed. It was Kelly's goal to reach that stage of perfection. He had a long way to go, but as the *Commando*'s actuators shifted from stand-down immobility to live flexibility and he felt the machine beneath him stir and settle into an easy, natural stance awaiting his command to move, it felt right and natural. He knew he was on the path.

Some said that BattleMechs had originally taken their humanoid form to make the merging of man and machine more natural, easier to achieve. Kelly didn't know about that. Certainly he felt like the *Commando* was *his*, though not yet *him*.

Most of the Vigilantes' 'Mechs were distinctly humanoid. It was the "classic" BattleMech look, that of a caricatured giant in bulky, squared-off armor. Admittedly, Commander Veck's *Vindicator* had only one hand since its lower right arm was devoted to an Extended-Range Particle Projector Cannon, but that didn't affect the overall impression. They were a far cry from bird-like designs like the *Raven* or the almost alien types of machine that tended to look like stilt-walking crabs or scorpions. They had the "classic look."

Whatever their "look," all BattleMechs were beautiful to Kelly, and none more so than his own *Commando*. He set it in motion, marching smoothly forward to take his place in the lance formation. Veck's *Vindicator* strode among them, its head swiveling from side to side as the commander surveyed his troops. "Move out," Veck ordered as he led the lance out of the compound and into the rugged badlands of the Red Elk River.

It didn't take them long to lose sight of the base. It took longer to lose sight of each other, but that was deliberate. One by one they moved into their ambush positions among the boulders and outcroppings of the badlands. Each pilot chose his own spot. When they had settled in and powered down to maintenance levels, Veck moved his *Vindicator* across their front, surveying the position as he looked for anything that might betray a 'Mech's position. JJ caught a few blisters from the Whipmaster for his inadequate camouflage job. His second try met with Veck's approval.

"All right, you 'Mech monkeys. This is *your* ambush now. I will wait up on the butte at map ref seven-dash-niner-by-one-two. And before you start whining about being outnumbered by the OpFor, I'll tell you that you don't have to worry about Commander Chun's *Strider* on this run. He'll be developing a mechanical problem when I signal him that his chicks are heading for the bag. This one belongs just to you greenies. Good hunting."

Veck left them with a whoosh, superheated air billowing clouds of dust and gravel into a frenzy where his 'Mech had stood. As the *Vindicator* was rising out of sight on its jump jets, JJ came on the lance commo circuit.

"Hey, how are we supposed to know when to spring this trap?"

"Think I won't see them coming?" Slug asked.

"Know you will, my favorite Slug. But I lost line of sight on Mr. Chill when Veck moved me." The 'Mechs had been positioned to set up a chain of nearly undetectable, line of sight commo lasers to keep a communication link until they broke cover. They had planned to attack on a signal flashed from Slug when his *Raven's* specialized electronics said the OpFor were in the best position. JJ wanted to know, "How to I get the go code?"

Veck dropped into the circuit to remind them, "Radio chatter can be picked up."

"Sit tight, JJ," Kelly suggested. "Don't fire until we do."

"Unless they find you first," Sam amended.

JJ agreed, and the commo went quiet.

The plan was for the Vigilantes to get the drop on at least one of the Champion 'Mechs with two-to-one odds while the unfortunate Champion screened his lancemates from hitting the attackers. Take him out and move on, double or triple teaming their way through the chain of the OpFor, using their positioning to the Vigilantes' advantage. It would be harder to pull off without Veck. They needed the OpFor in close, almost knife-fighting range because almost every weapon the Vigilantes packed was optimal at short range. The lance's long-range weapon, the *Vindicator's* ER PPC, had gone along with the commander. At least the Champions were also going without their major long-range punch since Commander Chun and his *Strider's* LRMs were out of it, too.

Still, there'll be little chance of avoiding damage in the kind of dogfight we'll be having, Kelly thought ruefully. *More punishment detail for sure.*

Their best chance to escape damage to themselves lay in inflicting maximum damage in the first attack. Elementary tactics, but given a personal immediacy by Veck's work-for-damage program.

"Let them get kissing close," he lasered to Slug.

"Roger that." Slug was slow but not stupid, and if anyone dreaded work-for-damage more than Kelly did, it was Harry Trahn. It was the better part of an hour later before Slug zapped another message. "Get ready. They've entered the canyon." Kelly passed it on to Sam. A few minutes later, he did the same for Slug's "Drat all, they're spreading out."

So much for Plan A. Dispersed Champions meant the OpFor would have a better chance to react and return fire once the ambush was sprung. They might get the first one, but the rest would be a lot harder. They'd probably be taking on three of the Champions as a team, a tougher proposition.

Kelly waited, wondering which of the OpFor 'Mechs would come his way and whether he'd be the one to spring the ambush. Time seemed to stretch in the cockpit. The air grew stale and the temperature rose. It wasn't as nasty as swamping the 'Mech's heat dumping capacity with major weapons fire, but the badlands sun pumped out a good deal of energy itself and even a stationary 'Mech had to soak up some of that. His mind began to drift as he envisioned various scenarios of combat.

When the *Commando* first came into view, he spent a moment thinking it was just another imagining. A few hard blinks told him that it was real.

With his active sensors held in check, he wasn't getting IFF and the Whipmaster hadn't authorized personal markings for CSVB 'Mechs, so it took Kelly a few seconds to work out which of the two Champion *Commando*s he was seeing. It was Gunter Stübel's machine that was pacing toward his hiding place.

No word came from Slug, which probably meant that the other Champions were badly positioned. Stübel's *Commando* was at one hundred meters and closing. If he spotted Kelly, the ambush was blown.

At eighty meters and still moving cautiously, the *Commando* continued straight at Kelly, but the camo netting over the cleft in which he was hiding seemed to be holding up for the moment. Once Kelly popped the dampers and brought his 'Mech up to full capacity, the heat bloom would register on Stübel's sensors. Close as he was, it might actually be Stübel who got off the first shot.

Then Kelly's external mikes picked up the sound of a rock fall. Speakers erupted with the sound of multiple SRM launches. Nobody shouted a go signal and no lasers cracked, so it had to be out-of-commo JJ in his all missile-armed *Javelin* that had pounced. Stübel's *Commando* halted and turned toward the sound.

"Wrong move," he told Stübel. Of course, since Kelly

wasn't transmitting, Stübel didn't hear it. Neither was the OpFor pilot focused on Kelly's hiding place to register the *Commando* coming up to full power. He had Stübel cold.

Kelly popped his dampers as he sighted in the back of the OpFor 'Mech's head, swiveling his *Commando*'s torso and raising both of the 'Mech's arms to bring all weapons to bear. He dropped the laser target reticule over the center of Stübel's *Commando*'s back just as the Streak target lock-on pinged positive for his arm-mount launcher and the Artemis FCS registered a good firing solution for the torso-mounted 6-pack.

"I'm planning on a good night's sleep," he told the unhearing Champion pilot as he triggered his weapons.

Kelly's 'Mech shook. His eyes widening in surprise. That wasn't right! The umpires had insufficient control of a 'Mech's systems to simulate the shock of an actual launch. But smoke trails arched from the *Commando*'s chest and arm!

Dear God, his missiles had actually launched!

Without thinking, Kelly stomped the pedals and sent his machine forward. His laser shot had gone out full power, too! He could see where it had cored the unsuspecting *Commando*'s back. Missiles were already impacting on the hapless Stübel. There really wasn't anything he could do, but he rushed forward anyway.

Stübel's *Commando* staggered under the pounding. Kelly didn't count the number of missile strikes. He didn't need to. Any was too many. A *Commando*'s rear torso armor was light. It evaporated under the pounding. Fire flamed from its back. The *Commando* reeled like a drunken man, or like a BattleMech whose pilot was unconscious. Or worse.

Thankful that he wasn't piloting an armless 'Mech like a *Raven* or a *Strider*, Kelly reached out, intending to steady Stübel's *Commando*. If Stübel had survived Kelly's strike—*God, Buddha, anyone, please make it so!*—the fall could kill him.

But steadying wasn't enough. Stübel's machine went as limp as a passed-out drunk when Kelly's touched it. He managed a grip on one of the arms, slowing the 'Mech so that it crumpled to the ground instead of crashing. It landed face down, its ravaged back visible to God and all.

Kelly slammed his neurohelmet back into its cradle and ripped away his restraining harness. He was cracking the hatch when the commo channels began to buzz with chatter. He hadn't shut down the commo circuits. Cha, he hadn't shut down anything. It was against procedure, leaving a live 'Mech, but he didn't go back. The noise was faint as he dragged himself out of the cockpit. It grew fainter. He couldn't hear what they were saying, but it didn't matter; he knew what they were talking about. They had to have seen or registered his launch. Kelly shoved the voices from his mind as he clambered down the rattling access ladder.

He intended to drag Stübel out, to learn if he was still alive, but when he reached the ground, his feet seemed to freeze there. Even prone the *Commando* towered above him. Its shadow lay across his legs and he looked at it. Twisted metal and composites made tortured silhouettes against the bright sunlight. All he could do was stand and stare at the wreckage he had caused.

He didn't hear the other 'Mechs arrive. He never felt the thunder of their steps. The voices calling to him were nothing more than the buzz of gnats. Those things couldn't touch him.

He knew he should, but he couldn't bring himself to climb up onto the *Commando*. To look into the wrecked cockpit. To learn the truth of what he had wrought.

Veck had no such reticence. He climbed the wreckage more nimbly than any monkey. Cursing as he tugged on twisted wreckage, he forced open a passage. Then he disappeared into the dark cavern that Kelly had opened in the back of the *Commando*'s head.

Vigilante and Champion 'Mechs stood in a circle around the fallen *Commando*, much like mourners at a funeral. That was as it should be, for a frozen-faced Veck emerged from the *Commando*'s cockpit alone.

14

Mirandagol District
County Shu, Epsilon Eridani
Chaos March
6 January 3062

Kelly choked back a sob as Veck strode toward him. There was blood on the commander's hands. More blood spattered his legs and arms and there was a big smear of it across his cooling vest. It wasn't Veck's blood, of course, it was Stübel's. Gunter Stübel's. It belonged to the man Kelly had just killed. Veck's voice was chillingly cold, drifting in from some glacial planet that hadn't seen any warmth for a billion years.

"Did you, at any time, disable or tamper with the umpire in your 'Mech?"

Kelly couldn't bring up any words. He was deep inside in a dark place. From far away, he heard voices arguing. First, Sam saying, "Kelly wouldn't do that."

Then Veck, "I want *your* answer, Kelly, and I want it now."

Then Sam yelling, "I'm sure it was an accident. And I don't like you implying it was anything else." She continued to rant at him. Her obvious feelings for Kelly might have warmed his heart had he not been so deep in the cold place, speared by Veck's frigid eyes. When Sam finally stammered to a stop, Veck asked, "Done?"

"Sir."

"You're out of line, Liu." JJ and Slug prudently dragged the protesting Sam away. Veck waited till they were out of earshot before he whispered, "Well, Kelly?"

"I never touched the umpire, sir."

Veck's eyes narrowed slightly. "There will be an inquiry."

Of course there would. "I understand, sir."

"Understand this, Kelly. This *incident* happened on my watch. I don't like it, I don't like it at all, and I *will* see justice done. The person responsible for the death of Subcommander Stübel will be found out and will be brought to justice. And if the Count's courts can't do it, I will."

Veck left Kelly with his lancemates after that. They all sat in a patch of shade, shocked and silent, while Veck and Chun talked with the base. The equally quiet Champions sat in a separate patch of shade. They all waited until a flight of *Cavalry* VTOL transports blasted in for a dusty landing. The base personnel in the transports didn't have business with the MechWarriors, so they did some more waiting. Finally the recovery vehicle for the downed *Commando* rumbled into the canyon and the waiting was over. Kelly observed that Force Commander LaJoy-Bua was notably absent from the technical crew who hopped off and began to work on the downed 'Mech.

The dispirited trainees didn't pilot their 'Mechs back to the base. The "special manual" pilots who had come on the transports helped the techs do that. The MechWarriors went back in the transports, each lance in its own. Veck saw them all settled, then went forward to ride with the driver. He was on the commo to base before the pilot compartment's hatch shut and sealed him off from the main cabin.

Sam sat beside Kelly. In the thunder of the transport's engines, they might have been alone. She put her arm across his shoulder, but her warmth didn't do much to stop his shivering. Still, he was glad to have her near.

"Thanks," he said.

"For what?"

"For what you said to Veck. For being here. For keeping me grounded when I feel like I'm drifting away. But I can't agree with you here. I—well—thanks."

"Hey, what are lancemates for?" Her hand against his cheek suggested a somewhat more personal fondness. "We've got to look out for each other."

JJ and Slug sat opposite Sam and Kelly in the cramped confines of the transport, busy looking elsewhere. Kelly appreciated the discretion, barely. Even Sam's shift in attitude hardly registered. He kept seeing the rear of Stübel's *Commando* erupting in debris and flames. And for some reason, he heard his father's voice. *There's more to lose than just a leg.*

Back at the base, word of the accident had spread. Everyone told Kelly that is wasn't his fault. Everyone except Stübel's lancemates; they had nothing to say to Kelly. Sten had plenty to say and none of it complimentary, but Kelly heard little of the Blowhard's vitriol.

Kelly spent a long, sleepless night, not getting any rest until he stumbled during morning PT and Veck sent him to the infirmary where a medtech gave him something that laid him out for hours. When he awoke he was rested, but far from fit and ready. His mind remained shadowed in a way he doubted any Warrior House scion's would ever be.

Why did he feel so guilty? Stübel's death was an accident. Kelly hadn't deliberately killed the man. But his spirit seemed unable to accept what his mind told it. It told him so in nightmares and daily bouts of recrimination. He did his best to soldier on. He had to. Life, and training, weren't stopping and waiting until he was ready.

Sten's harassment went on, too, but one or another of Kelly's lancemates always seemed to be around to head Sten off. Usually Sam. Once she and Sten disappeared for a while. Both of them came backing limping and bruised. Sten stayed away from Kelly for a whole week after that.

Veck's promised inquiry began. Kelly had sessions

with officers in the uniform of Count Shu's security team. Scuttlebutt said the finger had been pointed when LaJoy-Bua was escorted off base by two guys from the security office. Kelly wished he could believe it, but he had trouble understanding how the tech could be the one who had jiggered the umpire. Sure, she had put the unit in herself. She'd made no secret of it. Such openness seemed foolish for a saboteur. Besides, she'd made plays for him regularly since his first test. Why would she want to see him in trouble?

He also had therapy sessions with the base chaplain, but neither spiritual counseling nor investigative analysis did much to cut down on his nightmares.

When Colonel Bua's ferrets came and took LaJoy-Bua away, some of the trainees predicted that would be the end of it, but the chief tech's departure didn't change life on the base much. There were still ferrets rooting about, though the interviews became more rare. Technical glitches got a little more common, but nobody else died, and that was good.

Veck's Vigilantes continued to go out on exercises, but they went short-handed. "Real-world roster exercises," Veck called them. *Yeah, sure,* Kelly thought. It was true that military units in the real world were rarely up to full strength at any given moment, but Kelly doubted there would have been any such thing had he not been prohibited from the M-v-M exercises.

Kelly's restricted military activity was a sure sign that he was not free of the shadow of Stübel's death. He was confined to the simulators and the firing range, and he got to work the latter only when he had someone riding in the jumpseat behind him. He would have been restricted even further except that Veck had stood up for him. The commander never said a word about it, but JJ's connections reported a royal knock-down-drag-out between the Whipmaster and the Phantom Major.

"Don't swell your head, Mr. Chill," JJ warned. "Word is that the paranoid Phantom Major wanted to put the entire lance on ice till the whole mes—er, till things settle down. The Whipmaster was fighting for the whole lance. Your improved situation is just collateral damage to the Major's position."

Kelly wondered how a Warrior House pilot might handle his situation. He didn't have anything to go by; those elite MechWarriors never seemed to get into such situations. At least not in vids or stories, and that was all Kelly had to go by.

He did what he could. He exercised and studied and ran with whatever training he was offered. His ratings on the firing range actually improved, but in simulator sessions he flubbed it any time the opposition forces included a *Commando*. That wasn't the sort of problem that could be allowed in a fighting MechWarrior. A House warrior would have been disgraced.

For the first time in his life, Kelly was sure that he was experiencing life as a House warrior would: he felt disgraced. Stübel's death hung on him. The counselors said it probably always would, but that he could put it in perspective. They said he needed "closure."

Like he was going to get that before the board handed down its ruling?

When he awoke, sweating, in the small hours of the night, he thought that even with a decision handed down, for or against him, he would go on seeing that exploding *Commando* in his dreams.

Yet there was a bright spot to his revised life. Sam. She was still as competitive as ever, still pressing him on the firing range and agility courses, but out of her 'Mech, she had a different, warmer attitude. She dropped hints that she was ready to help him back from the pit in any way she could. And Kelly, even in the depths of his bouts of remorse, knew that he was on the edge of falling into Sam's comfort. He wanted to, surely he did, but he wasn't willing to let himself go. Not before he was cleared. She didn't deserve the crap she'd catch if he did go down for Stübel's death. He didn't want her to have to live with being linked to a washed-out killer.

═══ **15** ═══

Grene District
County Shu, Epsilon Eridani
Chaos March
13 January 3062

One thing a prudent MechWarrior knew was that BattleMechs weren't the answer to everything, and the pilot
of the unmarked *Axman* considered himself a prudent
MechWarrior. This deep raid into County Shu was one
of those times when keeping the *Axman* out of sight was
the optimal use of it. So it sat in the best position he
could find to give it short distance routes to its three
possible action stations. The first was the target, the
sleepy town of Barrhead, where Snatch & Grab should
already be hard at work. The second was the high probability location, a suitable choke point on the mountain
road that eventually led to the Garret Cleft, the passage
through the Grene Mountains and down onto the west-
ern coastal plains through which someone looking to dis-
rupt the operation would come. The third was another
such route, the nearest ford over the Barr River, but it
was also the best way back to base. If everything went

well, that was the route he'd be taking and nary a laser to fire.

Bloody unlikely!

But until a call to action came, he'd be what he already was: bored. There wasn't a lot to do in a 'Mech that was shut down to standby status. Listening to the news passed the time as well as being informative, and that's what the pilot did. The Shoes, as they'd nicknamed the people in this county with derision, were falling all over themselves. He'd already heard the report about the bombing of the Trade Union Building, listened to the commentators gassing to fill the airwaves while they waited for something real to report, laughed out loud when they fell all over themselves to finger whoever was behind the call from "the Free Trade Underground" who were claiming responsibility for the bombing, and nodded with satisfaction at the early reports of rioting. From everything he heard, it was clear that the clueless Shoes of the Barrhead civil authority and emergency services were stretched to their limits.

As intended.

If all continued to go according to plan, Snatch & Grab and his scavenger team would be taking over the target warehouse. Once they secured the place, they'd begin loading the trucks that would empty the building. The loaded trucks would head out across the disrupted town, taking safe routes Sneak & Peak Four would give them. A quiet roll through the suburbs, then out into the countryside, but not on the roads. Once they got far enough out, they'd head out cross-country to the rendezvous: a big fat *King Karnov*, an up-sized variant of the *Karnov UR* transport aircraft that was just waiting for them to roll into her belly. Then she could waddle across the plain, lift, and carry the goods low and slow under the Shoe radar net to the base the pilot and his fellow raiders were calling home.

Unfortunately, when his commo crackled with an incoming message, it wasn't Snatch & Grab reporting success.

"Sneak & Peak Three to Slash & Burn. Do you copy?"

The pilot killed the news report. "Slash & Burn here. Go."

"We've got ants swarming on the horizon. Mag det says four marks, and the dust they're raising says they're in a humping hurry."

Three was the first, and so far only, scout to report hostile activity. She was watching the Garret Cleft, which meant the nearest local militia units were reacting, but apparently not all of them. "Just the one lance?"

"Roger that."

"Which lance?"

"They're just coming into visual." A pause. "I've got the lead vehicle. I make it to be a *Goblin*, Slash & Burn. Mag det says all four are same mass."

*Goblin*s were a bastardized combination of tank and armored personnel carrier. They weren't the best at either job, but they were popular with leaders who wanted to stretch their C-bills. Count Shu had a reputation as a penny pincher and from what the pilot could see the Shoe militia forces showed it. God knew he wouldn't have wanted to go to battle in the retread cast-offs that Shu foisted on his soldiers.

"So, we've got the infantry coming," the pilot observed aloud. That probably meant the Shoes were reacting to the civil disturbance. He curled his lips up in the grin his guys called his "eat 'em up" smile.

The road through the Grene Mountains wasn't exactly high traffic. It wasn't an easy route for heavily loaded transports, being steep and full of scenic vistas born of sheer-sided mountain slopes. It was, however, the shortest route for ground-bound vehicles, which the tread-laying *Goblin*s most definitely were. If they wanted to get to Barrhead some time before rioters burned the place down, they would have to take the road.

He roused the *Axman* and started marching it toward the spot the scouts had picked. On his way he got the "all trucks rolling" from Snatch & Grab. He checked the *Goblin*s' position. It would take them another half hour of driving time past his ambush point for them to reach the outskirts of Barrhead. Even assuming that they could cross the town in a timely fashion, the trucks and their loot would be long vanished into the bush. He could just pull a fade. The Shoes need never know he was here.

But what was the fun in that?

Just as he had when the *Vedettes* had closed on him back in Severagol, he put his money on the first shot being the best, but this time he had no fragile CargoMech to nursemaid. He didn't have to pop the hostiles as soon as they came into sight. He could safely wait and let the tanks close, the better to use the *Axman*'s big gun. The Luxor Devastator had an impressive punch, but its accuracy over any distance sucked more than a fusion-powered vacuum cleaner.

The Shoes obliged him, motoring fat and dumb right into him. He unloaded on the lead *Goblin*. The driver must have caught a glimpse of the ambushing 'Mech just before it fired because he reacted incredibly fast, slewing his vehicle to one side, trying to cut the penetration by offering fresh armor for the ravening beams. Both of the *Axman*'s big bore lasers clawed into the tank's side, making a mockery of the driver's attempt. And the kinetic mass of the Devastator autocannon shell was his doom, bursting the armored vehicle open like a squashed fruit. Physically displaced sideways across the road, the *Goblin*'s churning treads scraped asphalt into marbled pellets that it flung every which way. Its port tread shifted from clawing gravel to clawing air as it slid from the roadway and out over the sheer drop. The *Goblin* teetered on its belly, poised on the brink of a two hundred meter fall.

Need a little help?

The *Axman* moved forward. One massive leg swung back, then forward. The kick was all the impetus needed to send the tank over the edge. The *Axman*'s pilot started to turn his 'Mech away. He didn't need to see the *Goblin* fall; he could imagine it turning over and over, spilling dead and soon-to-be dead infantrymen the whole way till the sudden stop and all consuming fireball at the end. The explosion would echo very satisfactorily from the mountainsides.

Almost immediately the pilot regretted his move to

help the Shoe tank along. Doing so exposed him to the others, and they let him know it. Three large lasers speared out. Two took the *Axman* on the left arm. The third burned into its back, stabbing deep and boring into the internal structure.

Warning alarms sounded and the board lit red. Heat flushed the cockpit as shielding failed on the 'Mech's nuclear heart.

But only partially. Though the reactor was bleeding heat, the core hadn't been breached. The extra burden would make the *Axman* sluggish and any full weapon volleys would push the machine's capacity into the danger zone. Still alive and knowing how near sudden death he had come, the pilot spun the *Axman*, sidestepping to avoid the *Goblins*' next strike while picking the first victim of his revenge.

Goblin lasers snapped out again, but the 'Mech's sudden movement meant one only burned air. The other two went home. The first blasted shards from the *Axman*'s chest, and the second devoured the last of the armor on its left arm. The pilot snarled as the function lights winked out on his pulse laser.

Damn them! Damn those lousy Shoe turtles!

He triggered the Devastator, sending a massive autocannon shell into one of the *Goblins*. The target shuddered as a great gouge was ripped into its turret armor, but the autocannon shell failed to penetrate. Heedless of the heat cost, the *Axman*'s pilot loosed his right-arm laser array on another of the tanks. Ravening energy chewed at the glacis of the *Goblin*.

With clockwork precision that the pilot might have admired under other circumstances, the *Goblins* fired again. The *Axman* shuddered under triple assault. Shredding armor, it staggered back.

The pilot managed to keep the 'Mech on its feet, but it was obvious to him that close work was as advantageous to the tankers' gunnery as his own. These turtles hadn't spooked as easily as the *Vedettes*, and his heat load was running too high for a prolonged fight. He ripped off another shot with the Devastator as he ducked the *Axman* for cover. He didn't see if he scored, but only two ruby beams slashed the air where the *Axman* had been.

Crouched once again in cover, he considered the situation. The Shoe turtles were out of sight around a bend in the road. As time passed the *Axman* would dump heat and he'd edge away from the chance of an ammo cook-off, but the longer he waited, the more likely it was that the Shoes would be calling up reinforcements. The *Axman* had been roughly handled by the damned turtles. Still, he was sure he could take them, but it would be a cat-and-mouse game that would eat time and it would cost the *Axman*. Not a good trade.

Well, he had killed one and probably at least crippled another. They'd be a while working up their courage to stick their heads around the corner again. Which meant they had no chance to catch the scavenger team's trucks. Which meant he'd done his job. Which meant he had no good reason to trade shots with the Shoes. Which made his decision easy.

He backed off a bit and sent an autocannon round into the mountainside wall right at the bend. The explosion of rock and debris was gratifying. The pile of boulders, rubble, and fragments that slumped across the road was even more gratifying. The Shoes would be hours clearing that.

Satisfied, he turned the *Axman* and headed for home.

16

Mirandagol District
County Shu, Epsilon Eridani
Chaos March
13 February 3062

The days had dragged on for Kelly in an almost timeless progression, with still no word on an ultimate verdict regarding Stübel's death. He was still living in a gray limbo that was occasionally penetrated by moments of relief like the one he was in now. He was sitting in Hall A with Sam and Slug, knocking back some cold Kai Lung and gassing over how hard the Whipmaster had ridden everyone during the day's M-v-M and agility course. In the middle of the good-natured banter, JJ hustled in, dripping with the evening's storm. The conversation dropped as he slumped into a seat and announced, "A ferret transport just came in from the capital."

JJ meant Colonel Bua's people, the county's one-stop office that looked out for safety and security of Count Shu. They also handled matters of political and military security, including the investigation of deaths where sabotage might be involved.

"More questions." Kelly sighed.

"Don't think so," JJ contradicted. "These guys aren't working ferrets. They're electron wranglers fit only for herding forms across the trackless wastelands of the bureaucracy."

"Maybe the brass has made its decision." Slug sounded hopeful.

"They'll clear you, Tyb." Sam had been calling him that in private for a while now. Nobody else in the lance did, nor did anyone say anything about it, not even JJ. "How can they not?"

Kelly shook his head. "I don't want to be pessimistic, but how often have you known the brass to stumble on the logical conclusion?"

"Then don't be pessimistic," Sam chided.

The ensuing argument over attitude, with all of its good-natured insults and occasional pokes in the ribs, came to a sudden halt with the arrival of a grumpy clerk. The desk jockey presented a summons from Veck: Kelly was to report at once. The clerk said that he didn't know what Veck wanted, but his surly attitude didn't inspire confidence. Despite the sunny encouragement of his lancemates, a gloomy Kelly headed for Veck's office, expecting to take more heat from the incident. The storm rolling across the base seemed to have a more suitable take on the proper mood than Kelly's lancemates.

"Take a seat," Veck said as Kelly entered the office. Kelly looked for a clue as to his fate in the commander's face, but Veck's expression was as closed as ever. He barely waited until Kelly had lowered his dripping self into the seat before beginning.

"I have just been notified that you will be declared blameless in the death of Subcommander Gunter Stübel." Veck tossed him a chip. "I know the official word isn't the end of it, but it helps. The detail's all in there. Long and short, you are back on the active roster as of 0600 tomorrow."

Kelly was glad he was sitting. The relief flooding through him would have dissolved his knees. "I'm cleared."

"The investigation of the incident is over."

"I don't know what to say."

"You are not required to say anything. But if you must, tell me that you will be the best damned MechWarrior you can be."

That had always been Kelly's intention, and he didn't hesitate to say so.

"Good. I expect no less from my lance."

Something about Veck's attitude seemed even stiffer than usual. Kelly hadn't expected grins and slaps on the back from the commander, but Veck's distance seemed a little out of place for the good news he had delivered.

"There's something else, isn't there?"

Veck's eyes slid away from Kelly's.

"I do have something else to say." He waited for a long moment. "I'm not talking to you now as your trainer or even your lance commander. We're lancemates, Kelly, and there are times when that's more important than rank and relative experience."

There was another long, awkward pause while Kelly wondered what was rattling the commander so.

"I like you, kid," Veck said. "You've got a lot of potential. Keep your record clean and you might have my job someday. If you're unlucky, you might even get slapped with a higher rank. But I think you could handle it. You've managed this Stübel thing well enough, but you don't need to be setting yourself up for worse problems."

"What sort of problems, sir?"

"You know what I mean."

"No, sir. I don't know what you mean."

"Liu."

Veck had been riding Sam hard ever since she stood up to him the day Stübel went down. Was he saying that Sam was in trouble, and that anyone associating with her was going to catch some of that same trouble?

"What about her, sir?"

"Forget her."

"She's my lancemate, sir."

"I never thought of you as stupid, Kelly. Don't be."

Kelly bridled at the harshness in Veck's tone. He got

his emotion under control before he said, "Your, er, advice, sir. Is it a suggestion or an order?"

"It would be a stupid order."

Kelly agreed with that. Now that he was a MechWarrior in good standing again, there wasn't anything to get in between him and Sam. Except maybe Veck, and he couldn't do that legally. So, like Veck said, ordering him to stay away from her would be stupid. No officer ought to give an order he knew wouldn't be obeyed. And Kelly had no intention of giving up his connection to Sam.

"Anything else, sir?"

Veck's eyes once again drilled in Kelly's. The commander just shook his head, and the interview was over.

17

Port Tsing
County Shu, Epsilon Eridani
Chaos March
20 February 3062

Gabriel's people were not able to get President Benton to agree to a face-to-face meeting—an annoying breech of etiquette and a not insignificant show of disrespect. The president was supposed to be available to the regional administrators, but Pierre Benton had been avoiding speaking to Gabriel for weeks now. It had gotten so bad that Gabriel had come to see the arrangement of a private teleconference as an achievement. He shushed Romano when his secretary Pierson announced that the link was up. Determined to have justice done, Gabriel jumped right in when Benton's tired face appeared on the screen.

"Mr. President, I and my county—"

Benton waved away Gabriel's opening as he cut him off. "This is about your dispute with Duvic, isn't it?"

"Of course it is. As I was starting to say, I and my county have been victimized here. The Price woman is out of control. Something must be done. You must take positive action. If the Eridani Guards were to—"

"Now, now, Gabriel. We all need to show a little considered restraint here."

Gabriel bristled, not just at Benton's familiar use of his given name, but at the condescending tone as well. This was no childish squabble, but a deadly serious business. And besides all that, Gabriel as Count Shu deserved to be treated with respect.

"Tell that to Price," he sputtered. "She'll back down if you send the Guards—"

"Gabriel, you know better than that. You know the constitution prohibits direct federal interference in jurisdictional trade disputes."

"This is serious, Mr. President. It's only going to get more serious."

"And sovereignty issues are serious, too. You were still in school when we put together this rickety federation that we have the nerve to call a planetary government, but your father was a leader, an absolutely inspiring leader, in the process. I also have to tell you that the count was one of the strongest advocates for jurisdictional sovereignty. Hell, he was the one who insisted we put it in place for the palatines as well as the traditional fiefdoms."

Yes, he would have been. Gabriel's father had been a curiously democratic autocrat. "I understand that unity is important."

"Good. That's good. Then you should understand why I have to keep out of this. I've got a dozen lords and nearly as many palatines threatening to break the federation if I put planetary troops into this. As if I had them to spare. You know as well as anyone that bandit raids are up. And we have enemies out there, Gabriel. People who would be quite happy to see the end of an independent Epsilon E. What if these so-called bandit raids are some of those enemies testing our defenses? And things are not going well on Ingress, you know. We have to support our neighbor in their attempt to secede from the Duchy of Small. If they lose their fight, we may be next on Duke Small's list of conquests. This may require that we send more troops."

"Ingress can go to blazes. We stand at the brink of a civil war here at home on Epsilon E. Your first responsibility, Mr. President, lies here. You have to deal with what *is* happening, not what *might* happen or what some nebulous enemy *might* do. I believe that you must step in."

"Don't try preaching to your elders, boy. Don't you think I know we're looking at a civil war? I have nightmares about it. And if I dispatch planetary troops to you, that's exactly what we'll have, Gabriel. And it won't just be the Duvics and your people." Like a man shifting gears on his ground car, Benton put away his pique and put on his conciliatory face. "Look, Gabriel, there's been a lot of hot talk, and way too much saber-rattling going on. No, I am not accusing you. I am not accusing anyone. I would prefer if things are worked out peacefully. Do you understand? War would be bad for everyone."

"War is the last thing I want."

"Good. I'm glad to hear that. That being the case, this is what I want you to do. You, or your representative, will meet with Duvic's representative before the week is out. I have arranged a meeting place—neutral ground, of course. The Arousian Regional authorities have, ahem, volunteered and offered the Trade Council Palace in Dori. I understand Lake Arous is beautiful this time of year. Very peaceful and calming. And that's the very effect I hope it will have on this situation."

Gabriel agreed. Benton had offered another chance to stop the madness. What else could he do but accept? If there was an avenue open that led to a peaceful solution, it had to be taken.

"You're doing the right thing, Gabriel," Benton assured him.

Gabriel cut off the link and slumped in his chair. "Doesn't he understand that Price will not be mollified?"

Romano shrugged, rearranging the ice in her drink. "It could be that all the Duvic rhetoric and—what was the charming term our dear president used? Ah, yes, saber rattling—it could be that all this *saber rattling* is simply posturing to get a better negotiating position."

"Do you think so?"

"No. I think that if free trade passage won't serve, Presider Price will find some other *causus belli*."

"Are you certain of that, Romano? Are we doomed to this nonsense?" Gabriel didn't want to believe that they were, but it seemed inevitable.

"I will tell you one thing of which I am certain. I am certain that *you* cannot go to this meeting. It will be too tempting to certain people."

They argued well into the night about who would go. In the end, Romano got her way. As always. In the morning, Gabriel lit candles in the family shrine and asked his ancestors to do what they could to see that she did not become Presider Price's *causus belli*.

PART 2

An End to Innocence

≡ 18 ≡

Mirandagol District
County Shu, Epsilon Eridani
Chaos March
22 February 3062

Rumors had circulated almost daily since the ill-omened order to arm the BattleMechs. The Duvics had hired Wolf's Dragoons or some other high powered mercenary group. The Duvics had poisoned the upper reaches of the Barr River. The Duvics had bought up all of the *Lineholder*s that had come off the Kressily Warworks assembly lines for the past month. The Duvics were massing for an attack. The Duvics were dispersing, preparing to attack. The Duvics had demobilized.

And even when the rumor wasn't directly about the Duvic Palatine and its intentions toward County Shu, the Duvic shadow almost always lay upon it. The unit was to activate and they were going into the Palatine. The unit was going to be disbanded, because the Duvics had made nice. Prices were up in Port Tsing, because of Duvic counter-tariffs. The unit was to activate and stand guard, against Duvic incursions. A lot of rumors hinged on the unit being activated, though as far as Kelly could see that wasn't going to happen soon, unless the Duvics really did start something or the raiders struck somewhere nearby.

There were also lots of rumors about the bandit raiders, and those rarely included the Palatine as the puppeteers since everybody knew that the Palatine had its own bandit problem. There were lots of ideas as to who the raiders were, including the ludicrous suggestion that they were renegade Eridani Guard. Where they were going to hit next was a popular topic. Usually the target was the chief rumormonger's hometown. There was a lot of speculation on how tough they were, or not a little bit of gassing about how weak they were and how easy they would be to take out. Kelly paid more attention to raider chatter because defending County Shu and chasing down the raiders was why the County Shu Volunteer Battalion had been formed. It was only logical that the day would come that they would go out after the bandits.

And, of course, once a week or so, the scuttlebutt said they were headed off planet to support President Benton's adventurism.

With the Phantom Major's news black-out still in effect, the base didn't get much in the way of solid information, even family communications were censored. But the personal need to know what was going on couldn't be ordered away, and so people listened to gossip. The wild and not so wild reports swept across Veck's Vigilantes as fast as they hit the other elements of the CSVB, but most of them eddied to a stop at the breakwater of JJ, who made a practice of living up to his nickname of Ferret and having the straight skinny.

Veck's Vigilantes were showering down from morning PT when Slug passed on what he'd heard from a tech in Acevedo's lance. Supposedly the Vigilantes were about to be given an active duty assignment. Their Mechs had been repainted last night. Kelly admitted he thought he had smelled paint thinner drifting across the tarmac. When asked what it was all about, all JJ could say was, "I don't know." Kelly and Sam exchanged raised eyebrows. If JJ didn't know anything about what was going on, it was notable.

JJ might not have the word, but Veck did. The commander roared into the barracks, bawling for his lance to scramble into dress uniforms. Veck was already in his dress red-and-golds.

"Dress uniforms?"

"Questions later. Hustle NOW!" snapped Veck.

Hustle, they did. It still took a quarter hour before they had all their collars snapped down, boots laced up, creases creased sharp and tucks tucked away. A quarter hour in which an impatient Veck's only response to questions was to urge more speed and attention to the task at hand. When they were finished, the commander nodded his approval before leading them out onto the field.

Their 'Mechs were already out on the tarmac, moved there by the techs. Once again Kelly smelled paint thinner. Fresh paint gleamed wetly where the unit markings, identification flashes and numbers had been touched up. Selected panels had been outlined in white, just like for a parade.

The swelling drone of an approaching *Cavalry* dragged everyone's eyes to the sky. The aircraft wasn't in sight yet, but its engine noise meant it was near.

"Fall in at your 'Mechs, 'Jocks," Veck ordered.

Kelly was halfway to his *Commando* when he realized that, for the first time, Veck had not referred to them as 'Mech monkeys or some other demeaning term. It could mean only one thing: the unit really *was* active. Kelly wanted to howl his relief and pleasure, but he guessed that to do so would, at the very least, get him a loud, embarrassing dressing down from Veck. He settled for grinning as wide as he could as he snapped to attention by the access ladder of the *Commando*.

The *Cavalry* appeared, flying low over the badlands and headed straight for the field. It wore the red and gold livery of Count Shu. The pilot banked his craft as it reached the field, turning to line up on his chosen landing point. Dust danced across the field as the VTOL engines swung around into position for landing.

"All right, 'Jocks." Veck's voice was barely audible over the *Cavalry*'s hard-working turbines. "We have an assignment. It is not exactly a date with destiny, but make no mistake, your personal destiny may well be decided by how you perform. You are about to meet the individual who will have the greatest say in that evaluation. Look sharp. Be sharp. You get me?"

"We get you, sir!"

Veck gave a curt, satisfied nod and left them. He was standing at the aircraft's hatch when it opened. He ignored the security troopers who hustled out of the transport, but he saluted the next person to emerge.

Kelly recognized Romano Shu the moment she stepped into the *Cavalry*'s hatch. All the troopers had seen her gorgeous face on the newscasts many times. Some, as Kelly did, got closer looks occasionally—in their dreams. But it was a living, breathing Lady Shu who exited the aircraft and greeted Veck.

"Good to see you again, Commander Veck."

"I am honored that you remember me, Lady Shu."

"What kind of a lady would I be if I forget a gentleman like yourself? You are happy with the commission report on the tragedy, I hope."

"My unit is ready to serve."

"So I trust. I will meet them now."

Veck bowed assent and began Lady Shu's tour of the line with JJ and his *Javelin*.

In person, she conveyed an even more vibrant and alluring presence than she did on newscasts, and it wasn't just the way she was dressed, although that didn't hurt. She wore a sleek, form-fitting coverall of the sort flaunted by the more flamboyant 'Mech units. Though the outfit was in CSVB colors and trim, it was nothing like any Eridani military had ever issued. Had they done so, male pilots would have needed issues of extra coolant for their vests.

The hussar jacket slung over her left shoulder wasn't Eridani issue either. *Marik,* Kelly thought, and judging by the unit flash and by the trim, it had once belonged to a Knight of the Inner Sphere. The absence of House Marik or Free Worlds League affiliation patches made it clear that the jacket was a gift or trophy rather than a statement of belonging. Perhaps it had belonged to one of the lady's rumored MechWarrior paramours. Or maybe not. Its gold braid flashed in the light and drew attention to Lady Shu each time she moved. That would be reason enough for her to affect it.

Speculation stopped, as did nearly all of Kelly's higher cerebral functions as the lady approached his *Commando*.

"Ah, Subcommander Kelly."

Kelly barely noticed that she knew his name because he was too stunned that she was holding out her hand. The lady's gesture wasn't normal for cultures of Liaoist extraction, but that hadn't stopped ladies, including any number of nominally Liaoist ladies, from greeting MechWarriors on *'Mech Combat* using it. Kelly slipped his hand under the delicate fingers, and bowed over her hand. He didn't dare kiss it.

"My Lady."

"So gallant. One rarely meets such courtesy in these strident days. So much gruff attention to duty and too little to manners. How is it that you are here, my handsome young MechWarrior, and not simply playing a MechWarrior on the vids?"

"My pleasure is to serve."

"Really?" One eyebrow rose and a sly smile caressed her lips. "I am certain you will serve well, given the chance. And I think perhaps that the pleasure would not be one-sided." She chuckled at his obvious distress. "I am sure we will talk again. Commander Veck, please introduce me to the rest of your valiant MechWarriors."

As they moved away down the line, out of earshot, JJ whispered, "Medic, medic. MechWarrior down. Coolant overload."

"JJ?"

"Yeah, Mr. Chill?"

"Shut up."

When the inspection was over and Lady Shu was escorted away to the operations center, Kelly discovered that JJ wasn't the only one who had noticed his interplay with Lady Shu. Once Sam had wound down a bit, Kelly managed to say, "Drat all, Sam. I was just being polite."

"I was just being polite," she echoed, still in danger of a heat overload. "You were a puppy dog with your tongue hanging out."

"Chow-chow," JJ barked, imitating a dog.

Slug just smirked as Kelly's face grew hot.

19

Arousia District
Arousian Region, Epsilon Eridani
Chaos March
23 February 3062

The next day, Kelly and the Vigilantes found themselves on their first official assignment under active duty, marching along the rosy beaches of the Lake Arous Resort, headed for the city of Dori.

"Commander, I've got 'Mechs on scanners," Slug announced over the lance link. He gave the coordinates. "Two count. IFF not responding."

An unknown force of 'Mechs was not the sort of business that the Vigilantes wanted to be dealing with, even if they outnumbered them two and a half to one. Their mission as Lady Shu's honor guard wasn't supposed to include combat. Just the opposite. The Arousia District was supposed to be neutral. Lady Shu was a peace negotiator, aiming to settle the differences between County Shu and the Duvic Palatine before shooting broke out.

"They ain't us," JJ pointed out unnecessarily.

"So who are they?" Kelly wanted to know. He checked

his scanners to ensure that Lady Shu's ground transport was secure. "Bandits or Doofvics?"

"They could be Eridani Guard," Sam observed "This meet is President Benton's show."

"Enough chatter," Veck declared. "Trahn, do what you can to refine the scan. And let me know if they show the slightest signs of interest in us. Meanwhile, we keep on course. And off the link."

Slug was able to peg the two unknowns as light 'Mechs, but no more. The machines showed no interest in the converging Vigilante 'Mechs, but the unknowns' destination seemed to be the same: the city of Dori. Just before the two bogeys disappeared into the scanner clutter that was the city of Dori, Slug announced he'd picked up two, maybe three, more BattleMechs, bigger ones, already in the city. One of the new contacts was an assault 'Mech, a mechanical monster that would outmass at least three of the Vigilantes' machines by itself.

"Think it's a trap?" asked JJ.

"They're not doing a good job of hiding, if it is," replied Kelly. There was nothing else to do at the moment but proceed.

A kilometer or so from the city limits, they encountered what at first glance appeared to be a roadblock. It was, in fact, a welcoming committee, complete with media coverage. Romano Shu exited her groundcar to bask in it, and Veck dismounted to join the party, but the rest of the Vigilantes remained in their 'Mechs and stood sentinel. Kelly ratcheted up his external mikes so he could hear what was going on.

"Kwai!" Lady Shu beamed at the head of the welcoming delegation, a man in a conventional business suit that stood out among the ceremonial robes of the Arousian officials. "In person! Now I know this little *tête-a-tête* really has President Benton's support."

"A pleasure as always, Lady Shu." Minister Kwai Jame's body language didn't match his warm tones. "The city elders of Dori requested that I accompany their delegation to greet you and welcome you to the city. They thought it wise that I, as the senior representative from the capital, be the one to make the formal introductions. If I may, I will do so, after which we shall enjoy a small ceremony."

"I would be happy to meet the distinguished delegation, Kwai, but if you're going to be speaking I would rather pass on the ceremony."

Minister Jame's face darkened at the slight.

"Oh!" Lady Shu sounded distressed. "I misspoke, didn't I? I meant to say that *unless* you were speaking I would pass on the ceremony."

Jame calmed his ruffled dignity and started the introductions. Kelly saw what the minister missed: the wink that Lady Shu sent to Commander Veck. Introductions completed, the "small ceremony" began. Forty minutes later, Federation Minister Kwai Jame concluded his welcoming speech and signaled that the vid crews cease recording. He took a reader from a waiting aide and presented it.

"The pad has details of the security arrangements for your guard captain to look over. I am sure everything will be satisfactory. Since I am also sure that your ladyship would like to rest from her journey, we can proceed with no further delay."

Lady Shu nodded for Veck to take the reader, and said, "Her ladyship would like to meet with the Duvic negotiator as soon as possible."

"Minister Waterhouse has stated that he will be available for a mid-morning meeting tomorrow."

Veck looked up from the reader. "Who belongs to the BattleMechs?"

"Those are Minister Waterhouse's honor guard," Jame replied off-handedly.

Veck wasn't satisfied with the answer. "Both groups?"

"Both?" Jame blinked like a bird that had just rammed a window. "Yes, of course. Who else would they be?"

"If they are both part of the minister's honor guard, why did they arrive separately?" asked Veck.

Jame sighed. "I wouldn't know. Some military necessity, I suppose. Isn't that what it always is? In any case, why shouldn't they arrive separately? The machines belong to two separate mercenary groups."

"What units?" demanded Veck

"I don't know, Commander. They are just mercenaries. I don't think that their unit names are important. This is not a war zone, and they are not here to fight. Perhaps all of you MechWarriors should go out for a drink together and toast the coming peace. Now, Lady Shu—"

Romano cut him off. "Lady Shu thinks that the commander's question is a good one. Who are these mercenaries? And why don't you know? Price sends mercenary units and you do not even think to ask after them?"

"I already told you that—"

"What you already told us is unimportant. Especially since you are about to tell us that you will get the information and get it now."

"This is—"

"An outrage? Of course, but only a minor one. Certainly, in civilized circles, it would hardly compare to sending mercenaries instead of household troops to an honorable conference, but we weren't speaking of that, were we? We were talking about my outrageous behavior. I am so sorry, Minister, but being outrageous is part of the job of a hereditary ruling family like mine. I find it hard to help myself. It must be my genetic heritage. Now, you come to your position by choice, do you not? An act of will and dedication. No prisoner of genes are you. You have risen through the ranks of bureaucrats by skill and ability. How sad for you that the job of a bureaucrat is to follow orders, especially those given by an outrageous hereditary chieftain. It will be even sadder if such a chieftain has to have a word with President Benton if she doesn't get her way. Am I clear, Minister Jame?"

Apparently she was, for the information was forthcoming.

It turned out the units were one that styled itself "the 48th" and another that didn't seem to have a *nom de guerre*, but was simply known after its commander, Kingston Crawford, as Crawford's BattleMechs. Colonel Bua's ferrets had already noted the presence of both units in the Duvic order of battle, so their presence wasn't a new and unknown factor. Not that there was much known about those two units. The ferrets had dug up precious little solid information about them beyond the names of their commanders, but what there was the Vigilantes shared on the lance commo circuit as they moved on.

Crawford's BattleMechs, according to a JJ-approved rumor, was a splinter faction of the Tooth of Ymir, MechWarriors who had refused to carry on with the rest of their unit under Liao paymasters. That was a stance worthy of respect. Crawford's 'Mech strength was unknown, although two lances were supposed to be on the Duvic payroll. Colonel Bua had yet to share what, if anything, he had learned about specific BattleMech models. But there was a rumor that Crawford was running some kind of shell game because the lances never seemed to have the same machines in them and 'Mechs of the same model were reported in multiple color schemes. JJ thought the lances might be understrength and that the repaints were to make the unit appear stronger than it was, although with an assault 'Mech and several top-end mediums in the line-up, Crawford's MechWarriors were not an insignificant force.

The 48th, according to ferrets official and not, was an all Kuritan unit. Sam thought that might mean that they were *ronin*, warriors whose lord had died and left them unprovided for, thus condemning them to make a living selling their skills as warriors. The 48th was supposed to be all light 'Mechs, suggesting an outfit that specialized in operations like scouting and light raiding. It might be that the mercs, if they were *ronin*, just couldn't afford anything heavier.

The *ronin* phenomena had been pretty common once, but now, most Kuritan survivors from a shattered unit just got transferred to another unit. Like owner-operators, warriors demonstrating such unswerving devotion to the samurai ethic of undying loyalty were becoming things of the past. Kelly thought that sad and hoped that rumors he'd heard of a revival of samurai sentiment among certain Kuritan elements was true.

"I wouldn't put too much faith in the poor *ronin* theory," JJ advised. "Word is that this '48th' touched down in a pretty hefty DropShip. An *Overlord*, I hear."

"That's not confirmed," Veck said. "We have better things to do than worry about rumors. Let's get to it."

Getting to it amounted to joining a parade as Minister Jame's cavalcade took them on a route into the city that had been approved by the city authorities. People lined the streets in spots, many looking confused or worried at the presence of the BattleMechs. Some of the kids cried as the mighty machines tramped past, but most stared in silent awe. Some few had to be restrained from running close to the machines and getting underfoot.

The route included the finest civic sights of Dori, including several spectacular views of Lake Arous's sapphire waters. It also took them past the lot where two of the Duvic 'Mechs were parked. Minister Jame confirmed that they had a second vehicle park elsewhere.

"Trouble in the chain of command?" speculated JJ.

"Possible rivalry," agreed Veck.

"Useful if we have to fight them," Kelly said.

"We're not supposed to be fighting them," Sam reminded everyone. "This is a peace mission."

The two 'Mechs were the lights that Slug had spotted heading for the city: a *Panther* and a *Jenner* that Minister Jame said belonged to the 48th. Both designs were thiry-five-ton BattleMechs and both were often considered Kuritan designs, having made up the bulk of the Draconis Combine's light 'Mech forces since well before the birth of any of the Vigilantes. They didn't show any of the latest upgrades, but they looked well cared for, suggesting that the *ronin* had pride, if not mountains of C-bills.

When the parade finally passed Crawford's BattleMechs, JJ was the first to react.

"Look at the size of that monster!"

The monster was a one-hundred-ton *Pillager*. Massive shoulder assemblies and a low narrow cockpit between them gave the machine a thuggish look, calling to mind one of the bruisers who habitually threatened the heroes in crime vids. Spikes on the knuckles of its battlefists reminded one of tiger's claws or brass knuckles and only added to the sinister effect.

"I've never seen anything quite like it," Slug said in an awed voice.

That wasn't surprising. The *Pillager* had the smooth and rounded surface armor commonly associated with older designs, the sort that had fallen out of production when the Star League fell. Though once common, the venerable machines had fallen to the advance of time, just like the League, though now, like the Star League itself, such designs were enjoying a new lease on existence. ComStar had brought hundreds from hidden storage facilities and many old designs, gleaned from an ancient memory core recovered by the Grey Death Legion, were being brought back into production. As yet, backwaters like Epsilon Eridani had seen few of them.

"Think it's vintage or a new build?" Sam asked.

"Dunno" was the consensus.

Ton for ton, Star League style machines were faster, stronger, better armored, and better armed than the BattleMechs the Successor States had been limited to during the long, slow decline since the original League's collapse. They weren't up to Clan standards, or even those of the newest Inner Sphere OmniMechs, but they were plenty tough. Vintage or newly built, this *Pillager* was undoubtedly a mighty 'Mech. It mounted a large laser on the right forearm and paired mediums on the left. Slug said it had two more mediums as well: one in the torso where the designers must have found some spare space and one in the head where it would have a little extra traverse. But its primary armament lay in the twin gauss rifles embedded in its thick torso, paired magnetic railguns that could fire nickel-plated ferrous alloy slugs capable of tearing the limb from smaller machines or coring into the heart of larger ones. It was a true engine of destruction, and it dwarfed the fifty-ton *Enforcer* and forty-ton *Clint* parked beside it, let alone the light 'Mechs of the Vigilantes.

Though he didn't join in the excited chatter of his lancemates, Kelly was as deeply dazzled by the machine as they were. When Veck didn't cut off the awed-teenager babble, Kelly wondered if his radio had gone out. "Commander, you on-line?"

"On-line, Kelly. Just thinking."

"How to beat a *Pillager*?"

Veck's answer caught Kelly by surprise. "There was an *Enforcer* among the bandit 'Mechs that attacked the Amalgamated Mining facility out at Comaton Bluff. A *Clint*, too."

"An *Axman*, too," JJ put in.

"What about *Pillager*s, *Panther*s, or *Jenner*s?" Slug wanted to know.

"Not that I heard," JJ said. "How about you, Commander?"

"Presider Price didn't send all of her BattleMechs here any more than Count Shu did."

"Are you saying these guys are the bandits?"

"Careful, Commander," Romano Shu cautioned, revealing that she had a link to the lance commo. "Well-honed paranoia might be useful in many places, but mis-aimed paranoia is more dangerous than any enemy. You are edging toward the sort of talk that ignites wars. We are here to stop one."

What stopped was the Vigilantes' speculation, but Kelly was sure that the others, as did he, wondered and worried about the commander's misgivings.

20

Dori
Arousian Region, Epsilon Eridani
Chaos March
24 February 3062

The next day, with Lady Shu safely delivered to Dori, Kelly figured they'd fulfilled their orders, leastwise until she was ready to leave. With the 'Mechs in shutdown as per the terms of the meeting, there wasn't a lot for a MechWarrior to do—not officially anyway—and he was looking forward to seeing some of the city with Sam. At least he was, until JJ popped in with word that the Vigilantes had more duty ahead of them. He said that they were to escort Lady Shu to the negotiating sessions, but it turned out that he didn't have the story completely right. Only two of them were to accompany the lady to the meeting site: Veck and Kelly.

As he and Veck were on their way to meet the lady, Kelly had to ask, "Why me, sir? I'm no diplomat."

"We're none of us diplomats, Kelly. We don't have to be. That's what Lady Shu is here for. We're supposed to be honor, which is to say bodyguards, but what we really are is just set dressing and status symbols. Even so, you wouldn't be going to the negotiating session if Minister Waterhouse hadn't insisted on having both commanders from the mercenary units accompany him. Minister Jame says that we get two to balance them. I go because it's my lance. As to why you," Veck shrugged, "Lady Shu requested you."

Kelly wasn't sure what to make of that, but he was glad Veck hadn't said it where Sam could hear.

When they arrived at her suite, Lady Shu was radiant and cheerful and ready to get down to business. Kelly soon forgot to worry what Sam would say. The lady and her team spent most of the trip to Trade Union Palace, the site at which the negotiations were to take place, reviewing the situation. Kelly got lost fast in the discussion of the intricacies of taxes and trade regulations and jurisdictional issues. He stopped listening, sat back, and just watched the lady, letting himself get lost—in an entirely different way—in her presence.

His reverie didn't last long. The bustle at the Trade Union Palace meant business and time to be onstage. The other parties in the process were present. Minister Jame made formal introductions, Lady Shu to Minister Waterhouse, but no introductions were done for the MechWarrior escorts. In short order, Jame led the lady and Waterhouse and their top aides into a private conference room, leaving the vid crews, further bevies of aides, and their MechWarrior attendants standing around with little to do but wait.

Veck attracted some attention from the media and while the commander was fending off their questions, Kelly found himself effectively alone. He took the opportunity to look over the opposition commanders, as they too were besieged by the press. The big flamboyant one he took to be Kingston Crawford. His suspicion was confirmed when the reporters addressed him as Major Crawford. The newsies addressed the other as Major Namihito, but they were soon ignoring the laconic commanding officer of the 48th in favor of the easy-talking Crawford. Kelly figured they were missing a bet. Namihito looked far more an officer than the piratical Crawford, and Kelly figured that if either of them had the real story, it would be the Kuritan.

Impressed by the man's look and by the way he evaded

the reporters to find a place away from the crowd, Kelly wanted to talk to him. He hesitated. The man was a foreigner, and a higher-ranking officer in the opposition military. No, that second part wasn't right. Yes, Namihito was high-ranking—intimidation enough—but the Duvic Palatine wasn't the enemy; they were a polity of Epsilon Eridani just like County Shu.

So why shouldn't the two of them talk? Weren't they both MechWarriors? Didn't that give them something in common? Still, he hesitated. What finally got him moving was realizing that he would never hear the end of it if JJ found out that he had been in the same room as the Duvic commanders and hadn't tried to learn something about them.

Namihito looked older up close. The close-cropped, iron gray hair showed hints of white and there were wrinkles in the mahogany skin around his eyes and mouth. The sudden appreciation of the Kuritan's age daunted Kelly a bit, but he got a sense of acceptance or maybe brotherhood when the man turned to face him as he approached. Yet there was a feeling of distance, too, like the Kuritan lived in a place to which Kelly had yet to travel. Kelly had sometimes gotten a similar, less intense impression around the veteran Veck and it was quite a bit like what he'd imagined it would feel like to be in the presence of a master MechWarrior from one of the Warrior Houses.

Kelly cleared his dry throat and introduced himself, bowing in the old, formal Capellan way.

"You must be Major Namihito. I'm Tybalt Kelly, County Shu Volunteer Battalion."

The Kuritan officer bowed back, less deeply, as befitted a superior greeting an inferior, despite the fact that his dark gray uniform bore no rank tabs.

"I am Namihito."

"Isn't a lance a little small for a major to be leading?"

"Convention would have it so."

"And you're not conventional?"

"An officer leads his troops. Troops know their officers. What matters rank?"

"It matters a lot where we come from."

"So ka."

"I'll just bet you do understand. You're Kuritan, aren't you?"

Namihito's eyes bored into Kelly. "You are inquisitive."

"Just trying to be friendly.

"We are not friends." His eyes slid away.

Kelly scrambled to recover the ground he'd apparently just lost. "We could be soon. The negotiations, I mean. We're supposed to be settling whatever it is that got Presider Price's shorts twisted around. This time next week all this trade nonsense will be old news, and our units could be hunting bandits together before the month is out."

"Shigatta ga nai."

Whatever, eh? Kelly decided to try another tack to crack Namihito's reserve. "I've heard it said that Kuritans are the best individual MechWarriors, and the most honorable."

"I have heard that said as well."

"Would you say it was true?"

"House affiliation has nothing to do with individual skill or achievement or, most especially, honor."

Kelly detected an edge of bitterness behind the Kuritan's calm, soft delivery. "You don't sound like you care much for your homeland."

"I am a mercenary MechWarrior. I have no homeland, only a contract."

"So you are *ronin*," Kelly mused, belatedly realizing that he had spoken aloud when Namihito turned a cold stare on him. "I am sorry. I meant no offense. I have nothing but respect for the old codes and the warriors who follow them. I meant no disrespect."

"You are young. I was once young myself. It is a painful time."

Was that a crack in the reserve? "Ain't that the truth?"

Namihito made no reply.

"Listen. This whole conference deal is about being good neighbors. Good neighbors don't have to be friends, but it doesn't hurt to be friendly. What say we do our part for better relations and have some drinks or something? We're all MechWarriors and that's gotta count for something. We can trade war stories or rag on the politicians or whatever you want.''

The Kuritan remained silent.

"I'll buy,'' Kelly offered in desperation.

"Public bars are loud and disturbing to the *wa*.''

Which wasn't *exactly* a "no.'' "I heard there's a good club in the old town, down near the lake front. Club Hoodedoo. They have private rooms. Quiet places where people can talk.''

Namihito studied Kelly's face, unguessable thoughts moving behind his impassive expression. Kelly tried to look friendly. And respectful.

"Fraternization is not forbidden in my contract, but I do not find it conducive to good discipline,'' Namihito said. "Will your officer be there?''

"I can try to talk him into it.''

"If you can do so, I will meet with you.''

"Consider it done,'' Kelly promised. Rash, he knew, but he was *pretty* sure Veck would go for a chance to schmooze the Kuritan. "Club Hoodedoo, okay?''

"I will find it.''

They agreed to make it a "lancemates welcome" deal. Kelly figured that wouldn't hurt his pocket too badly since the Kuritan had only one lancemate in town and Kelly, for sure, wasn't buying for his own 'mates. He started developing a plan to get them, especially the news hungry JJ, to chip in on the cost.

Getting Veck to agree turned out to be easy, much easier than getting his lancemates to agree to chip in on the bill. Unfortunately, finding Club Hoodedoo proved not so easy. Kelly and his lancemates arrived well after the appointed hour.

"What a dump!'' Slug had been complaining about the neighborhood for the last three blocks. Now it seemed that he liked their destination less than the journey.

Kelly had more important things on his mind. A quick look around the club's crowded main room only ramped up his worry that Namihito had given up on them and left.

"Looks like we got stood up,'' said Sam.

"Hey, I'm dying of thirst here," Slug complained.

"There's the bar." JJ pointed out the rack of bottles, which was all that could be seen past the elbow-to-elbow mob seeking refreshment. "It looks open to an assault."

Slug didn't jump at the chance. "I came because you all said we ought to meet the Kuritans. I didn't really want to come here."

"What you don't want to do is to pay for a drink," JJ concluded.

"And you do?"

"No, I don't. Not for you anyway."

"Which is spot on for you, JJ. You don't care about anyone but yourself."

Kelly didn't know what had gotten into his lancemates, but he couldn't stand it any more. "All right, all right. I'll buy you both drinks if it'll shut you up while I try to find them."

"Crowd will take some working," Veck said as Kelly arranged drinks for his fractious 'mates.

"They won't be in the crowd," he told Veck. "I'll check the private rooms."

"Want company?" Sam asked.

And a witness to what was going to be an abject apology for tardiness? "No, thanks. If I find him, I'll come back and get you guys."

Kelly made his way to the back of the club. The private rooms were curtained alcoves off a narrow corridor that started in one corner, circled around, and emerged in the other corner. There was only space for a dozen or so alcoves, and if he didn't mind butting into other peoples' parties, it wouldn't take long. But he did mind; it was bad manners—and potentially dangerous. The first three were empty, curtains drawn back, so he didn't have to face his dilemma until the fourth.

As he stood, trying to decide whether manners—and good sense—outweighed his need to find Namihito, a man emerged from the alcove and barged right into Kelly. As they jostled in the narrow corridor, the man's cowled trenchcoat slipped open, revealing an elaborate tunic trimmed in a style Kelly recognized as belonging to a Word of Blake adept. The hall was dark and the man's face was shadowed in his hood, but his voice, raised in cursing Kelly's clumsiness, fixed itself in Kelly's mind. Adepts were usually soft-spoken in public, and the strident tone of the man's unjust accusations jarred. Kelly did his best to get out of the man's way, but he got no thanks, only a final insult as the man stalked off, brushing aside the curtain and vanishing into the crowded club.

The departing adept's coat had caught at the alcove's concealing curtain as he exited. Kelly had only gotten a glimpse into the badly lit space, but he had seen two men remaining in the room. One was a big, bald guy in a cooling vest and the other a cocoa-skinned fellow in civilian clothes. He thought the bald guy looked like Crawford, but hadn't gotten a good enough look to be sure. He was sure that the second man wasn't Namihito; his skin tone wasn't dark enough.

If it was Crawford in there, could the Kuritan have come with Crawford? Could he be in there? No, the room was small, and there was no place for the Kuritan to be sitting that Kelly wouldn't have seen a foot or an elbow or something.

Kelly checked the other alcoves. Two more were open and empty. He'd have to deal with interrupting the people in the closed-off ones. How? He decided to be straight forward and just ask for Namihito at each of them. He mostly got "no" for an answer, some polite, most not. A couple of the responses were obscene and included suggestions as to what he might do with himself. In the best Warrior House tradition, he let those responses simply pass through him. But from none of the alcoves came an affirmative. He didn't bother with the one occupied by the Crawford look-alike and his friend.

Namihito wasn't present. Kelly had blown it.

Dejected, he returned to his lancemates.

Veck had an answer. "So we're here, and they're not. It's still a bar, isn't it? Let's get to it. First round's on me."

They managed to find a table, but they hadn't gotten through that first round before a dark shadow occluded the light. It was Kingston Crawford, in all his hairy-chested splendor. Crawford had two other MechWarriors in tow, but neither one was cocoa-skinned. One was a tall, lanky blond with strong Scandinavian ancestry and the other a compact female with dark hair and an olive complexion. Each wore a Tooth of Ymir unit patch with a red bar across it. One didn't need to be a ferret to figure that these two were Crawford's lancemates.

"Well, well, lookee here," Crawford bellowed. "We've got Count Shu's baddest boys out on the town. Four cubs and one tired old lion. You must be Veck."

"That's right."

"Surviving being a nursemaid?"

"I'm surviving. I find being a nursemaid is better than needing one. How are you surviving?"

"Oh, that's good. Nice return volley. You're okay, Veck."

Crawford snagged a chair from a nearby table, dumping the occupant in the process. Crawford's size and the presence of two back-ups seemed to convince the displaced patron that there was no reason to make a quarrel over it. Crawford seated himself in his purloined chair next to Sam.

"Hello, pretty thing."

Sam rolled her eyes and shifted her chair away from him and closer to Kelly's. She leaned into Kelly, wordlessly making her point.

Crawford was philosophical about it. "Maybe later, sweet. When you're looking to upgrade."

He introduced his companions. The blond was Powell Jorgensson, the *Enforcer*'s pilot. The woman was Adelaide Tobin who ran the *Clint*. Jorgensson just nodded, but Tobin had something to say.

"Hello, Jeremy," she said to Veck.

"Hello, Addy," Veck responded.

"You two know each other?" asked Kelly.

"We've met," Veck stated.

"Still a man of few words, eh, Jeremy?" Tobin shrugged. "Yeah, kid, we've met. Long time ago. Another planet, another life."

"Did Major Namihito come with you?" Kelly asked.

Crawford guffawed. "The Kuritan stick? This place has got too much life for him and his crew. He and his shadow blew outta here ages ago."

"His shadow? He was being followed?" JJ was always looking for intrigue.

"What? Naw. I was talking about—what's his name—his number two."

"Duvorshak," said Adelaide.

"Who the hell cares about them anyway? Ya know, I saw you guys over here and I thought there's some MechWarriors; maybe they can help me out."

"What sort of help?" asked Veck.

"It's my unit. The name, ya know. A good unit's gotta have a good name. I'm thinking of calling it the Claw of Ymir," he said, tapping his prosthetic hand. "Some of the guys have a nostalgia for the old unit, ya know. Seeing that we fight tooth and claw, I thought, we could play off that. Whaddya think?"

"Not our business," Veck said.

"You're as stiff as that Kuritan board." Crawford looked around the table and focused on Kelly. "What about you, kid? Whaddya think?"

"I'd heard your unit split from the Tooth of Ymir over political differences. I don't see why you'd want an association in your names. Unless, of course, you're still part of the Tooth."

"Still a part? Ya mean like a crown or a filling. Maybe ya mean a cusp or a root."

Tobin and Jorgensson laughed at their boss's bad joke. The Vigilantes were silent. Crawford pressed on.

"Maybe I should just go with Kingston's Killers, eh? 'Cause I'm Kingston, and we're all killers. Simple. Ta the point. And it's got that alliterative ring."

"So would Kingston's Kute Kitty Kats," JJ suggested, bringing a snicker from Sam.

"Har, har." Crawford's eyes held no humor. "I think Killers it is. Y'all will be finding out about that soon enough."

21

The next morning dawned without any sight of the sun. Dark clouds ruled the sky, swirling and jostled by rising winds. Rain lashed against windows, drumming a hard, harsh beat, as the storm gathered strength. The storm, grown from an unusual coagulation of thunderstorm cells, was a big one, a true thunder tempest covering a sizable portion of the continent. Weather forecasters predicted a blow for the record books while ticking off similarities to notable storms of the recent past. Well-experienced in such things, many public facilities in Dori were shutting down to wait it out. MechWarriors and aides gathered in the lady's suite, waiting for word from Minister Jame's staff as to the fate of the day's session.

The party-like atmosphere that had arisen from the sudden prospect of a day of relief from the tensions of negotiations evaporated when JJ reported a rumor that Duvic forces had made a sneak attack on a Shu target.

Details were vague, but JJ assured them that word was circulating all over the hotel.

Lady Shu's attempt to reach her brother and Veck's try at getting through to headquarters were both frustrated by a storm-related communications blackout. The hotel staff assured them that failures in long distance communications were ordinary occurrences during storms of the magnitude of the one they were weathering. Trahn, the closest thing to a commo expert they had, agreed and warned that local commo was going to get worse before it got better.

"I don't like it." Veck looked worried. "This is too good an opportunity for trouble."

"Don't be ridiculous, Commander. The Duvics will be having every bit as much trouble as we are." Romano waved her hand at the turbulent sky. "Who could coordinate an attack in this?"

"They're not attacking *here*."

"We do not know for sure that they are attacking anywhere. We cannot jump to conclusions. Just because the sky here is gloomy, we cannot let that cause us to take a pessimistic attitude to the situation."

"If the Duvics have started a war, we could be in serious trouble. We have hostiles here in Dori. We are outmassed and out-gunned."

"And we are in the dark." The hotel lights flickered as if to emphasize the lady's words. "Soon we may be so literally."

That got some nervous chuckles from her staff, but Veck remained grim. "My lady, we—"

"We must discover just what is *really* happening, Commander."

"And if we are at war?"

"We cannot fight it here. We must get back to County Shu."

"Then we should leave now."

"And if it is all a false alarm? Would you like to explain to my brother why we abandoned the peace negotiations? I didn't think so."

"My lady, we must do something."

"I understand your frustration, Commander. We must continue to determine the truth, any way we can. Meanwhile, you may take whatever precautions you deem necessary, but I do not want you doing anything provocative."

"Understood." Veck began giving orders. "I want all 'Mechs prepped and ready for fast start. Trahn, I want you in your bird. Stay put, but see what you can pick up. I don't want us getting blindsided."

Veck went with them to see that the 'Mechs were ready. Once he was satisfied, he sent Kelly, Sam and JJ back to the hotel, while he stayed with Slug in the hope of getting a link with headquarters through the *Raven*.

When a soggy Kelly and the others got back to the lady's suite, she was complaining about Minister Jame's "prissy reluctance to get his feet wet." Over warm drinks provided by the staff, they heard about Lady Shu's conversation with the minister. It seemed that Jame wanted to cancel the day's session, something Lady Shu opposed, concerned as she was to "find out what Waterhouse knows about any and all troubling rumors." They had argued, Jame's concerns over propriety and convenience against the lady's pique. Apparently, Jame didn't share the lady's concern over the rumored attack. He had denied hearing any rumors of an attack by Duvic forces, although he'd heard something about a bandit raid at Severagol near the County Shu-Duvic Palatine border, he seemed to think it was just another minor incident. The minister's diffidence had vandalized the lady's attitude and she now sat fuming, given a wide berth by her aides.

"A bandit raid could just be a cover for the Doofvics," JJ suggested quietly to his lancemates.

"A concern," Lady Shu remarked, revealing that her hearing was quite good. "Well, MechWarriors, how valid a concern is it?"

"Hard to say, my lady." JJ shrugged. "We just don't have enough hard data."

"Very well then. Perhaps we can get ourselves some data. Trish," she called, "get Minister Waterhouse on the line."

It took Trish several tries to get through. Apparently local communications were indeed succumbing to the storm. As she handed over the phone, she said, "The static is bad, my lady."

Lady Shu's voice was all honey when spoke.

"Minister, I have just heard the oddest thing." She listened for the briefest of moments before her expression soured. "What? Where is the minister?"

The person on the other end tried to explain, but Lady Shu clearly found the explanation unsatisfactory.

"What do you mean he is unavailable? Do you know to whom you are speaking?"

A brief pause.

"Very well, then. He *will* be available. Do you understand?"

She slammed her hand down on the desk.

"I don't care how sorry you are. If you don't get your superior in communication with me right away, you will be sorrier yet before this day is out."

Lady Shu slammed the phone down in a very unladylike way and said a few choice words.

"Something is going on," she told them. "And I don't like it."

Veck, water still dripping from his storm gear, arrived and confirmed the lady's suspicions.

"There's a lot of military traffic on the net. We're just getting snatches of it, but it sounds like we've got units moving toward Severagol."

"Then the attack is real."

"I think so," Veck agreed. "Unfortunately, nothing I heard confirmed the identity of the attackers."

Resolve shone in Romano Shu's face. "Very well, then. Pack your bags, everyone! We'll be leaving soon. Selina, I'll be wearing my uniform. Trish, see that everyone has storm gear and do make sure this fleabag has a cover over the walk to the limousine."

"Limousine? It won't travel cross-country," said Veck.

"We won't be traveling cross-country for a bit, Commander. First, I have a visit to pay. I want to see Waterhouse's face when I break off the negotiations. I want to know if he's a dupe in this or part of the plot."

"I'm going with you," Veck stated. "Kelly, Jurewicz, you're with us."

"What about me?" Sam asked.

"Back to the 'Mechs. You and Trahn are the cavalry if we need it."

"I don't think that will be necessary, Commander. There's little chance of gunfire here."

"Your pardon, my lady, but you didn't think the Duvics would attack Severagol."

"We still don't know that they have, but I take your point. An honor guard for my visit to the distinguished representative of the Duvic Palatine seems in order."

The trip across the city to Waterhouse's hotel had more than a few exciting moments as the vehicles skidded on slick pavement under the buffeting of the gale, but they arrived intact. Despite fears, no BattleMechs loomed out of the driving rain to stop them. The party bundled into the lobby, steaming and spraying water everywhere as they doffed their storm gear. Lady Shu formed up a phalanx of her aides and headed for the elevators. The Vigilantes were rear guard simply because they hadn't moved fast enough. As Lady Shu entered the elevator she said, "Trish, time to let Kwai know where we are."

The aide headed for the main desk to use the building's circuits for the call.

"Kelly, stay with her," Veck said. "Follow us up."

The lights flickered, then dimmed, while Trish was delivering her message. It didn't seem to affect the connection, although Kelly noted that the lobby clock had stopped. He mentioned it to the clerk behind the reception desk.

"Must be the storm," the clerk said. "It was fine a moment ago."

By the time Kelly and Trish made it upstairs, Lady Shu was in full cry, berating the Duvic flunkies in the anteroom of the minister's suite. There were no Duvic

MechWarriors in sight. The nervous, frightened aides were very reluctant to speak to the Shu people, but they clumped before the minister's private rooms, refusing to let the lady see their boss.

"We'll worry about the niceties later," she decided. "Commander Veck, clear these people out of my way."

There were a dozen Duvics. They were clerks, personal aides, valets, and other underlings—not a soldier or security officer among them. As the three CSVB MechWarriors advanced on them, they gave way under the mere threat of violence. Lady Shu strode to the doors and threw them open herself.

Then she stopped in her tracks.

Minister Aaron Waterhouse, representative of and negotiator for the Duvic Palatine, lay on the floor of his chamber. He was tangled in his dressing gown. The rich carpet beneath was stained dark, and the stain was growing like a living thing.

Veck barged past Lady Shu. After a quick scan of the room, he knelt by the body.

"Dead," he announced. "Murdered."

There were gasps and outcries from the lady's attendants. She simply stared at the corpse and grew pale.

Veck ignored all that.

"Where are Crawford and Namihito?"

He shouted his question at the cowering Duvic functionaries, but no one had an answer for him.

"Not good," he concluded.

"It's going to get worse," Lady Shu predicted.

Everyone looked where she pointed. Clutched in the dead man's hands was a scrap of yellow-trimmed burgundy fabric in the exact shades of the County Shu livery colors.

22

Dori
Arousian Region, Epsilon Eridani
Chaos March
25 February 3062

Trish whispered in Romano Shu's ear, "The police have arrived, my lady. They have questions."

"Let them get in line."

Kelly looked at the two plainclothes officers in the doorway who were talking with the deceased minister's aides and trying to make sense of their excited babble. "How did they get here so fast?"

"Maybe they're just hotel security," JJ suggested.

"Even if that's all they are, they got here pretty quick." Kelly moved to the window, intending to see if there were any police cruisers on the street below. Fleeting reflections on nearby buildings indicated that vehicles with emergency lights were approaching, but so far none were parked in front of the hotel. As he pondered the situation, a lightning flash showed him something more ominous: a BattleMech moving several blocks over. The chunky humanoid shape was too big to be a *Commando*, so it wasn't Sam. Too big, too, to be the 48th's *Panther*.

It had to be the *Enforcer* or *Clint* belonging to Crawford's unit. He called Veck over and told the commander what he'd seen. Veck didn't waste any time trying to confirm Kelly's sighting.

"It's a set-up!" Unceremoniously, he grabbed Lady Shu's arm and started hustling her towards the door. "We've got to get you out of here. Now!"

The officers at the door objected to anyone leaving, and a hot argument ensued about noble license, diplomatic privilege, and the law. Kelly whispered his intent to JJ and got the lady's staff moving past the knot of disagreement and down the hall to the elevators. It was their good fortune that the "police" didn't notice until they'd gotten the last of the aides out of the suite. Lady Shu caught on quickly and turned her argument into a debating retreat. A shove from Veck removed one officer's restraining hand from the elevator door long enough for the doors to slide shut, but not before a last hurled threat of arrest and prosecution for leaving the scene of a crime joined them in the car for the ride to the lobby.

"They'll be adding assaulting an officer to the charges against you, Commander," predicted Romano Shu.

"I expect they will," Veck said calmly. "It won't mean anything if they don't catch me. Somebody has put a good bit of planning and arranging into this morning's affair. Best we can do to screw it up is to not cooperate. The truth will come out eventually. We need to make sure we're around to help it along."

"I fear that the commander is right." Kelly guessed that Lady Shu was speaking more for the benefit of her aides than herself. "Right now time and distance are our best allies. Getting wrapped up in legal coils is not to our benefit. We have to get out of this town and give the county's lawyers a chance to go to work. Commander Veck, I hope you have a plan to ensure that we remain at liberty."

"I'm working on it. The first thing we have to do is get out of this hotel without using lethal force on any of the supposedly neutral local authorities. If we're fast enough, and if the goons upstairs can't get a call through to have us cut off, we have a chance."

As it turned out the local police hadn't yet arrived. Kelly knew it wouldn't be long before they did. At Veck's sharp orders, he and JJ chivvied the civilians across the lobby and into their storm gear at the double quick. The MechWarriors' drawn sidearms discouraged any interference from the hotel staff. As they were cramming everyone back into the limousine, one of the aides balked and pointed.

"The police, my lady!" he shrieked.

"In!" Veck manhandled the aide to help him along.

But the man was right. The first cruiser, no more than its lights visible in the storm's gloom, had turned on to the street fronting the hotel. It was still blocks away, moving slowly, careful of the tempest. Apparently, no word had come down for them to hurry. Whether that was due to luck or the storm, Kelly didn't care. He figured that they might still get away before the oncoming police realized who they were. Then he caught a flaw in Veck's plan.

"The driver's still in the hotel."

"Then you drive," Veck said as he helped Lady Shu into the vehicle.

"What about the driver?"

"He's local. We leave him. We roll now." Veck shocked Kelly into motion with another, "Now!"

Kelly threw himself into the driver's seat and slammed the door. His action killed the overhead light and he promptly lost track of the controls. "Interior lights," he called, hoping that the vehicle's systems included a housekeeping computer. It did. A soft glow filled the driver's compartment, more than enough for him to find and identify controls. With a lurch, he got them rolling.

"Maybe I should drive," JJ said.

"Maybe you should just shut up." Kelly had too much to deal with to add JJ's smart remarks. "Be useful. See if they're stopping."

JJ cursed. "Lights didn't stop. They're following."

Kelly checked for himself. It looked like the police cruiser was picking up speed.

"Lose him," Veck ordered.

Kelly wondered how. The stretch limousine wasn't made for a high speed chase, and it certainly wouldn't take any tight cornering. Given the weather conditions, fancy maneuvers could be suicidal, seeing the road was hard enough. With the city in effective blackout, most of the light was what a vehicle threw out for itself, and that didn't go far. He was keeping tabs on the pursuit by its flashing lights. And there, perhaps, was the way.

Kelly killed the limo's lights, guided it to what he hoped was the center of the roadway, and accelerated. The limo did have power, and he didn't spare it. With luck, the cops behind them would presume that he'd gone dark to hide which way he turned. Certainly no one would just keep driving straight ahead when pursued by a faster vehicle.

If they were really lucky, they wouldn't ram something in the dark.

Kelly divided his attention between keeping the limo moving straight and steady down the wide boulevard, watching the rearview screen, and praying for deliverance. The police cruiser didn't take the first turn. To Kelly's relief and amazement, they took the next left. According to the limo's map screen, that would head them in the general direction of the hotel where the Lady Shu's embassy had been staying.

Kelly slowed to an only slightly insane speed for the conditions and snapped the lights back on. None too soon. He corrected the vehicle's course away from the curb they'd been approaching tangentially.

"What now?" Kelly looked at Veck in the rearview mirror. "We can't go back to our hotel; they'll have someone waiting."

"I never intended to go back," Lady Shu declared. "We go to the 'Mech park, to which I already sent the transport crew. Once there, we fire up the vehicles, and we leave this place."

"The transport moves out as soon as it's hot," Veck agreed. "I'll be escorting it, and Lady Shu rides in my jumpseat."

"I want to stay with my people."

"I want you inside the best armor we've got. It stinks, but I do anything else and the count will have my head. I'm not taking complaints on this. You got them, you give them to the count when I deliver you. Till then, you're a passenger. Got it?"

The lady's lack of response made it clear that she understood, but her expression promised Veck a bleak future. He didn't seem to notice.

"Kelly, Jurewicz, the rest of the lance is rearguard. You screen our exit. Buy us some time if necessary, but minimal contact with hostile forces."

"You sure one 'Mech's enough to guard the lady?" asked Kelly, as he turned a corner and came into sight of the 'Mech park. The sight of the giant machines standing stolid and uncaring in the driving rain raised his hopes, but didn't totally allay his fears. "If they come after you, you won't be able to fight them alone."

"The whole lance isn't enough, but we've got to play the hand we've been dealt. Maximum force to the rearguard; there's too much hostile tonnage out there for anything else. Kelly, it's your job to see that I get the lady out. Soon as you think we're clear, you cut and run. Head for Severagol unless you get other direction from headquarters. If the Duvics are attacking, the major will want all 'Mech forces to concentrate there. Got it?"

"Got it, sir."

An anxious Sam was waiting for them as they piled out of the limousine. "Slug says he thinks some of the Duvic 'Mechs are on the prowl."

"Old news," commented JJ. He filled her in on what had happened at Waterhouse's hotel before heading for his *Javelin*. Sam was ready to mount her own 'Mech, but Kelly held her back. Surely they had a few minutes for him to let her know how glad he was to see her again. Their clinch was interrupted as Veck slapped his shoulder.

"Damp it down. We've got work to do." Veck headed for his *Vindicator*, Lady Shu in tow. "Fire up the tin men. Lock and load."

Kelly and Sam ran for their machines. The scramble up the ladder almost ended his MechWarrior career when his foot slipped on a slick rung. A quick grab arrested his fall, but earned him a wrenched shoulder. He climbed more carefully after that. He reached the cockpit, entered his password while settling in, and began the start-up sequence.

The other 'Mechs were vague, blurry shapes in the storm, save for Veck's *Vindicator* standing beside his *Commando*. Kelly could see the commander helping a rain-drenched Lady Shu into the cockpit. She was now their mission. The political assignment had soured, and the honor guard had become bodyguards as the mission went military. No Warrior House pilot could have asked for a more clear cut, honorable task. No 'Mech combat soldier could have asked for a more romantic one. Kelly found himself floating in an odd mixture of satisfaction, calm, and trembling terror.

As the machines were warming to full operating capacity, Veck sketched his minimalist plan for Sam and Slug. With no new data, there wasn't any way to refine it, but now everyone had the same grasp of the situation. Once Veck got the ready from everyone, he started his 'Mech into a trot.

"Good luck, 'Jocks," he called as the transport swung behind him. 'Mech and ground vehicle vanished from sight behind the storm's veil. BattleMech sensors tracked them somewhat farther, before losing them in the clutter. Moments after the *Vindicator* faded from their screens, a new blip appeared. This one set off alarms.

"Bandit closing on us," Slug announced. That much everyone knew, but his *Raven*'s Beagle suite offered him additional data. "It's the *Pillager*."

"He got his buddies with him?" asked JJ.

"Don't wish for trouble," Sam adjured. "He's bad enough by himself."

"Magnetic field spiking!" Slug cut in. "He's loading the gauss!"

"Time to move." Kelly put his *Commando* into motion on reflex. His eyes snapped to the local map on his screen. They needed a rally point. *There!* "Boxly Park. In five. Move, move, move!"

'Mechs scrambled like a covey of bushquail spooked by a hunting dog. It wasn't coordinated. It wasn't pretty. But it must have worked. The *Pillager* didn't fire, having lost its targets.

Kelly suddenly realized that he had taken on his first unit command.

He also realized that they were a forlorn hope—in the worst sense—if they tangled with that hundred-ton monster.

Slug confirmed that the *Pillager* was trying to follow them.

23

Dori
Arousian Region, Epsilon Eridani
Chaos March
25 February 3062

The Vigilantes reassembled in Boxly Park. Sam was already there when Kelly arrived. Slug and JJ came in together, late but intact. Slug reported spotting the *Clint* and the *Enforcer* a dozen blocks to the west and moving north. The hostile 'Mechs had been going slowly, so his guess was that they were searching.

"But they're not headed after Veck. That suggests that they don't know where we are or what we're up to," Kelly concluded. "That's good."

"The Kuritans are unaccounted for," Sam reminded him.

"And they could be on Veck's trail. I know, I know. We've got the *Pillager* on our tail, and the rest of Crawford's people are stumbling around the city. If we can confirm that the Kuritans are looking for us and not Veck, our job will be half done.

"Survival is the key,.people. We don't have to beat the Doofvics today. They out-gun and out-mass us, but we're faster than most everything they have, and we have Slug's electronics to help us out. So we let them see us, then we scoot."

"We could gang up on one of their lights if we can get it alone," Sam suggested. "Get in a few good shots and let those Doofvics know they've poked a hornet's nest."

"Not our mission. I think drawing them east and south would be best. Once we get them following us, we work to spread them out enough that we can pick our point, cut through them, and break away. Till then we work in pairs. Sam, you're with me. And we don't get separated too far. Commo is too chancy in a city and the storm isn't making it better."

"Where do we start, boss?" asked JJ.

"We head for the 48th's vehicle park. That'll put plenty of distance between us and the *Pillager* even if he figures out that we're going that way."

"What about the Kuritans?"

"It should be safe. They'll be out looking for us. Now let's get moving before our hundred-ton friend lumbers his way here."

As it turned out, Kelly was wrong about the Kuritans. Both of their BattleMechs were still standing in the vacant lot that was their vehicle park. He didn't need Slug's "They're cold" to tell him that the two machines were not powered up. Even his *Commando*'s standard sensors could read the fact that neither the *Panther*'s nor the *Jenner*'s fusion hearts were up to operating temperatures. At least not fully. But it was plain that the pilots were aboard and getting their 'Mechs ready to move.

"I don't get it." JJ sounded as confused as Kelly felt. "Crawford's people were on the move immediately."

The reasons why didn't really matter at the moment. Sitting in front of them was a gift. The *Clint* and the *Jenner* had the potential to be their biggest headache since each was fast enough to catch Veck's *Vindicator* and big enough to give it a fight. Though Kelly had told the others that their mission didn't involve taking on the hostiles, here was a chance to catch the fastest of the hostile 'Mechs with its pants down. It was too good an opportunity to pass up.

"Target the *Jenner*," he told his lancemates. "We scratch it before we go after the *Panther*. Let's make sure they never get up and running."

JJ and Slug acknowledged as Sam whooped her enthusiasm.

Having given the order to fire, Kelly dropped his targeting crosshairs on the *Jenner*. A faint flicker of motion within the cockpit made him hesitate. The Kuritan aboard the *Jenner* was defenseless, but it was his side that had started this fight. He was a legitimate target.

Wasn't he?

His companions' energy weapons flashed. Missiles roared out.

Kelly's finger tugged on the trigger. His thumb stabbed down on firing buttons. His *Commando* shuddered as missiles launched. Heat flushed across his cockpit. It was a familiar sensation, and it sent a familiar feeling clawing icily down his spine.

The *Jenner* tottered under the pummeling it received. Twenty or more missiles ripped into its armored hide. At least three lasers tore past what remained of its armor and speared into its innards. Fires started, too hot for the rain to extinguish. The *Jenner* streamed and smoked. It tilted. It fell, crashing to the broken pavement.

Kelly tried not to think of the pilot who lay dead, or dying, or at least wounded in the wreck of his machine, but he couldn't do it. Duvorshak was the man's name. Kelly, however, imagined Stübel's face, screaming his pain.

There was a pause. Kelly's lancemates halted their fire, seemingly as stunned as he in seeing the sudden destruction they had wrought. The *Jenner* was wrecked. Kelly no longer saw any movement in the cockpit save the flicker of sparks and fire.

The lull ended as a PPC blast, wild lightning crackling around the ionized particles, came sizzling through the air. The *Panther's* pilot had gotten his machine on-line.

The shot caught Sam's *Commando* high on the torso. It went down in a cloud of steam and smoke.

"Sam!"

Kelly was terrified that she had been killed.

"Sam!"

There was no reassuring response.

JJ and Slug were engaging the *Panther*. Kelly knew he should be helping them but he shifted his machine in Sam's direction.

He had to know.

As he got closer, he could see that the *Commando* was still moving. It could only be so if Sam was still alive to direct it. The machine was scrabbling its leg against the pavement, as Sam tried to get it rolled over enough that she could use the arms to help push it upright. Kelly moved his *Commando* in to give it something to brace against, calling all the while to Sam.

She still didn't answer.

Once the *Commando* was on its feet again, she raised one battlefist to tap a finger against the machine's head in the ages-old gesture for a commo failure. Her signal indicated that she could still receive intermittently, though. He rocked his *Commando*'s head to signal that he understood even as he told her so.

Kelly could see that much of the left side of her *Commando*'s head had been torn up. Clearly her transmitter had been shredded. The shoulder assembly on that side had been mauled, too. It was affecting the arm, causing it to move jerkily, but her *Commando* ought to be able to fight on.

Apparently Sam was ready. She started the *Commando* toward the fight and gave him a "let's go" wave.

They ran their machines to support JJ and Slug. The Kuritan had cut across an alley to a main street. JJ was in close pursuit and Slug was racing down a parallel street. Kelly led Sam a block over then up another parallel. If they could surround the *Panther*, they had it.

The four-on-one fight should have been a foregone conclusion, even in the midst of the storm and the confines of the city, but it wasn't. The pilot of the *Panther* seemed to lead a charmed life. Time after time he just managed to avoid fire from the Vigilante 'Mechs. The way he broke target locks made Kelly think that the Panther had to be running some sophisticated electronic countermeasures, but Slug said it wasn't so.

"He's just a heck of a pilot."

If he wasn't using electronics, he was, indeed, a heck of a pilot. The Kuritan ducked his machine just as Kelly and Sam caught him in a laser cross fire. They nearly nailed each other with the beams. He cut behind a building just before a full flight of JJ's missiles reached his position. Most uncanny of all was that every time Slug tried to nail the *Panther* with a NARC beacon, the pilot grabbed cover or disappeared around a corner or sent enough fire down range that Slug ducked and covered himself, costing him the shot.

They did hit the Kuritan, though. With as much fire as they were pouring out, they had to. But they were only scratching him. The *Panther*'s fire was even less successful, but Kelly suspected that it wasn't because the *Panther* pilot was a poor shot.

Several times he had seen the Kuritan pass up clean shots at one or another of the Vigilantes. The *Panther*'s arm-slung particle projector cannon rarely spoke and when it did, it toppled a sign or a wall to dump debris in the path of an advancing Vigilante, forcing the machine to slow or pause. Inexplicably, the Kuritan never pressed any advantage, seemingly preferring fleeing over firing.

And so, the chase went on. The *Panther* moving wraithlike through storm and city, always one step ahead of them.

"What gives?" JJ wanted to know. "He's moving north and east."

"Yeah, why isn't he leading us back into his buddies?" Slug asked.

"Maybe he thinks he's drawing us away from ours," Kelly suggested.

"He's got to be wanting help from Crawford's 'Mechs," JJ predicted. "He can't take on the four of us."

Watching the eerily smooth motions of the *Panther* made Kelly wonder about that. If the Kuritan wanted help, why was he moving so fast in the wrong direction?

Kelly thought he knew. "Let's try something. Everybody halt."

The Vigilantes followed his order, but the Panther kept moving. The Kuritan didn't slow down to let them catch up or fire a shot to keep them in the fight.

"He's not leading us anywhere. He's trying to get away." Kelly felt they were lucky that was the case.

"Or we're where he wants us," JJ added.

"If it was a trap, he'd turn back on us. He's not badly hurt." Kelly felt sure of it. There was something else he was sure of as well. "But our little fracas will have almost certainly advertised our location to anyone who cares. That's good news and bad news. Good news: Crawford's people will be heading this way and not after Veck. More good news: I think we've bought the commander enough time, and we can give up on this soggy burgh. Bad news: we've got a longer road home."

The Kuritan had led them well out around the curve of Lake Arous. They had to move back south before they could cut west toward County Shu. Kelly shunted his plotted route to his lancemates. They hadn't been moving long when Slug commed.

"Heads up, everybody. Action on our seven."

In that direction, the fading flare of jump jets revealed a BattleMech incoming.

A burst of autocannon fire from their three announced another.

24

Dori
Arousian Region, Epsilon Eridani
Chaos March
25 February 3062

Kelly swiveled his *Commando*'s torso right, firing the chest-mounted Coventry launcher before the Artemis system had a solid lock. He didn't care. His main objective was to get the enemy's head down. Through the exhaust trail of the spiraling incoming missiles, he caught a glimpse of the opponent. It was the *Clint*. He raised his *Commando*'s arms, waited for the ping of the Streak system locking on, and gave the Duvic 'Mech a pair of SRMs and a blast from his laser. He didn't linger to gauge his accuracy. Starting his *Commando* moving, he snapped the torso back to its normal facing as he shouted, "Move! Cover!"

The Vigilantes scattered, Slug's *Raven* shedding armor plates. It had been the autocannon's target and the Duvic MechWarrior had scored on the *Raven*'s right leg. Sam didn't move with the rest. She stood and sent a flight of missiles at the *Clint*.

What did she think she was doing? "I said head for cover!"

This time her *Commando* moved to his command. Whether she hadn't heard his first order or had just ignored it to get a shot off at the enemy, he'd find out later. For now he sent a six-pack of his own missiles to cover her.

"Sam's got it right," JJ proposed. "We got another four-on-one, and I'm betting this *Clint* pilot isn't half the MechWarrior that Kuritan was. We can take him."

Maybe they could. The *Clint* was the other opposition machine that had a chance of overtaking the fleeing Veck and Lady Shu. Crippling or killing it would ensure the lady's escape. Unfortunately, JJ wasn't right about the odds. The jump jets that Slug had spotted meant there was another enemy within striking range. It could be the Kuritan returning in his *Panther*. The Kuritan's return wouldn't change the mass equation too badly, but it would shift the piloting equation far too much. It was strange to be thinking that they'd be lucky if the incoming 'Mech was the *Enforcer*. If it was, though, it would really be bad news, since that 'Mech massed as much as both *Commando*s combined. Worse, the unknown might be the *Pillager*, which would leave the Vigilantes hopelessly outclassed.

"Forget it," he told JJ. "Mission first. Covering fire only. We're moving out."

A thumbs-up from Sam's *Commando* signaled that she had gotten his orders. The Vigilantes moved out.

The *Clint* used its speed to dog them hard, but Kelly kept his people moving and using the city to shield them from the pursuit's fire. They took some hits, but it was all minor stuff, and BattleMechs were made to take a lot of punishment. The Vigilantes doled out some hits as well, but the *Clint* still came on. Its pilot wasn't easily discouraged. Still, Kelly figured they were doing well. They were covering ground, cutting across the northwest quadrant of Dori, and they seemed to have lost the other hostile among the maze of the city's buildings.

Until Slug called out, "Jets at one o'clock."

Kelly cursed. They hadn't evaded the jumping 'Mech. It had moved to cut them off. This time the unknown was close enough for Kelly to get a gauge on its mass as it landed, covered from their fire, behind a parking structure. It was a medium 'Mech, presumably the *Enforcer*, and that was trouble.

The Vigilantes moved in response, trying to get out from between the two hostiles. They weren't fast enough. Blue-tinged lightning ripped past JJ's *Javelin*.

The jumping 'Mech had fired a PPC. The *Enforcer* they'd seen didn't have a particle cannon, and the PPC-armed *Panther* wasn't a medium 'Mech. Kelly's momentary confusion almost sent his fast-moving *Commando* into an office building. So who was this new enemy?

No enemy at all, it turned out.

Veck's voice crackled on the lance circuit. "Trahn, Jurewicz, flank right. Kelly, Liu, flank left. We drive this dog back to her masters."

Kelly spun his *Commando* and triggered both launchers. JJ loosed a full volley as Slug used his paired lasers. Sam was a little slow in shifting over to the attack, but when she did, she unloaded everything onto the *Clint*'s position.

Like a hound whose quarry had suddenly transformed from running hare to enraged boar, the *Clint* backed away. The Vigilantes furious assault didn't score much damage as far as Kelly could see, but it turned the tables. The *Clint*'s pilot was happy enough to chivvy a gaggle of green MechWarriors, but facing a well-commanded lance was another matter. The *Clint* booked.

Veck didn't let them pursue the fleeing *Clint* very far. He halted the Vigilantes in a small plaza and called a conference. They cracked their cockpits so Sam could be in on the catching-up.

Veck told his side in short clipped sentences. Intermittent pick-ups from the civil broadcast network had informed him that there were BattleMechs fighting in Dori. Having gotten Lady Shu safely out of the city, he'd sent the transport on, as much as a decoy as to get the lady's staff to safety and stashed the lady herself in a safe place before coming back. He'd expected to find the lance in deep trouble. Kelly thought he detected concern in the old MechWarrior's voice, but knew better than to mention it. "Looks like you 'Jocks learned something after all. All right, Kelly, report."

Kelly followed Veck's example and kept it short and simple.

"Good work," Veck said of their handling of the Kuritans, but his mind wasn't on the past. "This hide-and-seek city fighting works into Crawford's strengths right now, and I won't play his game. We're going to get ourselves some open space and take advantage of our ground speed. We've still got a mission. Once we're clear, we secure the lady and head home. No unnecessary combat. Got it?"

They said so, loud and clear. Kelly was relieved to have Veck back in command. It felt right, the way it was supposed to be.

When everyone was buttoned up again, Veck turned them toward the lake. Slug reported the *Clint* shadowing them.

"She won't take us on alone," Veck assured them.

He was right. The *Clint* didn't close on them until Slug reported a new contact, an incoming medium 'Mech landing atop a three-story building to their front. This time the jumper really was a hostile, and it had cut them off. Laser and autocannon fire poured down on the Vigilantes as the *Enforcer* joined the *Clint*'s attack.

Veck wasn't having a stand-up fight.

"Cut south," he ordered.

The Vigilantes found themselves in another running gun battle. Under Veck's direction, they worked the cover that the city offered, all the while trying to edge back toward their intended route. Veck himself stood rear guard, sending PPC blasts and the occasional laser pulse at the enemy to keep them at bay.

Kelly thought it was fortunate that Crawford's people were as reluctant as the Vigilantes were to come in for a serious brawl. Maybe they'd had their own version of

Veck's lessons on what damage to your 'Mechs meant in a campaign, and a campaign was what they were going to get now that the element of surprise was lost.

The winding roads of this quarter of the city tended to weave and thread across the wide boulevards that made up the main arteries. It meant the Vigilantes were rarely out of sight of each other for long. Kelly saw Slug's *Raven* as it came racing among the trees of one of Dori's innumerable small parks to join him. Veck's *Vindicator* appeared at the mouth of an alley. As Sam and JJ moved into the park, the *Enforcer's* shadow flickered across a wall of one of the boundary buildings. Veck's particle cannon spoke and the shadow drew back.

"Through this park to West Shore Boulevard," Veck ordered. "We can use the boulevard to cut back to the warehouse district. There'll be faster going alongside the lake."

West Shore was a true parkway, its broad median strip filled with trees and decorative plantings. The sodden vegetation whipped in the storm's winds, seemingly waving good-bye to the passing 'Mechs.

Without warning, Slug's *Raven* exploded. One leg cartwheeled away as thirty-five tons of unguided missile that used to be a BattleMech plowed into the boulevard's trees in a spray of splintered wood, fragmented armor, and shredded machine parts. The fireball disintegrated stately oaks in bursts of superheated steam. Lasers clawed into the twitching wreck. More explosions sent parts of the *Raven* into the wind-driven rain on tails of sizzling smoke.

Stunned, Kelly staggered his *Commando* to a halt. "Harry?"

There was no answer. Nor would there ever be.

Numb, Kelly looked for the killer. The *Pillager*, author of the lethal destruction, stood a dozen blocks away on West Shore, recycling its weapons. The wide avenue gave the monstrous 'Mech a perfect firing lane.

"Scatter, scatter, scatter," Veck ordered the lance. "Reform on the other side of the lake."

On reflex, Kelly heaved the *Commando* into motion.

The other Vigilantes were obeying Veck's orders as well, evacuating the boulevard.

The *Pillager* reacted to the sudden scramble, charging toward them. Kelly stowed the rendezvous coordinates Veck sent and dodged left, looking for cover. The *Pillager* fired its gauss rifles again. The magnetically driven slugs tore the air, but failed to score against the rapidly moving Vigilantes. Bricks and shattered concrete pelted Kelly's *Commando*. Lasers dug into the buildings beside him. Only his quick response to Veck's command had saved him from the enemy's shots. He hoped the other Vigilantes would be as lucky.

The *Pillager* stalked the lake shore, firing occasionally. Its long-range armament let it rake any target that showed itself along the shore, as Kelly learned when paired ferrous-nickel shells nearly caught him trying to use the shore to make time. He barely avoided Trahn's fate. Shrapnel from the building that had caught the shells peppered his armor. Raking beams from the *Pillager*'s laser array slammed into the *Commando*'s left arm. Armor exploded. The impact spun his machine around. Kelly tried, but he couldn't keep the *Commando* upright. It toppled, smashing hard on the pavement and slamming his head against one of the cockpit's structural members. The neurohelmet kept his skull in one piece, but only barely. He forced the pain aside and, groggy, fought his way upright. He stumbled the machine forward, barely managing to avoid another gauss round as he ducked back under cover. The *Commando* paid his ticket to safety with more armor lost to flying debris.

After that, he traded away the speed that the shoreline offered for the cover the waterfront buildings afforded. He pressed on, losing track of his lancemates. From time to time his external mikes picked up the supersonic crack of the *Pillager*'s gauss rifles firing. Someone had attracted fire. He prayed that it wasn't Sam, but whoever it was, he hoped that they stayed lucky. He tried the lance channel, but the storm and the city weren't letting the separated 'Mechs communicate. He thought about trying to see who was taking fire, but didn't go. There was still the mission, and that required survival. So he did his best to avoid giving the killer 'Mech another chance at him. He couldn't afford to expose the *Commando* if he wanted to reach the rendezvous point.

The shot he'd taken had ripped away nearly all the armor sheathing the *Commando*'s arm and torn up a significant amount of the internal structure. The *Commando*'s laser was out of commission, and he was reading intermittent malfunctions on several activators. Armor was down fifty percent or more in most locations. Veck wouldn't approve. Kelly's battered *Commando* was hurting, but at least it was still functional, and he concentrated on keeping it that way while heading for Veck's rendezvous point.

He was congratulating himself on managing to do it as he reached the rally point. Until he counted heads. Only Veck's *Vindicator* and JJ's *Javelin* were present.

"Where's Sam?"

Kelly's heart chilled as he remembered the banshee scream of the *Pillager*'s gauss rifles echoing across the lake.

25

World Spine Mountains
Arousian Region, Epsilon Eridani
Chaos March
25 February 3062

"We have to presume she went down," Veck said heartlessly.

"No!" Kelly protested. "Her commo was out. Maybe she's trying to get back to us. We need to—"

"What we need to do is be realistic. If Liu is still operating, she will join us when she can. Meanwhile, we have a job to do. We can't afford to go back into that slaughterhouse to get her. It's time to be a soldier, Kelly. We move on before the Duvics catch us. You got me?"

Kelly mumbled his affirmative reply. Mercifully, Veck didn't demand he repeat it with enthusiasm.

The surviving Vigilantes headed their 'Mechs away from Dori and through the verdant shore region and out into the foothills of the World Spine Mountains north of Lake Arous. It was rough country, much broken up by valleys and canyons, many of which were inundated by the storm's water. They avoided the worst of the flooding and crossed the numerous tempest-frenzied streams where they could. It wasn't an easy passage and the dying storm made it no easier. The trek was a test of their piloting skills. Fortunately, no one failed.

Though Kelly kept checking, he saw no sign of Sam following them. But there was no sign of the Duvic 'Mechs either. They had achieved their escape.

At what cost?

The storm was finally ebbing by the time they reached the old minehead where Veck had stashed Lady Shu. She emerged from her shelter as the 'Mechs stomped into the narrow-mouthed canyon. The rain-laced wind whipped her coiffure into disarray but did nothing to dampen her regal composure as she greeted the dismounting MechWarriors. She listened gravely to Veck's synopsis of the action, giving Kelly a sympathetic glance when the commander described their losses.

Kelly and JJ both set up the two-man shelters from their 'Mechs' emergency kits. Veck's was already up and in use by Lady Shu. Dinner was ration meals. Veck set JJ on first watch, posting him high on the canyon wall where he could command the approaches to their hiding place. Then he snagged a commo unit for himself and headed for even higher ground.

"With the storm blowing itself out, I should be able to get through to command. Either way, we're moving out at first light. Get some rest."

Veck's suggestion was good. Lady Shu retired to her shelter, but Kelly didn't bother. He knew he wouldn't be sleeping. He huddled by the dying cookfire, seeing images of death and destruction in the flames, but unwilling to give up its faltering warmth. When there was little more than embers, he heard a soft footfall behind him. It was Lady Shu.

"Couldn't sleep," she said sheepishly.

"I know what you mean."

Lady Shu settled beside him. She was a warm, comforting human presence that reminded him that he was alive. Still, he couldn't quite shake the chill that shrouded his feelings about the day's events. He got the feeling that she would understand. He wanted to talk to her about it, but he didn't know how to start. She sat, quiet and undemanding, until he found his voice.

"It's cold, isn't it?"

The lady slid closer and laid a comforting hand on his leg. "It is always hard to lose comrades."

Her instant understanding touched him. It also pointed to a hard knot of emotion that was twisting inside him. She had said "comrades." First, Stübel. And now, today . . . As much as he hated to admit it, he had begun to see that his father was right. He really hadn't understood what was at stake. But he was beginning to.

Something else was bothering him too. Two Vigilantes had fallen today, but Kelly didn't have the same reaction to both losses. He ought to, oughtn't he? "I saw Harry go down. We were friends. I feel bad but not as bad as . . . I've known him a lot longer."

"You will mourn for him. I think the difference you feel is because Samantha Liu was more than a comrade."

"Yeah." He felt a little odd admitting that to the lady. "Veck tried to warn me to stay away from her."

She gave him a sad smile. "I think Commander Veck was looking out for you. He can be crude and awkward at times, but his heart is kind. Not that he would be happy to hear me say such a thing to one of his soldiers, but I think it is important for you to know. He has lived a MechWarrior's life for a long time. He knows that to lose a comrade is a hard blow, and that to lose a lover is harder still. To lose both in a single person can be shattering."

Kelly was getting a first-hand taste of that. "I feel like maybe I should have done something more, something different."

"You did all that you could, and all that could be expected of you."

"Maybe it should be me lying back there in the wreck of my machine."

"You must not blame yourself because you survived, and they did not. It is as it is. You must embrace life, for if you turn your back on life, you make their sacrifice meaningless." Lady Shu spoke with pure and utter conviction. "I cannot believe that you think so little of them."

"I don't—I mean, think little of them." He couldn't dishonor their memory, could he? "I just keep thinking that—"

She put a finger to his lips. "No. You will put this behind you."

"I can't forget her!"

"Of course not. You won't forget Harry Trahn either. Your feelings honor you and them. Accept your loss, but accept life as well."

She leaned against him, putting her head on his shoulder. Her presence was comforting, a strong, warm reminder of life. They sat quietly for a while, Kelly soaking in her vitality. Feeling her beside him made him understand that he *was* alive. He had survived his first combat. Life was indeed going to go on. *He* was going to go on.

"Strange, isn't it?" she said dreamily.

"What?"

"I could not sleep thinking of all that has happened, and dreading all that is to come. My tent was so empty that it seemed to echo my very breathing, and I came here looking for a little company and, perhaps, a strong shoulder that I might lean on for a moment, and instead I find myself being such a shoulder."

"Thanks," he said. His response was clumsy and blunt, but he hoped that she understood that it was heartfelt. He wished he could do the same for her. This wasn't the sort of situation he was used to. After all, what did he have to offer to a high-born lady? "I, uh, I can listen."

"A kind offer, and I thank you for it, but not now I think." She sighed, long and soulfully.

Tentatively, he put his arms around her. She melted into them. Slowly, her scent filled his head. She looked up into his face, and he down into hers. He saw need there, desire too. He felt it himself. Her lips parted. His dipped to meet them. Their kiss was hungry, eager after the spark of life, seeking to reaffirm the truth of it.

"The tent," she suggested when they came up for air.

Hand in hand they scrambled into his shelter. Fingers

fumbled in the dark, finding, losing, and finding again, in a needy, impatient rush.

"I think," she said, opening the first clasp on his cooling vest. "That perhaps you should call me Romano." Adding as she opened the last clasp, "At least when we are alone."

He finally did call her Romano and she smiled in that tense-abandoned way that one has in ecstasy.

He was alone when JJ woke him for his turn on watch.

"Where is she?" he mumbled.

"Who?"

"Ro—Lady Shu."

"In her shelter. Why?"

"I, er, just wanted to make sure she was safe."

"Dreaming again?"

Could it have been a dream? No, her scent still lingered. It hadn't been a dream.

Kelly sat his watch through the waning night, unable to grasp all that had happened in the last twenty-four hours. Luckily, exhaustion spared him his torturous thoughts.

Finally, a gaunt-faced Veck called him down as the sky started to gray. The commander had indeed gotten through to headquarters, but the only report he gave his lance was "things don't look good." All else was reserved until Lady Shu finished her conference with the capital. Then the whip cracked, and the MechWarriors scrambled to make what few field repairs they could. They needed to be ready to fight. After all, who knew what the day would bring?

When Lady Shu returned, she looked tired, but she still offered him a small, private smile. It was a sad smile and something about it struck Kelly as odd. She asked for a moment to speak to him.

"Samantha is alive," she said. "Captured."

Kelly started to say something, what he wasn't sure because his brain was awhirl. Romano put a finger to his lips.

"No. Don't say anything you will regret." She caressed

his cheek. "And don't regret anything that you've done. I don't."

"But Sam—"

"Need never know. We must step into the roles that the fates decree for us, even when they hand us parts we do not care to play, and that they have done."

He looked into Romano's sad eyes. He felt the brief touch of her hand as she offered him a resigned smile. Then she called the others over and transformed into the brisk and efficient Lady Shu.

"A state of war now exists between Duvic Palatinate and County Shu," she announced. "Severagol is indeed under attack. Fighting has been intense, but the situation is undecided. There have been other attacks as well. Minor in scope, but they've hurt us. County Shu has been rocked, but we have not been taken out of the fight.

"Our dear, sweet president is doing nothing but calling for more negotiations." Lady Shu smiled bitterly. "I suppose we should be grateful that he's not siding with the Duvics. They are claiming that we started this mess. That we assassinated Commissioner Waterhouse. That we fired the first shots."

"How can that be?" JJ wondered. "Their 'Mechs were hunting us before we found out Waterhouse was dead."

"ENN is running footage showing comital BattleMechs firing on Duvic 'Mechs that are not yet up and running. A *Jenner* was completely destroyed. Sound familiar?"

"Someone caught us taking on the Kuritans."

"Exactly."

"But Crawford had already come after us," Kelly protested.

Lady Shu scowled. "*That* doesn't seem to have been recorded."

PART 3

Command
Burden

26

**Port Tsing
County Shu, Epsilon Eridani
Chaos March
26 February 3062**

The intercom sounded with its well-bred and ever so annoying chime, making Gabriel Shu look up at the clock, fearful that it was time for his meeting with the council. It wasn't. He tapped the intercom button.

"What is it, Pierson?"

"You said that you wanted to know when Lady Shu and her escort reached the city, your excellency. They are entering the eastern gate now."

The good news cracked the shell of his funk. When the first garbled reports of fighting in Dori had come in, he'd known something had gone terribly wrong with her peace mission. He'd feared for her safety, especially when word came that Minister Waterhouse had been murdered and that she was missing. The little bits of data leaking through the storm-disrupted communications only confused things, making visions of revived Capellan unification plots and anti-autocrat uprisings race through his head. And then the word of the invasion had come.

The turmoil, confusion, and outright panic that had swept through the county and especially through his government, was appalling.

Dear Lord, he'd missed having his sister at his side these last few hectic days.

When he'd first heard that she had escaped the fighting in Dori, he'd been relieved. Of course, hard on the heels of that news had come word that Palatine Price was calling for a full investigation into Waterhouse's murder and what she called "the County Shu connection." *Infamous!* Though Price didn't name names, she hinted at high level persons being involved, which could only mean that Price wanted Romano blamed for the crime. It was utter nonsense, but Price's rhetoric roused the fears of the anti-autocrat factions, something that didn't seem difficult on Epsilon Eridani in these post-Federated Commonwealth days. They stood in real danger that reason might lose out to unwarranted fear. What *was* the woman thinking? She didn't seem to appreciate how dangerous her assertions were to the underlying framework of the planet's political structure. Did she truly think that the autocratic governing system was useless? Hadn't it served the planet well for centuries?

One thing she and he agreed upon was the need for an investigation, but one didn't need to rouse a rabble to get an investigation started. Price spoke as though Gabriel was trying to stop it and seemed to be making the masses believe her, but reality was quite to the contrary. He didn't have Price's knack for playing the media, but he'd put in his own request that President Benton urge the Dori authorities to expedite the matter. No matter who the guilty party, it was best for everyone that the murderer be exposed. Sure as he was that the villain wasn't any of his people, he felt that when that truth came out, a lot of the wind would go out of the Duvic sails. People might even see Price for the slanderous troublemaker she was.

But that was for the future. The present held Romano's return.

At Romano's insistence, the three BattleMechs had

been cleared to enter the palace grounds. She intended to arrive home as she had been spirited from the disaster in Dori. Roads cleared for the machines and crowds encouraged to attend to make a better picture for the media. After all, this was the triumphant return of rescuers, saviors of the county's designated heir. There would be no slinking, and the soldier heroes would be celebrated, no matter what sort of insidious defamatory distortions anti-Shu factions might put on it.

Gabriel, accoutered in ceremonial robes, met them in the courtyard. On the steps of the Summer Palace, he stood beaming as the BattleMechs clanked and rumbled into line. Cockpits opened and access ladders rolled down. The three surviving MechWarriors scrambled down as nimbly as monkeys. Romano appeared a moment later. Gabriel noticed that Romano had managed to have her hair dressed so that just a hint of her wild adventure showed. She waved to the crowd (and the cameras), and made her own way down the ladder.

Suppressing his desire to hug her, he greeted her formally. She played into his chosen presentation, showing herself to be every bit the proper lady despite the unladylike military uniform she affected. She introduced her rescuers simply as MechWarriors of the County Shu Volunteer Battalion, and he greeted them, naming them "heroes to the Shu family."

Commander Veck led his soldiers in a traditional bow, before saluting and saying, "We were just doing our job, your excellency."

"Your devotion and sacrifice is beyond simply 'doing your job.' You will be rewarded, all of you."

One of the three soldiers looked unhappy. His name tag read 'Kelly.' "You have a concern, Subcommander Kelly?"

"Has there been any further word on Subcommander Liu, sir?"

Gabriel looked over the earnest, but nervous, soldier. Subordinates were often nervous when speaking to the count for the first time, but this man's eyes shifted away from Gabriel's stare with unusual frequency. Gabriel noted that the MechWarrior's mobile eyes alit often on Romano. She seemed not to notice.

"Beyond her capture and injuries," he told the soldier, "we have heard nothing certain."

"Injuries? What injuries?"

"I am not certain. Pierson, get the information for Subcommander Kelly."

"At once, your excellency," Pierson said in his best put-upon grumble.

"And no dawdling," Romano added.

"Indeed," Gabriel agreed. "This man has earned our regard. Easing his concerns is the least we can do. Come. We will speak more inside."

As they stepped into the portico's shadow, a voice called to him. "Your excellency?"

"You, too, Commander Veck?" At least the officer had waited until the media glare was averted. "What can I do for you?"

"Approve my request for compensation to Subcommander Trahn's family."

"Trying to take advantage of my good mood, Commander?"

"If that's what it takes, your excellency. Dead men have little use for medals, and their families have less. Harry Trahn earned better."

"As, I am sure your formal report will bear out. Pierson, see to that as well."

Pierson, apparently infected by the rampant outspokenness, started to protest. "But the council needs to—"

"The council needs a lot of things, but Commander Veck's request needs only my approval. Make payment from the private fund until the council approves drawing the funds from the public accounts."

Gabriel's statement seemed to make the soldiers happy, and so he contrived to leave them that way, excusing himself and his sister. He hoped he'd feel happy about what he had ordered after he wrangled out the details with the council. The members of which, Pierson reminded him, were awaiting his pleasure. Romano raised an eyebrow as he shooed the disgruntled Pierson away. The council members would not be in a good mood with him delaying the meeting, but his pleasure was to speak with Romano first. He pulled her into a private drawing room.

"The meeting sounded pressing," she observed.

"Everything is these days." And he was tired of it. "But, you know, what I fail to fathom is why, if everything is so pressing, is so very little actually happening?"

"This war is no little thing."

"I didn't mean to say it was. I meant how the war is going. Last week Duvic forces attacked at several places along our border, focusing on Severagol. This week Duvic forces are sitting still, though they are still attacking in Severagol. Oh yes, and we are counter-attacking. But you know, Colonel Bua's maps look little different than they did last week."

"That doesn't sound right. I was told that the Volunteer Battalion had been sent to the front. Surely, with nearly half the Duvic 'Mechs chasing me around Lake Arous, the estimable Major Ling-Marabie has achieved something with her locally superior forces."

Gabriel sighed. "I expected as much myself when I dispatched the major's BattleMech force after the first reports of hostile action, but so far the Major has declined to commit her troops decisively. Something about strategic imperatives that I don't quite grasp when she explains it. To tell the truth, I think she has lost her nerve and become overly cautious, especially since the Old Guard was rebuffed nearly as soon as she sent them in. We are fortunate that the Duvic forces are showing no real aggressive tendencies. On the whole, it appears that we are settling into a protracted siege situation. Which, I might add, is how I feel about council meetings lately."

"I can imagine. You are planning on getting me back up to speed, aren't you?"

"If you don't have something better to occupy your time."

She shrugged. "Nails. Facial. Hair. A real, long, hot bath and a massage. The usual affairs of state."

He laughed along with her. It was indeed good to have her back.

"Before you get down to the big business, my brother, let us start with some more trivial honesty. You were holding back something when you told Kelly about Subcommander Liu. Are her injuries, perhaps, worse than you let on?"

"It's not that at all."

"If not that, then what?"

"I'm afraid it is what you might call 'big business.' The Duvic Palatine is holding Liu, not the Arousian authorities. They allege she is a criminal, having killed a Duvic soldier prior to the commencement of hostilities. They refuse to turn her over to neutral authorities until they are assured that she will be tried. We, of course, have been insisting that she is a prisoner of war and not subject to criminal trial."

"And this has all gone before our dear, sweet president?"

Romano's flat, angry tone made her question a statement, but he answered it anyway. "It has. Benton is temporizing, giving Colonel Bua and Major Ling-Marabie something to agree upon. They both say that Benton will stay sitting on the fence, not wanting to be on the bad side of whoever comes out on top in our struggle with Duvic."

"Picking no side might be worse for him than picking the loser," she said in the chilling tone of a threat.

"Nevertheless, he is trying to avoid playing favorites. For example, the remains of Liu's *Commando* and Trahn's *Raven* are to be returned to us at Benton's insistence and against the claims of Palatine Price. At the same time, the dead mercenary's *Jenner* goes back to Duvic, as the employer of record. Neither side is being allowed to claim salvage rights on its kills."

"That would seem to legitimate Price's claim that the skirmish was not part of the war and to open Liu to the criminal charges. Kelly won't be happy when he hears."

Again she referred to the MechWarrior without his rank. Gabriel recalled the handsome face and tall, lean body. "Subcommander Kelly was rather solicitous of you. He was the person Veck left in charge when he spirited you from Dori, was he not?"

"Yes."

The brevity of her answer surprised him. She was rarely so laconic unless—"Now you seem concerned over his concerns. Another conquest?"

"Not exactly."

"What does that mean?"

"I don't know," she replied, gazing off into the distance.

"I think I understand," he said.

She turned and gave him the smile that said he didn't have a clue as to what was going on in her head.

27

Shu-Duvic Border
Epsilon Eridani
Chaos March
27 February 3062

Veck's Vigilantes—what was left of them—moved out almost immediately to join the rest of the County Shu Volunteer Battalion at its new forward base, but not before JJ managed to scrounge up the skinny on why Sam hadn't been returned to County Shu. It left Kelly with a serious mad on, and he took it out on any Duvic soldier who came under his guns when the unit headed out for a sweep of the surrounding countryside. The ground-pounders of the 17th Duvic Militia were no exception.

Men scattered as the *Commando* stalked into the dell that had been their camp site. Ferro-fibrous armored feet ripped through shelters, kicked over sand-bagged revetments, and trampled emplaced weapons—and their crews. Articulated battlefists snatched communication arrays and, with the immense strength of myomer pseudomuscles, shoved vehicles over on their sides or backs, leaving them as helpless as stranded fish. SRM launchers spat their deadly flights. The Defiance B3M swept ravening beams of ruby fire across anything that crossed Kelly's path.

The Duvic infantry were Lilliputians to his maddened Gulliver. The groundpounders were armed with little that could harm a 'Mech. And, barring a lucky shot, what they had would do little more than flake off a few armor plates.

Kelly knew that well. He'd been a groundpounder once.

When he saw the SRM teams scrambling to set up their launchers, he recognized one of the few threats the infantry had to offer. He didn't give them a chance. His own launchers spewed death, and the infantry teams disappeared in explosions, fireballs, and rising clouds of acrid smoke.

"Mr. Chill," JJ called. He was commo relay, needed because the lance was strung out in the disruptive hills. "Veck says we got 'Mechs incoming."

"How many?"

"Two. Both of them lights."

"Let them come. We'll serve them the same as we dished out here."

"Veck wants us to close up."

Kelly surveyed the smoke-shrouded hell he'd made of the camp. It was quiet now. Nothing moved, save a few wounded gropos crawling for cover.

"Sure. Why not? I'm done here anyway."

Veck's reports guided them in toward his position. He identified the hostiles as a *Panther* and a *Firefly*, probably the Kuritans, and in short order reported exchanging fire with them. Nothing serious, though. The Kuritans were being cautious, quite reasonable for two light 'Mechs taking on a medium. As soon as they picked up the weapons fire on their external microphones, Kelly suggested JJ jump his *Javelin* to a vantage point and try for a visual.

"We want to get the drop on them if we can," he added.

The *Panther* was nearest. JJ gave Kelly a vector, but before Kelly could close, something spooked the Kuritan. The *Panther* backpedaled and Kelly barely caught a glimpse of it disappearing behind a hillock. The Vigilantes mounted a pursuit, but couldn't manage to close with either of the Kuritan mercenaries.

Veck called off the chase, but when he set the lance back toward their patrol route, the Kuritans reversed again and closed. The Vigilantes turned to give battle, but the hostiles gave way again, refusing to be engaged.

Three times the farce played out before Veck called a halt to all attempts to fight the mercenaries. Kelly protested, but Veck shut him down.

"We are not going to give them any more satisfaction." There was a hint of grudging admiration in Veck's voice as he added, "Bastards. We chase them, they run. We go back to our mission, they follow and we can't cover much ground because if we separate, they'll pounce. And if we get involved in anything halfway serious, they'll be sitting there on our butts."

"Well, they're not accomplishing anything either," JJ said.

"Aren't they? They're tying down three 'Mechs with two."

"What about splitting and suckering them into a trap?" Kelly suggested.

Veck thought it worth trying, which they did, but the Kuritans didn't bite.

"Doesn't really surprise me," Veck admitted. "Namihito's not stupid."

The Vigilantes went back to their sweep. They covered ground, but not as much as they could have, saddled as they were with maintaining a tight formation. The Kuritans shadowed them all day, always close, but never close enough to put under the gun. Eventually it was time to head back to the barn. The Kuritans departed at some point—Kelly wasn't sure when—and the Vigilantes marched into the CSVB base camp.

There was mail waiting. Now that they were at war, the Phantom Major's training camp censorship had been replaced by general censorship. They were allowed to see the news, and some letters got through, though from his sister's messages, it was clear that not all his letters made it home, and those that did probably didn't include everything he'd written. But today, all Kelly had waiting was a note under the county seal.

"Count Shu seeking your advice again?" quipped JJ.

"No. It's from Lady Shu. She's apologizing for not being able to get Sam released."

Kelly wasn't sure what to make of the contents or even the fact of the letter. He was sure that he felt a little queasy about his night with Ro—Lady Shu. Sure, he'd believed Sam dead at the time, but Sam wasn't dead. Lady Shu had done the proper thing, the noble thing, and pretended that what had happened between her and Kelly had never happened. But she hadn't seemed happy about doing so. Honestly, Kelly wasn't happy about it either, but he wasn't clear on why he wasn't happy. Romano had been so—well, maybe it wasn't good to think about that. Now Lady Shu seemed to be in charge of the negotiations to free Sam. Could the lady be facing her own conflict of interests?

"I wish I knew what was really going on in the Palatine."

"So do we all, Mr. Chill. I'll see what I can do."

What JJ could do was scrounge up a broadcast receiver and, with a little judicious tuning, rig the command hut's commo unit to dump Duvic public airwaves into it.

Kelly soon found himself remembering the old saw about being careful of what one wished for.

Most of what they picked up was Duvic propaganda, which brought derisive jeers from the MechWarriors and techs that gathered around the receiver. That was fine. In fact Kelly was quite enjoying it until they hit on a speech by Palatine Price. Playing split-screen with the politician's harangue was footage of the Vigilantes' attack on the Kuritan bivouac in Dori. Price went on about how it was a criminal act and how it had taken place before any Duvic troops had violated the county border, and the date-time stamp on the footage backed her up.

"The true criminal in this matter is the Shu officer who ordered the massacre," said Price as though she were speaking directly to the comital soldiers. "That is his BattleMech you see firing first on the recording. We have learned through sources, which cannot now be revealed for fear of reprisals, that the criminal officer is one Tybalt Kelly. This criminal is still serving in the County Shu military. He has actually received a medal from Count Shu for his actions in this crime. Instead of punishment this killer is receiving acclamation. Indeed, he is about to be—"

"Shut that thing off!"

Like mice before a pouncing cat, the soldiers scattered as Veck stomped in and executed his own command. Only Kelly and JJ stood their ground. JJ tried to laugh off the Duvic accusation. Kelly looked to Veck.

"What do you think, Commander?"

Dour faced, Veck shrugged. He snatched up the receiver and tucked it under his arm. "What do I think? I think that we don't need to be listening to this crap. We know who the real bad guys are. We'll fight. We'll win. And none of this will matter."

"The Whipmaster seems pretty sure we're coming out on top in this one," JJ whispered as the commander departed.

"If he's not worried, I don't see why I should be," said Kelly, willing himself to believe it.

28

Kelly sat in the cockpit of his *Commando*, waiting. Over two weeks of patrolling and very little actual combat were wearing on him. Count Shu was willing to confine the fighting to military objectives, but the Duvic 'Mechs were rarely seen. It had turned into a frustrating game of hide and seek.

The morning sun was creeping above the distant mountains, beginning its daily effort to heat everything to uncomfortable levels, but for the moment the day was cool. Not that Kelly could feel it, cocooned inside his cockpit. The live fusion engine beneath him spread its heat through the 'Mech like the morning's coffee had done for Kelly himself, and like the sun, the reactor was only getting started for the day. There would come a time when he would crave a bit of cool air, but for now he could sit comfortably, his cooling vest inactive. Once Kelly would have thought such a moment was one to be savored, or to use for a warrior's meditation. Today, he sat beneath his racked neurohelmet, wishing to be about the day's business. He chafed at the constrictive snugness of his restraining harness, reminding him as it did of the restrictions placed around everything in his life. He wanted to be out and moving. Doing something. Sitting still gave him too much time to think and thinking led him down dark and disturbing paths. Action was what he needed. When the Vigilantes went into action, he didn't have time to fret.

He considered running a systems check, but the last three hadn't differed save for a minuscule rise in overall temperature. There seemed little point in getting another report on another tiny and inconsequential change. He did it anyway. The button pushing offered the barest of welcome distractions.

He was contemplating another check when JJ's voice came over the lance circuit.

"Any idea what's holding up the Whipmaster?"

"Haven't a clue," he grumped. "Captain Lazlo pulled him aside as we were leaving the briefing hut."

"Yeah, I saw that. Must be some serious war news to hold up the commander for so long."

Wasn't it all serious news? "We shouldn't be doing this."

"Doing what, exactly?" JJ asked, confused.

"Fighting Duvic."

"And why not? We're the soldiers, remember? We fight the wars."

JJ's tone was unsuitably jaunty and irritated Kelly. "We shouldn't be at war. Duvic is a state of Epsilon Eridani just like County Shu. We're part of the same nation. We shouldn't be fighting each other."

"And we've got some divine exemption from civil war just because we're all from Epsilon E? The politicos are in charge, my friend, and when they disagree, it's fighting for me and thee."

"Civil war isn't right."

"Hey, the Great Houses of Steiner and Davion are headed by siblings, and they do it. Well, maybe that's not such a good example. Their fracas is more of a family squabble, than a real war."

"What makes it not a real war? Aren't people dying? You bet they are. That makes it just as real as our war," Kelly complained. "We're all Eridani. We're supposed to be under one government, aren't we? Aren't we supposed to be one, big, happy political family?"

JJ snorted a laugh. "Ah, the naïveté of the dedicated soldier. So, tell me. You never wanted to kill your brother?"

"I don't have a brother."

"Your sister, then."

"Not for real," said Kelly, despite having made numerous threats of mayhem up to and including murder. "I'm serious."

"You're serious, all right," JJ agreed, shifting to a serious tone himself. "But we're not arguing about what's worrying you."

"What do you know about what's worrying me?" snapped Kelly.

"You're afraid Sam won't be coming back."

And wondering what it will be like if she does. "Yeah."

"Listen, Mr. Ch—Listen, Kelly, we're all afraid for Sam. Best we can do is what Veck says. We win this thing and everything will turn out okay. You'll see. Too bad we don't have one of their MechJocks so we could do a trade. At least it would give us a better hand to play in the negotiations."

It might at that, but Kelly had been made very aware lately that wanting what you didn't have wasn't a way to sleep well at night. "Hard to win a war when the enemy won't stand and fight and your own commanders won't let you go pry them out."

"Opportunities may soon present themselves," JJ said in his best fortune cookie voice. "Look."

Veck was crossing the field towards his *Vindicator.*

The commander was in no hurry to get underway. Neither was he receptive to questions about the delay. Kelly sat. He rechecked his systems yet again. The *Commando* was every bit as ready for action as it had been all morning. If anything, Kelly was more ready.

The lances of CSVB's Second Company moved out. Even First Company's other lance, Lazlo's Old Guard, usually the last to be sent on patrol, marched into the wilderness, but Veck's Vigilantes remained sitting in base camp. They had companions in idleness, of course; Third Company had once again been assigned as strategic reserve, which in practical reality meant they had drawn sentry duty. Although seeing Blowhard Sten's one-armed *Caesar* sitting idle sparked a small bit of cheer, it wasn't enough to dispel Kelly's growing gloom. Being able to see the *Caesar* collecting dust meant Kelly was sitting on his butt, too. Which he didn't like at all. He wanted to be out there, hunting the enemy, where he didn't have to think about anything but running his 'Mech and doing his job.

Finally Veck gave the order and they started their sweep. They were supposed to check the canyons west of the Green Banks bend of the Barr River, looking for Duvic troops. Intel said there was a mechanized infantry company operating in the area, and the gropos were the Vigilantes' target. *If* they could find them, *and* if the Duvic 'Mech forces didn't intervene.

Kelly hoped they would. After all, BattleMechs were the rightful opponents of BattleMechs. So far, the kings of the battlefield had yet to meet in serious combat. The Palatine's own small regular force of 'Mechs had seen as little action as CSVB's Third Company. When the Duvics committed 'Mechs, they sent in their mercenaries instead, and those hirelings seemed to have little interest in the sort of 'Mech versus 'Mech combat that Kelly had dreamed of, trained for, and now wanted.

It was his misfortune that the enemy wasn't cooperating. Crawford's people, Kingston's Killers as the press was calling them now, seemed to prefer picking on Shu conventional forces and melting away from BattleMech response forces. In some ways, they were more elusive than the Kuritans. At least the Kuritans traded a few shots before bugging out.

Two hours into their approach march, Kelly noticed

that Veck had them veering away from the Green Banks region. "What's going on, Commander? This heading is taking us off our sweep path."

"We got a lead on a Duvic supply camp," Veck replied. "We get it if we can. Intel's weak on this zone, so you 'Jocks keep your eyes open."

Veck had replied in the clear, which made Kelly curious. The new objective was curious, too. The lance hadn't received any transmissions from base, so Veck's lead must have come up in his conference with Captain Lazlo. The commander usually covered their objective *before* they left camp. Something was up. Kelly wanted to question Veck, but JJ beat him to it.

"Jurewicz," Veck snapped, cutting off JJ. "I said eyes open, not mouths. No commo unless you've got something to report."

At 1317, JJ reported a Kuritan shadow. A *Firefly.*

"Ignore him unless he starts something," Veck ordered. "We don't need distractions."

Forty-two minutes later, the Kuritan did start something. The *Firefly* lit up JJ's *Javelin* with lasers. Armor fragmented, flowed and burned. The *Javelin* crouched, then launched itself into the air to escape the fire. A particle beam screamed through the space it had occupied as Namihito's *Panther* rose from behind rocks two hundred meters to the lance's right flank.

"They asked for it," Veck shouted. "Hit 'em hard, Vigilantes!"

His *Vindicator*'s PPC crackled, burning a hole in the air between it and the *Panther*. But the Kuritan moved his machine with supernal grace. The charged particles ripped a scar across the *Panther*'s left arm, but expended most of their fury on the rocks behind the 'Mech. Steam and debris billowed. The *Panther* disappeared into the cloud.

Kelly launched at the *Firefly*, giving JJ covering fire. Craters opened in the 'Mech's armor as missiles slammed home, but the *Firefly* shrugged off the damage, backpedaling and launching his own salvo of LRMs amidst a trio of emerald laser bursts.

Veck led the Vigilantes after the Kuritans. As usual, the mercenaries faded back from the fire, but the Shu MechWarriors pressed them hard, staying on their tails. They exchanged shots when the opportunity arose, but the broken terrain gave such chances only rarely. Energy weapons blasted and missiles exploded, but they mostly chewed up the landscape. With fire and movement, the Vigilantes countered every attempt by the Kuritans to slip across their front and escape. The running firefight moved down into a broad canyon. Massive columns of banded rock to either side threw deep cold shadows across the valley floor. The 'Mechs lit those shadows with fire.

Kelly spared a glance ahead, and saw that the terrain was starting to close in. It would be taking away the Kuritans' room for maneuver. He grinned savagely. There, among the deep shadows, they would bring their opponents to bay.

Then he saw a shadow move.

"Ambush!" he called, seeing more shadows shifting ahead.

A seventy-ton *Cataphract* emerged into the sun. A pair of *Lineholder*s followed it. One of those two fifty-five-tonners alone matched the mass of JJ's *Javelin* and Kelly's *Commando* put together. Another 'Mech, a small bird-legged type like the *Firefly*, strutted behind them. The crackling sensor static which suddenly bloomed suggested that the fourth was a *Raven*, using its electronics to shield its companions—as though the massive machines striding toward them needed any help making scrap of the Vigilante 'Mechs.

The Duvic regulars had finally come out of hiding.

"We're in the pot!" JJ yelled, sounding scared.

He had every right to be.

29

Shu-Duvic Border
Epsilon Eridani
Chaos March
14 March 3062

The Vigilantes broke formation without need for an order. Veck's drilling on the practice fields had built in reactions that didn't always need conscious thought. It didn't hurt that the natural human reaction to seeing that much heavy metal coming towards you was to run and hide.

Their fast reaction to Kelly's warning made all the difference. The barrage from the Duvic 'Mechs only caught them in its periphery, which meant they were only mauled by the net of laser fire, the thunderous explosions of long- and short-range missiles, and the blasts of multiple calibers of autocannon shells, instead of being annihilated.

"Easy," Veck called. His voice was as steady and solid as a glacier. His PPC blazed back at the ambushers. "Let them come on."

Was he crazy? Kelly was scrambling his 'Mech out of

the line of fire, too, but he was sure his voice wasn't as steady. "We can't go toe-to-toe with these guys."

"We're not going to. Fall back on rally position zeta. Do you copy my map update on position zeta? Acknowledge." Both Kelly and JJ confirmed. "Fire at any and all targets as you go, but keep max range. Don't let them close. Don't let them sandwich you."

They shouldn't have had much of a chance, especially with Veck keeping the Vigilantes together and tying the swifter *Commando* and *Javelin*, the fastest machines in this battle, to the *Vindicator*'s lower—suddenly potentially lethal—top speed. Had Kelly been commanding the opposition, he would have pushed forward hard. Aside from the massive armor and weapon advantage held by the Duvics, their slowest machine was the ancient *Cataphract* and even it could match Veck's *Vindicator*. The *Lineholder*s were swift enough to sweep over the commander's machine like he was no more than a paper tiger, leaving the surviving Vigilantes to rout, if they could survive the weight of fire that would be falling on their heads.

But fortune favored the Vigilantes, and the Duvic commander—Veck identified him as "Red" Shang, commander of the Palatine Protectors—didn't share Kelly's tactical analysis. Or if he did, he didn't care. Shang kept the 'Mechs of his Protectors clumped together under the EW umbrella of their *Raven*, hording them like a fragile and precious resource.

Kelly offered a prayer of thanks for Shang's timidity. He figured that it was the real reason the Vigilantes were still alive, though a look to their right flank told him that condition might soon change. The Kuritan *Panther* and *Firefly* were going wide, working their way around to cut off the Vigilantes.

"Keep out in front of the Duvics," Veck ordered.

He was gone in a blast of his *Vindicator*'s jump jets. His particle cannon fired before he landed, catching the *Firefly*'s pilot by surprise. The Kuritan had delayed his dodge too long. Ravening energy chewed away the armor on the *Firefly*'s right leg and gnawed into the endosteel bones. That leg bent on the *Firefly*'s next step. Wobbling wildly, the machine staggered sideways, leg bending more with each step, until the pilot lost control completely and the *Firefly* crashed to the ground.

Namihito's *Panther* responded to the counterattack. Man-made lightning flared from the muzzle of the *Panther*'s PPC. The beam caught Veck's *Vindicator* cleanly, high in the left chest. Kelly expected to see the commander go down, but apparently the hit was against undamaged armor. Veck kept the *Vindicator* upright, sending his own PPC shot back at the Kuritan. Veck's aim wasn't as good as his opponent's and he missed. Still, the shot seemed to intimidate Namihito, and the *Panther* eased back toward his advancing allies.

At least the Vigilantes weren't going to get cut off.

Veck rejoined the lance, and the sniping and skulking went on. Several times Kelly thought he saw places where there was enough cover that the Vigilantes could have made a run for it, but Veck never called for a full out retreat. Kilometer by kilometer they played their deadly hide and seek with the Duvics.

Soon it was apparent that the reprieve Veck had bought from the Kuritans wasn't permanent. Namihito's *Panther* once more edged wide, threatening to make another attempt to cut around the Vigilantes' flank.

Veck shifted more to their right flank, but he didn't go after the *Panther*. He just made his own threats whenever the *Panther* looked to be starting a move. Mirroring Shang's caution, Namihito hung on their flanks, a distraction and potential danger.

Kilometer by kilometer the rally point drew nearer. A shaky-voiced JJ pointed out the problem.

"How can we rally at zeta? They're still pressing us!"

"Steady, 'Jock. New rally point, designated X-ray. Take my feed."

The new rally point was another kilometer away. Kelly didn't understand it. The Duvics had harried them for kilometers already. What was one more?

Their desperate retreat continued. Kelly's head rang, not just from hits against the *Commando*, but from far too many near misses and just the general concussive nature of the continuous barrage. Somehow, the Vigilantes were keeping their machines moving. It was a miracle that couldn't last.

"Steady, 'Jocks." Veck himself was starting to sound despairing. "We make it a bit further and we're free."

A bit further? Free?

Half a kilometer more of battering brought them to a stand of tremendous pines. The boles of the mighty trees offered a respite from the Duvic fire. Kelly's topographical map showed it would only be temporary. Beyond the pines lay a wide loop of the Barr River and open ground. Once the Vigilantes were forced onto that killing ground, it would soon be over. The enemy saw the same thing. Shang's lance upped its speed like dogs closing for the kill.

"Make it worthwhile," Veck said quietly.

For a moment, Kelly thought the commander was ordering a death stand, then he saw that not all the giants in this forest were trees. Massive shapes stepped from behind trunks wider than they. Kelly nearly fired on them, but stayed his finger in time as he realized that he wasn't getting a "hostile in proximity" warning. These new BattleMechs were friendlies!

There was a *Cataphract* and a *Lineholder*, then two more *Lineholder*s and another *Cataphract*. It was the Old Guard. Lazlo's First Lance was about to ambush the ambushers.

"Well done, Vigilantes," Captain Lazlo commoed. "Leave them to us."

The Old Guard advanced to the edge of the treeline and opened fire. Facing a new threat, one more powerful than they, the Protectors lost all interest in the Vigilantes.

"Let's get our butts out of this losing game and deal ourselves into something more our speed. Kelly, down the riverbed at top. Jurewicz, you jump with me. Time to flush that annoying Kuritan kitty cat."

Attempting to comply with his orders, Kelly found he couldn't bring the *Commando* up to full speed. Heck, he couldn't even get halfway. Each time he tried, the 'Mech's stride developed a wobble that threatened to crash him. His board showed green on gyro and leg actuators, but that couldn't be right. He had to have taken some kind of damage down below. His money was on the right knee actuators since the *Commando*'s armor was nearly scoured off over most of that leg.

He wouldn't be able to keep up in the slash-and-run firefight of a light 'Mech battle. Both enemy and friend would soon outdistance his weapons.

The day's long grueling retreat had left him seriously wanting to hurt something, and now mechanical failure was robbing him of the chance. Like it or not, he wasn't going to be part of hunting Namihito.

He slammed his fists against the cockpit walls. There had to be something he could do! Shu BattleMechs were finally engaging their opposite numbers on something like an even basis, and he was gimped out by a bad actuator.

He refused to be sidelined.

Chasing fruitlessly after far more agile light 'Mechs wasn't the answer. Then he remembered that there was a light nearby. He turned his *Commando* around and headed back to the spot where First Lance was engaging the Palatine Protectors. He made sure he came in from behind the Protectors' position.

The Old Guard's ambush had turned into a slug-a-thon. The Guard's gunnery didn't seem to be matching that of the Duvics. Despite their numerical advantage, they were getting the worst of it. From the crackling static on all bands, Kelly knew the *Raven* pilot was still jamming.

Somebody had to do something about that.

He found the *Raven* hanging back and staying low. The Duvic pilot was doing what a light 'Mech pilot ought to do during a brawl between his betters. He was using his assets to support his lancemates while keeping his own personal asset out of the line of fire.

Kelly decided that it was time to invite the *Raven* to play with someone in his own tonnage class, and he knew just how to phrase the invitation. The Artemis FCS whined about lack of target lock and the Streak system refused to confirm target. Kelly dropped his crosshairs on the *Raven*'s antennae housing, lining up the shot as well as he could. He triggered. SRMs boiled out on smoky trails and his laser flashed. At least half of the missiles splashed on rock, but his shot was good enough.

The *Raven* heeled over and went down.

Sensor channels cleared.

Kelly felt the tightness of a grin stretch across his face.

Lazlo's Old Guard seized the opportunity Kelly's coup offered. Their suddenly more accurate fire poured down, and all the Duvic machines took hits, even the downed *Raven*.

Legs scrabbling wildly, the *Raven* shoved itself against a talus slope and up the incline to a favorable rock face. With a heroic effort, the light 'Mech's pilot managed to get his machine back on its feet. In a somewhat less heroic moment, he apparently decided it was time to be elsewhere. Kelly let him go. It wasn't like he could chase the fleet-footed machine.

Free of the *Raven*'s interference, weight of fire began to tell. The Duvic 'Mechs started a grudging retreat. But Shang wasn't going easily. The Duvic officer was fighting far better than his lancemates, and he was dishing out more than he was getting.

Shang's *Cataphract* edged closer and closer to Kelly's position. Either the heavy 'Mech's pilot was unaware of the *Commando* or considered it an insignificant threat. Or maybe Shang just had more pressing things on his mind.

There wasn't a lot that a *Commando* could do to a *Cataphract*, and that little had to be done from a range likely to be unfortunate for the *Commando*. On the other hand, Shang's *Cataphract* was in a place that was unhealthy for him and was starting to show it. Even a puppy could bring down a big dog if that dog was wounded badly enough. Lazlo's people were doing their best to wound the Duvic dog.

In a sudden flash, Kelly saw opportunity. "Red" Shang

was Captain Lazlo's opposite number in the Duvic 'Mech forces. If such a high-ranking MechWarrior could be captured, surely the Palatine would want him back. A prisoner exchange would be virtually certain.

The only problem was that the Old Guard seemed intent on blowing Shang into enough pieces to send one to each of the Buddhist hells.

Kelly started calculating. He could join the party and continue the shoot-em-up against Shang, but that course had too high a chance of losing Kelly what he wanted. If the *Cataphract* could be brought down, Shang would have to surrender. But how?

Ramming or kicking a leg out from underneath it were classic ways to drop a BattleMech, but neither approach from a twenty-ton *Commando* would make much of a dent in a seventy-ton *Cataphract*. There had to be something Kelly could do, some way to take advantage of his flanking position.

If he had a more equal 'Mech he could have tackled the *Cataphract* like a blitzing linebacker catching a quarterback. But he didn't. He was sitting in the equivalent of a child, not a bruising hulk of a ballplayer. He needed the solution of the weak against the powerful.

Then he saw it. BattleMechs, with their human mimicking form, suffered some of the same weaknesses as the human form. The massive power of myomer bundles could be shocked into failure just like the muscle they emulated. A blow to the back of his knee, dropped any man, big or small. Surely a BattleMech could be dropped the same way.

He'd find out.

Barreling his *Commando* from its cover, he charged at the back of the *Cataphract*. He pushed his speed, trying to cover the ground before Shang could react or his lancemates cover Kelly with fire. The *Commando* wobbled. It listed to the right, but Kelly fought it back on course. Struggling to maintain control, he watched the distance narrow.

Fifty meters!

Forty! The *Cataphract*'s torso started to turn.

Thirty! Kelly goosed the *Commando*, reeling from the vertiginous feedback from his neurohelmet.

Twenty! Autocannon fire ripped from the *Cataphract*'s right arm.

Ten! Shells cratered the ground behind the *Commando*.

Five! The *Cataphract*'s massive cannon housing shifted down.

Three! The *Cataphract*'s bulky, backward-jointed legs filled Kelly's view screen.

Time stopped for him as he realized his mistake. The *Cataphract*'s overall humanoid shaped had gulled him into forgetting that it was one of these rare hybrid-form BattleMechs. There were no vulnerable backs to this BattleMech's knees for his hurtling *Commando* to—

Impact!

Kelly's face met the visor of his neurohelmet with paralyzing force. His world somersaulted. Metal shrieked like a man under torture. He tumbled, helpless, until something whacked his helmet hard enough to send him into darkness.

30

Following the path of aches and pains to his bruised and battered body, Kelly dragged himself up out of the darkness. Time had passed. His *Commando* was sprawled, head turned to one side. Through the viewport he could see that he hadn't been out for long.

The Old Guard was advancing across his position, past Shang's downed *Cataphract*. Had he succeeded? Or had he just distracted Shang long enough for the Old Guard to finish him?

Whatever the case, with their leader's *Cataphract* out of the battle, the rest of the Duvics had lost their enthusiasm for the fight. The *Lineholder*s, belying their name, were turning tail and scampering after the long gone *Raven*.

As Kelly worked to get his *Commando* back on its feet, Veck and JJ returned, reporting Namihito's *Panther* in retreat. Yi Cha-song, Captain Lazlo's second in command, signaled that the captain was injured and ordered the company to stand down from pursuit.

"We've got them on the run," Kelly protested. "Let's get them while we can!"

"Damp it," Veck told him.

"We can take down more of them."

"Really?" Veck sounded disbelieving. "With what?"

That was when Kelly realized his status board was glowing a nearly solid red. The comp had even finally figured out about the actuator damage. The *Commando* could still move, slowly, and the reactor and ammo bays were intact, but that was about it.

Sobered, he looked around. The Old Guard were battered. Captain Lazlo's *Lineholder* showed internal structure on all limbs and had nasty gaping holes in its torso. Another of the *Lineholder*s was missing an arm, one of the *Cataphract*s was shuffling along, its right leg locked, and the other showed so much damage around all of its torso weapon ports that it was a good bet its main armament was out of commission. Veck's *Vindicator* wasn't exactly unscathed either; Namihito had caught him with at least one more PPC shot. Of all the Shu 'Mechs, JJ's battered *Javelin* was least damaged, and it bore a fair resemblance to the sort of gunnery range target Sam used to leave behind.

But they'd won.

And when he saw Red Shang crawling out of the cockpit of his fallen *Cataphract*, Kelly knew *he'd* won.

"You've got one thing to be thankful for, you sorry son of an order-disobeying, reckless 'monkey," Veck told him.

Kelly figured he had more than one thing. There was Shang. And Kelly was alive to see it. "What's that, Commander?"

"That the repairs to the wreck you've made of the BattleMech that was entrusted to you ain't coming out of your pay."

"Oh, I'm thankful for more than that."

Veck scowled. "We'll see. I saw what you did here, Kelly. Believe me, you're going to regret it."

Kelly stubbornly refused to let Veck's gloom infect him on the long, slow troop back to the base camp. He went to bed with his wounds dressed and aching all the way to his bones, but happy.

His attitude changed when the morning briefing brought news that Captain Lazlo hadn't done well in surgery. It nose-dived when he was handed the word that the Vigilantes were being pulled out of line as depleted now that Kelly's *Commando* was sidelined for repairs. Two partially functional BattleMechs did not a lance make as far as the Phantom Major was concerned.

As they walked out of the briefing into the noon sun, Kelly wanted to know, "How are we supposed to win the war now?"

"We're not the only troops in this thing," JJ pointed out. "You know, Mr. Chill, you keep going with this fired-up, gung-ho stuff, and we'll have to get you a new nickname."

"So change it."

"Not so fast. You're still cold steel under fire. It's just this between missions stuff. You need some serious chilling time, I think. What say we inspect the rec tent and see if they've managed to import some decent beer? A cool brew will help the time pass, and it's not like we got anything better to do."

The offer held an allure, but it was not enough to overcome Kelly's need to do something. "We could help the techs repair our 'Mechs."

JJ reeled back in mock terror. "You want to annoy the techs by getting in their way, go for it. Me, I know better. I'm taking the dividends on a hard-earned rest. The beer's just a first installment. I know you've got a high technical aptitude, but are you sure you want to beard the real techs in their lair?"

"I'm sure I want my 'Mech up and running ASAP."

"Do what you have to, Mr. Chill. When you've eaten enough grease, you know where you can find the beer to wash it down. I'll even make sure one gets chilled while you hose down."

Kelly reconsidered JJ's offer as he walked out to where the BattleMechs where parked. Maybe he was overdoing it. How much *could* he reasonably expect to do? It wasn't as if he could win the war single-handed.

But he couldn't sit still. He hadn't been able to do so since he learned that Sam was still alive. There was guilt in his restlessness, but there was more than that. He wanted Sam back, even if she hated him for his moments with Romano. Did it really matter that he'd thought Sam dead at the time? It did, and it didn't. He wasn't sure that he'd ever sort it out.

Someday—as soon as he could make it happen—he'd see Sam again. Then what would happen? Conceivably—probably—Sam would tell him it was all over between them, but he longed for their reunion nonetheless. He needed to see her free and alive.

But that was for the future. The present held a field of mauled BattleMechs and the technical staff trying to make them battle worthy. Most of the techs were gathered around the 'Mechs of the Old Guard. Kelly didn't see a one attending the comparably battered machines of Veck's Vigilantes. Privileges of rank and station, he supposed. It didn't make him happy. The sight of his *Commando* lying prone and spread-eagled, looking about as helpless as a BattleMech could look, only intensified his unhappiness.

BattleMechs were supposed to be the shining knights of the battlefield. This knight looked dead.

He could only hope it had given its "life" in a good cause. There was still no word whether Captain Shang would be ransomed back to the Duvic Palatine. He began to worry that Shang might not be the key to opening Sam's cell after all.

Kelly dragged his thoughts from possible futures to present realities, forcing himself to gaze upon his ravaged *Commando*. From a distance, it was hard to tell the weapon hits from the open access ports. Up close, that wasn't a problem. Access ports didn't have burn marks and jagged or slagged edges. Up close he also saw something he'd missed from a distance.

From one port, the one offering access to the Coventry SRM-6 rack, a rear end and a pair of legs protruded. There was something familiar about that shapely bottom that Kelly couldn't quite place. He shouldered the thought aside in his relief to see that someone was doing something to get him back on the field.

"Hey, Tech, what's the word on my machine?"

Something muffled and unintelligible wafted from within the *Commando*'s innards. The legs shifted, found purchase, and backed their owner out of the machine. The grease-smeared face was familiar, too. It was Meryl LaJoy-Bua.

Kelly's hand slid down to his holstered Sternsnatch Python. LaJoy-Bua's hands went up, though one remained covered in a filthy red rag.

"At ease, Mr. Chill. I'm on your side."

"Really, traitor? I remember the ferrets hauling you off."

"Yeah, they did, but they were wrong. Yeah, imagine that. What are the odds, eh? Of course, I'd still be sitting in one of their holding pens if I hadn't done half their job for them. But like I always say, you want a job done right, heft the tools yourself."

The tech jumped off the *Commando*. Kelly eyed her cautiously but didn't do any more than unsnap his holster. Everything about LaJoy-Bua seemed unthreatening, but the old anger at Stübel's needless death made him wary. *She had to be telling the truth, didn't she? She wouldn't be here otherwise, would she?*

"So you're not the saboteur?"

"Oooh, this 'Jock's a bright one. There's a mole in the count's garden all right, but it ain't me."

"Colonel Bua's people thought it was you. Did they change their minds?"

"Sometimes a girl's got friends, you know? The sort of people who recognize a frame when they see it and do something about. This particular girl had a friend slip her some computer access so she could heft some tools. Get it?"

He didn't and said so.

"Okay, maybe not so bright. The ferrets thought I was the one who fritzed the umpire in your 'Mech. The old means and opportunity thing, and they just wouldn't believe that I didn't have a motive, which I didn't. Since someone had to prove it to them, I did. I hacked the beautiful sunny Camp Red Elk's database and showed them how the umpire had been doctored and when. Seems the jiggering was done hard-docked to a computer in a supply shed while I was on the other side of the valley in the middle of a staff meeting with twelve other senior techs, including the Phantom Major's personal tinkerer. Q and an E and a D, I couldn't have done it."

Her story sounded good. She certainly told it fast enough, but Kelly thought he spotted a hole.

"If you hacked the database, couldn't you have planted false records?"

"Such a suspicious boy. That's just what the head ferret said. Only his pet spiders crawled all over the net and back and couldn't find any signs of tampering. Now, I'm good, but not that good. Nobody is. Hide your sig, change your modus, sure, but never leave a scratch? Not the way it happens. They had to believe me."

"So they let you go free?"

"Free? Send me back you mean. There's a war on, remember? The brass still have my grease-covered hide under contract, and they ain't about to let an able body sit idle."

Kelly's eyes strayed to his battered *Commando*. LaJoy-Bua followed his gaze.

"Unless, of course, they have to," she added.

"So you're cleared and back to duty."

"Cleared and back, aye. Miss me?"

He had to admit that the *Commando* hadn't run as well since she left, but the nervous edge to her patter made it hard to allay all of his suspicions. "Veck didn't say anything about your reassignment. You got paperwork?"

"You mean like a get out of jail card? Get real. If the Whipmaster ain't said anything, maybe it ain't come through yet. You know the bureaucracy around this place makes a slug look like it's got a Kearny-Fuchida drive."

He stifled a laugh at the idea of a slug with a space-warping drive, knowing her evaluation was not inaccurate. But jokes didn't make her story true. Or untrue. Someone had sabotaged the umpire and gotten Stübel killed.

"So, who is the saboteur?" he asked.

"You got me," she said with a shrug. "The ferrets are still having a happy time hunting. Sooner or later they'll track him down. Let's hope sooner.

"They wanted me to help, of course, but I convinced the brass that I'm of more use to the war effort doing what I do best, which is to say making the big tin men go. I thought they agreed too quickly and I saw why when I got here. The job has gotten tougher recently 'cause certain MechJocks can't seem to keep their toys in one piece, always straying into the line of fire, I hear. Even tackling 'Mechs three times their mass. Shame, ain't it? Such lack of respect, but what ya going to do? Patch 'em up and give 'em back to fumble-fingered pilots. It breaks a tech's heart, I tell ya, to see how little care some people take. All our sweat, tears, hard work, and brilliant technical wizardry treated like so much toilet paper."

She stopped abruptly and craned her head around as though to look at something behind Kelly.

"Hey, JJ, good to see ya," she called. "That right foot pedal still sticking?"

"Still," JJ hefted his beer in salute. "You're looking good, LJ-B."

JJ's off-hand attitude caught Kelly off guard. "Is she telling the truth?"

"About?" asked JJ, looking confused. Kelly forestalled LaJoy-Bua's attempt to retell her tale and offered a summary. When he finished, JJ was matter-of-fact. "Yeah. Thought you knew."

"He wouldn't believe me," LaJoy-Bua accused.

"But that's not the news," JJ said before the tech could launch a tirade.

LaJoy-Bua's pique evaporated. She leaned forward. "Spill, 'Mech boy."

"Lady Shu wrapped Shang around her little finger. She's arranged for an exchange of prisoners." He turned to Kelly, beaming. "Sam is coming home."

"What?" Kelly muttered. He stood for a moment, stupefied, then he let out a whoop. Sam was coming home. He'd worry about the problems with it later. Sam was coming home!

"Swell," LaJoy-Bua said frostily. "*Her* 'Mech came back in a box. Ya think she'd have the grace to do the same."

31

Red Elk River Training Center
County Shu, Epsilon Eridani
Chaos March
18 March 3062

The cease-fire that accompanied the prisoner exchange wasn't scheduled to last long, but it provided an opportunity for the scattered lances of the CSVB to come home to the Red Elk River training center. No one wanted to miss Sam's homecoming, not those who had to be wheeled out from the hospital, not even Sten. He was the Blowhard and a butthead, but he understood the need to send a message of solidarity, not just to the enemy, but also to the new recruits and the replacements for those who had fallen. The MechWarriors of the County Shu Volunteer Battalion stood by their own like true House Warriors.

The sight of the gathered MechWarriors, all turned out in their best uniforms and standing in the cool shadows of their prettified 'Mechs, stirred Kelly's heart. It wasn't the flash and glamor that touched him. It was the spirit of these men and women.

And they *were* men and women. The war had made

them that. Some wore decorations earned in sharp actions, more wore the count's Honored Service medal for wounds acquired in action, and all wore that look of hard use. The boys and girls who had come to Red Elk were gone away, leaving veterans standing in their places. Kelly felt proud to be among them.

This was the first time that the unit had come together since the Duvics had attacked. They had not gathered for Captain Franny Lazlo's funeral, as they had not for Harry Trahn's. There had been no cease-fire for those solemn occasions.

Gone but not forgotten, Kelly vowed.

Lazlo's ashes had been scattered to the wind, but Kelly thought he sensed the captain's presence in the breeze that flitted across the tarmac as though the fallen warrior wanted to be here for the return of one of her lost soldiers.

There was a stir on the far side of the field as the dignitaries for the day made their way onto the podium. Among the welcoming committee were Romano Shu and Major Ling-Marabie. Seeing their faces shifted Kelly's mood in differing directions. It was the first time Kelly had seen Romano since their return from the Arousian District and the jumble of emotions the sight raised in him was confusing him, dimming ever so slightly his eagerness to see Sam again. He was much clearer about how he felt about seeing the Phantom Major in the flesh for the first time. He was sure that any officer who only bothered to be with her troops when the media was around to record it hadn't earned the right to stand on this field with honorable MechWarriors.

Sound rumbled down from the sky. Kelly looked up and caught a flash as the approaching transport banked on its final approach.

The ten minutes it took the aircraft to land, taxi back across the field, and roll to a halt a short ten meters from the podium seemed longer than the three weeks since that horrible night in Dori. Another eternity passed before the hatch opened and ground crews rolled up the stairway. Time entered another dimension entirely as Sam appeared in the hatchway.

Kelly's throat clogged. The garments she wore, clearly Duvic rags, hung on her like a sack. She had always been lean, but now she looked more like a dog that had been forgotten in a dead master's house than the lithe tiger he remembered. She moved forward, awkwardly leaning on a cane. The tiger's stalking grace was gone, too.

But she was, he thought, the most beautiful thing he'd seen in a long time.

When the speeches ended and Sam was released from the public relations ordeal, she made a beeline across the tarmac to where the Vigilante 'Mechs stood. Kelly started forward to meet her, then recovered himself. He was still supposed to be under military discipline.

"Go ahead, son," Veck said. "Take point."

It was all the permission Kelly needed. He broke ranks and ran toward Sam. Her smile dissolved the distance between them. Catching her up in a spinning embrace, he heard her cane clatter to the ground. For a glorious moment they were alone in the world. Her eyes sparkled. Their lips met. He tried to hold her close enough that she would never go away again.

"Easy, Tyb, or you'll have me the rag doll the medics say I am."

He eased her to the ground, suddenly afraid of aggravating her injuries. She snorted at his sudden change of demeanor.

"Hey, I'm not glass. I'm functional, even if the medics won't okay me for active duty. But I'll get that fixed," she declared.

"If you're still—"

"I *am* still. Ready to serve, that is. Believe me when I tell you that I'd rather be wearing a uniform than these things." She plucked at the taupe tunic she wore. "Have you ever seen such terrible taste in clothes? Yeesh.

"Enough about me. Look at you! I go on vacation and you sneak up the ladder while I'm away. A commander!" She lowered her voice and smiled warmly. "I'm so happy for you. Congratulations."

Vaguely embarrassed, Kelly told her, "Happened just a few days ago. Captain Veck's got the company now.

He's second in command for the battalion, too, right under the Phantom Major.''

"I'll bet he wouldn't even like being on top of her."

"Who would that be, Subcommander Liu?" Veck asked as he came up.

Sam cleared her throat.

"No one important, sir."

Veck pursed his lips and nodded. "I see. Well, glad to have you back in the county, Liu. In some ways your absence has been more detrimental than your presence."

Veck saluted her and excused himself, needing to talk to the major. As he walked away, Sam whispered to Kelly, "Was that a slam or a compliment?"

"It was Veck," JJ answered for him. "Who can be sure?"

"JJ!" Sam threw her arms around him. "Where's Slug? Too busy reading to come to the reunion?"

Kelly and JJ exchanged doleful glances. Kelly didn't want to be the one to break the news, and it was clear that JJ felt the same. Sam picked up on the bad news anyway.

"They didn't tell me. I mean, I survived my wreck. I figured he did too, but that the Doofs didn't catch him. I didn't think he was—"

She started to sob and Kelly put his arm around her. She leaned into him, babbling about how sorry she was. It seemed she was almost as bothered by her loss of control as by Harry's passing. Kelly murmured reassurances to her until a slim man wearing the old traditional garb of Capellan physician arrived and suggested that Sam accompany him, saying, "Lady Shu wants to be sure that you have the best of care."

Sam wiped away her tears and shot Kelly a bemused look. "Hear that? Since when does the high and mighty Lady Shu worry about MechWarriors?"

JJ got a suddenly dry-mouthed Kelly off the hook. "A lot of things have changed around here. Didn't you hear that she negotiated your release? Won't do her public image any good to have you drop down sick as soon as you get back. From here on in the bosses can't claim what happens to you is the Doofvics fault."

"*That* I'll believe," Sam said, letting the physician lead her away.

With Sam back to safety, Kelly had to return to business.

Having been promoted, he was now a lance leader, replacing Veck as commander of Second Lance. In his office—*his* office, a concept that was more than a bit strange—he looked over paperwork and learned just how much crap Veck had been dealing with. There were little things and not so little things, as well as some things that he truly didn't think were the business of a MechWarrior. Consumption rates for lavatory supplies? He dealt with the petty things as fast as he could, but he didn't get through them that night.

By the next morning, they had multiplied. It wasn't until mid-afternoon that he could turn his attention to what he considered the lance's most pressing issue of the moment.

Second Lance was supposedly being brought up to full strength, but the paperwork covering transfers to the unit only listed two pilots. With Veck moved up, the Vigilantes were three 'Jocks down. So was he getting another assignee later, or was he being shorted? Or had the Phantom Major suddenly decided to revert to traditional lance strengths and hadn't bothered to inform a lowly lance commander? Or was it just a typical bureaucratic snafu?

While he was trying to figure out who he needed to see to get the information he needed, Sam and JJ walked into the office. They didn't knock.

Sam was back in uniform.

He frowned. "I thought you were still on convalescence."

"Light duty."

He pointedly looked at the cane on which she leaned. "The medics approve that status change?"

"That's what the computers say."

Kelly frowned at her. She looked away and whistled. He turned to JJ, who shrugged.

"A pulled string here and there," JJ finally admitted. "Maybe a twisted arm, but I assure you, Commander, no fundamental truths were harmed in the manipulation of the data. Subcommander Liu is truly the best qualified pilot on CSVB rolls to take a slot in First Company, Second Lance, Vanguard. She is a rated *Commando* pilot, and there *is* an empty *Commando* on our rolls."

Kelly was pleased at the spirit and initiative they had shown, but—"As commander of this lance, I can't approve of this."

"No need to, sir. You already have."

"JJ."

JJ looked offended. "I didn't do anything, *sir*. I'm a snooper, not a fixer. Takes a computer wiz to do any serious jiggering of the sort you seem to be implying has been done, and that's not me."

But someone else in the battalion was a computer wiz. "LaJoy-Bua."

"Now, *sir*, how could you think that a tech, even a senior tech, would have an interest in doctoring unit personnel records? Why I am certain if LJ-B were asked to do such a thing that she would refuse outright."

"But a pulled string or a twisted arm might achieve compliance?"

It was JJ's turn to look away and whistle.

A MechWarrior, even an implacable one from the great Warrior Houses, knew there were times when a battle could not be won.

"Light duty then."

"Yes, sir!" Sam beamed.

The three of them went to view the arrival of the newest soldiers of the CSVB. As they walked toward the orientation hut, JJ pointed out two unfamiliar machines near the maintenance hangars.

"The *Linebacker*'s my new machine," Kelly said, declining to add that it was Franny Lazlo's 'Mech refurbished. "Veck wouldn't give up his *Vindicator*. And because the Powers That Be demand that the leader of Second Lance have a medium 'Mech, they dug one up somewhere. The *Raven* could be ours, too. I don't know for sure, but I think we might be about to find out."

Meryl LaJoy-Bua was leading a woman in CSVB coveralls toward them. The stranger had a cooling vest slung over her shoulder. Offering a careless salute, the tech made introductions.

"This here is Sally Trahn, latest in a long line of family Trahn MechWarriors. Harry was her cousin. Sally—excuse me, I ought to show some respect—Subcommander Trahn, this is the old man. The guy's JJ Jurewicz, *Javelin*. And the gal's the prodigally famous captured MechWarrior Samantha Liu."

Trahn started a bow, aborted it, and made a sloppy salute. "I am honored to meet you, Commander, and to be a part of First Company. I will do my best to live up to the reputation of Veck's Vigilantes."

"Kelly's Vigilantes," said Sam.

Trahn looked confused.

"The official nickname of this lance is *Kelly's* Vigilantes," JJ said, exchanging a wink with Sam.

"The Vigilantes," Kelly said, deliberately omitting any possessive, "are pleased to have you. I am sure you'll do your family honor."

"I just hope I survive," Sally Trahn said candidly.

32

Port Tsing
County Shu, Epsilon Eridani
Chaos March
5 April 3062

Gabriel Shu stared at the display screen, letting the silence drag out. Some of his hesitation to speak was petty. Hadn't his counselors dismayed and distressed him with their reports and presentations? Didn't they deserve a bit of discomfort as well, waiting in suspense while their lord and master considered the reports and proposals? Yet more than such petty considerations tied his tongue. In truth, he felt more than a little lost among all he was hearing, overwhelmed by the reality of County Shu at war.

Another three weeks had passed since the return of prisoner of war Liu, and still the battle dragged on with no appreciable change. County Shu had been primarily on the defense. The Duvics continued their running game, tying up Shu forces in a never-ending round of cat and mouse.

Major Essie Ling-Marabie cleared her throat, a not very subtle demand for a response to her presentation.

The major had grown self-important and somewhat pompous since the beginning of the hostilities, though her performance didn't exactly justify such attitudes. Still, her forces had stalled the Duvic attacks, even though they had failed to recover much of the county's real estate. Certain voices whispered that she should be replaced, but those same voices suggested no one better qualified to lead the county's military forces. At least no one Gabriel could appoint and still satisfy political considerations.

The major again cleared her throat, a bit louder this time. It was a justified call back to the realities of the council meeting.

"So," he began. "This Operation Bagration is your great plan to end our travails, is it? A broad-front assault on the Duvic capital?"

"A decisive offensive," Ling-Marabie responded enthusiastically. "With the Duvic BattleMech forces drawn to our diversionary attack against Lushon and the demonstration at Severagol, we can easily slash our way through their lines, smash our way to the capital, and bring them to their knees. We can force them to call off their war."

Gabriel was all for an end to the war, but this method didn't seem right to him. "The attack on Lushon bothers me. They have no military presence there. Is that not correct, Colonel Bua?"

The stone-faced colonel replied, "Nothing significant. A small militia garrison. No more than a company of infantry and a battery of anti-armor support. Nothing that would pose a threat to a BattleMech assault. Their defense plan seems to rely on reaction forces."

Gabriel considered that. "So, our BattleMechs make themselves a threat by destroying the mining facilities and transport net, sowing devastation, and causing maximum confusion. The Duvics react to the threat and we force them off balance. Is that correct, Major Ling-Marabie?"

"Correct. We capture the enemy's attention and deprive him of strategic resources at the same time. Once the enemy commits to counter our thrust, our follow-up force advances on a different axis of attack, moving on the capital. Their field force is effectively neutralized as they will be unable to turn their backs on our forces at Lushon and Severagol. Once we reach their capital, the Duvics will capitulate."

Duvic capitulation sounded good, but . . . "It seems to me that this plan would entail significant civilian casualties and rather extensive collateral damage."

"Fortunes of war," Ling-Marabie shrugged. "They started it."

The major's callous remark angered Gabriel. "The people of the Duvic Palatine did not start this nightmare farce. They should not have to pay for it."

Ling-Marabie sat back, eyes narrowed. "Unless you expand the list of military targets, this war cannot be concluded."

Raising his hand to still the expected objections to and support for the major's position, Gabriel said, "Saving their lamentable attack on Severagol, Duvic seems to be willing to confine the fighting to military objectives. I would like to believe that Palatine Price has realized that our states have been manipulated into this war."

Gabriel ignored the suppressed groan from Justin Whitehorse. The old man had little faith in the outside agitator theory that Gabriel espoused. Truth to tell, Gabriel was losing faith in the theory himself, but this was not the moment to make public such doubts.

"We may be at war," he continued, "but we are at war on Epsilon Eridani. This is our home planet. What is destroyed hurts all of us. As count, I am the caretaker of my land and, to a lesser degree, the other lands of this planet. It is an ancient and venerated trust. We will not callously widen the circle of destruction while I am in charge. We will honor the bounds of war as long as the Duvic Palatine does the same."

"Restricting the war is a ploy on their part," complained Ling-Marabie. "They know their facilities are more vulnerable than ours. They are afraid of how much damage we can do to them, so they hide behind the conventions of war. They have a chance as long as they don't take on our 'Mechs in a stand-up fight.''

"What sort of chance?" Ismael Shu-Larabie wanted to know.

"Small, but not negligible. Our 'Mech force has a higher average tonnage and greater numbers, but they have the heaviest machines. Their strategy seems to rely on promoting individual encounters where they can apply a local superiority in tonnage."

"And you let them get away with it," Justin Whitehorse accused.

"It is not my choice," Ling-Marabie snapped. "They have veteran pilots who are running rings around the incompetents and under-trained novices with whom I am saddled."

"Are you sure it's not the MechWarriors who are saddled, Major?" Romano smiled sweetly as she fired her dart at Ling-Marabie.

"Enough," Gabriel ordered, shutting off the major's indignant reply. "We have ample problems without turning on ourselves. Colonel Bua, do you observe this sniping strategy?"

"Regarding the commitment of BattleMech forces? Yes."

"But you see another strategy in play using conventional forces."

"Of course there's another strategy for conventional forces," Ling-Marabie answered for the intelligence officer. "There's always another strategy for them. Doesn't really matter though, does it? BattleMechs are the decisive factor. It is what happens in the 'Mech conflict that will decide this war."

"Do you agree, Colonel Bua?" Governor Hall asked

"In part," Bua said, leaning in to the conference table. "BattleMechs can be decisive. Whether they will be in this conflict remains to be seen. We cannot ignore conventional forces when they comprise the great bulk of the armies involved. However, as I recall, the count asked for my opinion on the BattleMech strategy in use by our enemy, and there, I believe, Major Ling-Marabie has spoken truly. The Duvic BattleMechs are rarely seen operating in support of their conventional forces. They make attacks on our unsupported forces and evade our BattleMech concentrations. They do seem to be making a practice of ambushing lone or paired machines and luring away portions of a unit and counter-attacking with local superior force."

"We cannot allow this," Gabriel said.

"How can we stop it?" asked Whitehorse.

"We bring them to battle," asserted Ling-Marabie.

"They don't seem to be accepting your invitation, Major," Romano said. "Perhaps it wasn't properly engraved."

"Operation Bagration—"

"That operation is not one we will be undertaking at this time," Gabriel declared. "We will find other options. We will not allow the Duvic BattleMechs to continue mauling our conventional forces. We will not allow them to continue whittling down our BattleMech forces. And since we are fighting this war, we will start winning it."

The major huffed angrily. "Starting where exactly?"

"Their BattleMechs," Gabriel snapped back, angry himself. "You said they would be decisive. Deal with them!"

"Would the count care to share his wisdom and explain how?"

Gabriel sputtered, at a loss for words. Colonel Bua stepped in, his composure a shield behind which Gabriel could suppress his anger and begin to think again.

"Perhaps we might employ combat patrols," the colonel suggested calmly. "Since the Duvic MechWarriors are using tactics similar to those employed by the raiders, we might profitably deal with them as we were planning to deal with the raiders."

Ling-Marabie grumbled. "So it is still a game of hide-and-seek."

"Make it seek-and-find," Gabriel ordered. "And remember that it is no game, Major."

"War is my business, Count Shu. I do not need to be told to take it seriously."

The major clearly intended to say more, but Romano didn't give her a chance. "Serious business indeed, Major. Best you be about it, yes? I would wager that we all have business we ought to be about." She beamed at them all. "And since there seems little more will be accomplished here this morning. I would venture to say this session is over. Gabriel?"

Grateful for her cue, he confirmed, "It is closed."

His formal pronouncement left his counselors no choice but to fold their arguments away for another day. Their leaving seemed to freshen the air in the conference room. Romano, being family, wasn't required to leave. She didn't, and he was glad of that.

"Thank you for shutting Ling-Marabie down," he said.

"Not necessary. She's become such a pill. Every day I grow ever more weary of listening to her voice.

"What a flock!" she exclaimed. "But I suppose one doesn't get to choose one's political family in an autocracy. Counselors! Was there ever one born who did not grow up to be a moaning warbler, a dither chicken, or a storm crow?"

"They do seem to bring nothing but bad news," he said.

"Not all bad."

"You're right," he admitted. "All is not darkness among the reports. I see that your Commander Kelly seems to be settling in well. I gather he is not one of Ling-Marabie's incompetents or under-trained novices."

Romano's reply was a curt, "He's not mine."

"Is that a hint of pique I detect?"

"Is that a nose I see where it doesn't belong?"

"I am a concerned brother."

"And I am a concerned sister. I'm concerned that you are wasting your concern on unimportant matters. Don't you know there's a war on?"

He did know, all too well.

Just as she knew all too well how to shut him up. She left him then, and the weight of the count's burden settled again on his back.

33

Mirandagol District
County Shu, Epsilon Eridani
Chaos March
19 April 3062

The refurbished Vigilante 'Mechs, which was to say all of them, had no small amount of teething problems. Even Sally Trahn's "new" *Raven* was cobbled together from various chassis in the family's boneyard and included parts from Harry's ill-fated machine. Considering that replacement parts for just about everything that wasn't standard to a *Lineholder* was rarer than Steiner-Davion sympathizers at the Capellan court, the techs had done a pretty good job. Even *Lineholder* parts, though produced on Epsilon E, were in short supply. President Benton's Isolation Edict had seen to that. The edict laid heavy fines on any suppliers encouraging the internecine strife between County Shu and the Duvic Palatine by selling ammunition and any other goods or services rated as "military." It all meant that rebuilds and jury-rigs had been the order of the past month of refurbishing. As a result, not a one of their 'Mechs operated smoothly or without problems.

The good news was that each day they got better, because each night, LaJoy-Bua's team found and squashed some software bug, or integrated a hybrid subsystem more fully, or remachined some part to yield a smoother interface with its foreign mate.

The bad news was that with the fine details of their mounts changing underneath them daily, the new lance members were having trouble bringing up their skills. At least, Kelly hoped that was the problem.

Sally Trahn didn't seem to have her cousin's aptitude for 'Mech piloting. In fact, she seemed as klutzy in her *Raven* as she was out of it. The *Raven* did have a tendency toward slow response in its left leg actuators but that was an excuse, not a reason. A good MechWarrior could and would compensate for the lag.

Aldo Snell had inherited Kelly's *Commando*. Snell had been a groundpounder before becoming a "special manual" man. His record among the gropos had been admirable, and he brought the same dedication and earnestness to his new assignment. Unfortunately, like his fellow special manual men, he hadn't had a chance to hone any real BattleMech skills. With time, that would change. But no one knew how much time they had, and with JJ reporting rumors of stepped up Duvic activities, Kelly was sure that the Vigilantes, with five functional BattleMechs, wouldn't be sidelined for long.

The new additions had to be ready for combat, and ready soon. It was Kelly's responsibility to see that they were. It was a responsibility that, even with JJ and Sam buddying up to mentor the newcomers, he despaired of discharging well.

"Cha, were we ever that green?" Kelly asked aloud.

"Green as what?" Sam wanted to know. "You, Tyb? *Nobody* was ever that green."

Watching Trahn's *Raven* clip the corner of Hut 32 yet again, Kelly shook his head. "I wasn't this bad."

"Ah, the blessings of a failing memory," sighed JJ. "We were all that bad or worse."

Kelly sighed, too. Had Veck, when *he* was given a batch of green recruits, felt this frustrated and worried?

*   *   *

Three days later, Kelly rose before dawn. He was ready, if not eager, for yet another long, grueling, frustrating day of trying to turn his greenies into MechWarriors. After showering, he left Sam working on her physical therapy exercises and hiked over to his office to find that the brass had gotten up even earlier. Awaiting him was a message from the Phantom Major declaring Second Lance active again.

The elapsed time between that declaration and the first assignment was about three nanoseconds. The timing said less about the lance's readiness for combat than it did about the high command's eagerness to get units into the field.

Kelly looked over the assignment. At least the major had shown enough sense to make it a shakedown run. The Vigilantes were to take a recon turn to the east, down into the channel-cut prairie between the Red Elk River and the Caroloco. Intel had several points they wanted investigated on the ground: possible supply dumps, scout outposts, and the like. The 'Mechs were being sent because they were the nearest recon force. It was their speed and all-terrain capability that was wanted, not their combat power. Intel said that there were minimal enemy combat units in the area, and those were truck-born infantry.

"Ought to be a milk-run," Sam commented upon hearing of it.

"Assuming Intel's right," Kelly said.

"Aren't they always?"

This time it seemed that they were. The Vigilantes moved through their sweep zone without any sign of hostile activity, which suited Kelly fine. He found himself less eager for contact with the enemy as long as he had half-trained fledgling MechWarriors under his wing. JJ seemed less satisfied with the lack of action.

"So what are we doing out here?" he asked. "There's nothing but prairie and tumblebrush and sheeple ranches out here."

"Lots of sheeple dung," Sam said, demonstrating her

piloting skill by standing her *Commando* on one leg to mime wiping the excrement of the bioengineered animals from its left foot assembly.

There did seem to be nothing of immediate military interest in the area. It was nominally County Shu territory, but the local population had a history of short-lived independence movements. It had never been a significant issue because the area was so sparsely populated. Even the Duvics showed little interest in exploiting the non-existent defenses in the region as a way to cut around the committal battle lines. The Intel assessment that had gotten the Vigilantes out seemed to be an over-reactive concern on the part of some paranoid ferret. So far they'd found no more sign of the reported Duvic infantry than week old tire tracks that might or might not belong to Duvic trucks, and all of Intel's supply dumps had turned out to be sheeple feeding stations. There was one last site on the list and distant observation showed it to be a small and rundown ranch, a bit bigger than the feeding stations they'd scouted, but showing no more military activity.

Kelly led the way in. He saw a man notice the 'Mech, stare for a moment, then move into the low adobe structure that was probably the residence. A moment later, the man emerged again along with several more people. Kelly couldn't be sure, of course, but they all looked like sheeple ranchers. Some started to wave.

When the lance's *Commando*s emerged from the stand of pine trees that had covered their approach, the welcoming committee reacted. They ran away, scattering across the ranch compound. Most headed for a long, low barn, a few into the house and a couple just lit out toward a stand of adapted acacia trees on the far side of the ranch.

As Kelly's *Lineholder* closed to a hundred meters, the barn contingent reemerged, mounted. They spurred their horses away from the oncoming 'Mech. Two swung by the residence to pick up a couple laden with bags who ran to meet them, then urged their overburdened mounts to join the exodus.

Still unable to see even personal weapons, Kelly vetoed Snell's suggestion that the fleeing ranchers be taken
down. This was nominally County Shu territory, and even
with a disruptive history, the civilians couldn't be pre-
sumed hostile, despite running from comital forces.

"This isn't right," Sam opined.

"The guilty run when no one's chasing them," said JJ.

"You don't have to be guilty of anything to run from
a war machine stomping into your yard," Kelly pointed
out. "Still, I don't like the way it sits either."

He told Trahn to keep a close watch on her sensors
and set Sam and JJ on overwatch, while he and Snell
dismounted for a ground sweep of the ranch. For all his
time spent with Sam and JJ, Kelly felt better about having the newcomer Snell as a partner for dismounted
work. Outside his 'Mech, Snell neither looked nor acted
like a greenie, and he handled his Rugan K12 SMG with
easy familiarity.

They started their sweep moving in along the lambing
pens. A couple of gravid sheeple bleated unhappily about
their presence and strange smells. Kelly forbore making
his own comments about smells.

"House," Snell whispered as he scanned the horizon.

"Got it." Kelly, too, had caught a glimpse of motion
in the dark interior, but his interest also was seemingly
directed elsewhere. Whoever was in the house knew the
MechWarriors were there, but there was no reason to let
the lurker know he was spotted. There was also no reason to stay in the open since the lurker could be armed.

"You go right," he whispered back. "Now."

The two former groundpounders raced for the building. Kelly slammed his back against the wall, breathing
hard. Snell was there, too.

The house remained quiet.

A few short finger motions established the plan. Snell
nodded understanding. Kelly swung to the edge of the
open doorway, crouching with his Rugan ready. Snell
went through, moving as fast as possible to clear the
doorway. Kelly followed him into the untenanted room.

No one was present, but they were watched. Cold glass

eyes stared at them from every direction. In true rustic fashion, the place was decorated with taxidermed animals and animal heads.

The room was in disarray, as though the residents had been grabbing things for a fast getaway, as indeed they had. But someone was still here. Someone had attracted their attention. There were four other rooms to the residence. They found their man in the third, a bedroom. He was hiding in the back of a closet, beneath a tumble of blankets.

The man was dressed like a local, but Kelly noticed a medallion swinging under the lamb's wool vest. He pulled it out to see what it was. The shiny disc with its techno decoration was a familiar, though personally distasteful, symbol.

"Word of Blake."

The captive snatched it back and tucked it away. "I am a believer in the Blessed Blake's word. That is no crime."

Kelly looked into that arrogant face. The skin was lined around the eyes and mouth, from habitual frowns, Kelly guessed. But he didn't have the weathered look of a sheeple rancher.

"You're not from around here, are you?"

The man said nothing. He only deepened his frown and presented a passport.

Kelly thumbed through it. "Roman diMassi?"

"That's what it says, isn't it?"

The name wasn't familiar, but something about the man's face was. Or was it the way he held himself? "Have we met before?"

With an exasperated sigh, the Blakist looked away. "I don't think so."

The man's aggrieved tone triggered a memory. Kelly hadn't exactly met this man before, but he had run into him. Or to be more accurate, had been run into by him. This was the Blakist he'd collided with back in Dori at Club Hoodedoo when he'd been looking for Namihito.

What in god's name was the Blakist doing out here?

"Traveling. Sight-seeing," diMassi claimed. "Bringing the blessed word to the unenlightened."

"Your potential flock scattered like guilty crows when we showed up. You too. Why was that?"

" 'MechWarriors are men of violence. Is it any wonder that honest folks flee from them when they come astride their war machines?"

Kelly had said something similar himself. But these people had waved first, then something changed their minds about being friendly. It couldn't have been anything that the Vigilantes did, because they hadn't done anything but walk toward the ranch.

"Are you planning on holding me?" diMassi asked.

"For the moment we have to," Kelly told him. "We have reason to believe that there might be some enemy activity in this area. You sure the folk here are honest?"

The Blakist seemed to consider for a moment. "Well, since you mention it, no, I am not. Though I cannot see men's hearts, Commander. I do know that they were eager to hear my words and receive the wisdom of the Blessed Bla—"

"Okay, okay. Save the sermon. The fact that the ranchers fled raises suspicion. We will be searching this place for evidence of sympathizer activity. Your pardon, but your hiding from us is suspicious as well."

DiMassi exploded in protest. When Kelly could finally get a word in, he said, "Try and see it from our viewpoint, sir. It would be gracious of you to allow us to search you."

"As an ordinary citizen, I cannot claim diplomatic privilege against such an outrage." The man's attitude was bitter and outraged, but he submitted. They didn't find anything suspicious on him. "Satisfied, Commander?"

Bridling at the Blakist's surly attitude and suffering a nagging feeling that he was missing something, Kelly wasn't satisfied at all. "I am just trying to do my duty as I see it, sir."

Lips pursed, diMassi glared at him.

Kelly wished he really did have a reason to haul the man in, preferably clapped in irons. But he didn't. And though he did have grounds to question diMassi, unfortunately, he didn't seem to be doing a very good job. At the least, he needed cooling time.

Kelly opened lance commo. "JJ, I got somebody I want you to talk to."

While JJ was trying to interrogate diMassi, Kelly called Sam down, too, and sent her with Snell to check out the rest of the ranch. He sat in the house's main room, chilling from his encounter with the Blakist and brooding over the nagging concern that something wasn't right at this ranch.

It was diMassi that seemed most out of place. The Blakists sought converts all right, but they spent most of their time in the population centers and places where there were significant technology concentrations. A sheeple ranch wasn't that sort of place at all. What did sheeple ranchers have to offer the greedy Blakists?

Nothing Kelly could see.

So what was diMassi out here for? The ranchers abandoned him, not exactly the behavior of newly converted believers. Even so, if diMassi was an innocent bystander, why hadn't he run with the others?

He claimed that he hid because he was afraid, but his attitude when they'd hauled him out of his hiding place wasn't that of a frightened man. The Blakist had more the air of someone who'd been inconvenienced and put upon by his social inferiors.

Something was missing.

A tactile memory came to him. When he'd fingered diMassi's medallion, he'd felt a hollow in the back, an indentation the size and shape of a computer storage disk.

Might diMassi's remaining to be caught be due to his taking time to hide a hypothetical disk? If he'd delayed leaving in order to do so, he might have found himself trapped by the Vigilantes' presence.

Colonel Bua would certainly be interested in any data an out-of-place Blakist thought necessary to hide from comital soldiers.

So if it did exist, where would it be?

A hole dug in the adobe of the closet where they had

found diMassi? Too obvious for someone as duplicitous as Kelly suspected the Blakist of being. Somewhere else then. Kelly looked around the room. The cluttered place afforded innumerable hiding places.

The departing inhabitants had practically ransacked the place while grabbing whatever it was they had taken with them. Anything might be caught up in the debris, but that stuff was too loose to be a secure repository for anything important. So where could it be?

The glass eyes of the room's mounted specimens seemed to mock him, glittering in cold amusement at his puzzlement.

The heck with you, he told them. *Especially you,* he said to the canted form of a crested accipiter.

Canted? Someone might have brushed against the stuffed bird as it sat on its wall-mounted perch. It would have to have been someone very tall because the branch gripped in the accipiter's claws would poke Kelly in the forehead if he ran into it.

He walked over for a closer look. Tucked under the bird's talons, he discovered a shiny data disk with techno decoration that matched diMassi's medallion.

So, diMassi *did* have something to hide.

He popped the disk into the comp at his belt only to have the machine almost immediately announce that it was baffled by encryption. Kelly wasn't surprised that the small machine couldn't deal with the disk. He ordered a brute force copy, figuring that would preserve any data that might be damaged by decryption attempts by his 'Mech's computer, or even Intel's machines should the *Lineholder*'s brain be insufficient.

But then he had another thought. The Blakist had hidden the disk to keep it away from them. The best intelligence was intelligence that the enemy, or even just a potentially hostile agency such as Word of Blake, didn't know you had. With the copied data, he didn't really need the original disk to turn over to Colonel Bua's ferrets.

He slipped the disk back into its hiding place and did his best to make it look undisturbed. He was just finishing up when a shaky voiced Sally Trahn announced over the lance channel.

"I've got a bogey, probable bandit on scan."

Kelly didn't think there was any probable about it. He ordered diMassi tied up as he ran back to his *Lineholder*. Once in the cockpit, he took a look at the feed from Trahn's *Raven*.

"Confirm bandit. Everyone, mount up!"

"Lord, help us!" Trahn wailed as Sam, JJ, and Snell were scrambling into their 'Mechs. "It's a heavy! And he's closing fast."

34

Kelly got his *Lineholder* moving to intercept. Trahn, either game for the play or unwilling to be left behind, strutted the *Raven* at his side. It would be a few minutes before the others could get strapped in and follow.

"Talk to me, Trahn. What are we headed for?"

"I got a glimpse of it on the horizon and didn't recognize it, so I fed the image to silhouette recognition program. Computer gives 70 percent probability that it's an *Axman*."

"Only 70?" An *Axman* had several elements that made for a distinctive silhouette. The computer should have little trouble recognizing it unless something was missing. "Let me guess. No ax."

"Yeah. How'd you know?"

"I'm the commander. It's my job." No need to tell her that to the best of anyone's knowledge there was only one *Axman* on planet, the bandit machine that lacked an ax.

"So what do we do, Commander?"

The two of them outmassed an *Axman*. The rest of the Vigilante Mechs would more than double the heavy metal heading against the bandit.

"We catch him, if we can, and take him down."

He passed the same word to Sam and the rest, adding that he didn't want anyone getting too close to the *Axman*'s front. "He's got a monster autocannon in a torso mount that'll hole any one of you. Stay to his flanks or come in on his rear, but keep to cover till you're close enough to score."

"What cover would that be, boss?" Sam wanted to know.

The prairie didn't offer much to walking battle machines that stood six or more meters tall. The occasional stand of trees, like the one currently shielding their approach, was about it. Kelly checked his topographical map. There wasn't much in the way of trees along the converging vectors of the 'Mechs.

"Right. Spread wide and encircle then, but stay out of reach of that cannon."

"Two left, two right?" asked Sam.

"Negative. Two left. You and Snell. JJ to the right. He'll probably peg my *Lineholder* as the biggest threat." It was, after all, only ten tons lighter than the *Axman*. It was faster, nearly as heavily armored, and carried a long range punch the *Axman* lacked. "Trahn, you fall back behind me and prepare countermeasures to give us electronic cover."

The *Commando*s emerged from the relative cover of the pines first. Sam reported the *Axman* spotting them. A flash of laser fire from the hostile confirmed her report. The Vigilante 'Mechs were too far away for effective return fire, so they dodged and cut wider. Being fast and nimble, they managed to avoid being hit.

Kelly's *Lineholder* cleared the trees and he got his first look at the hostile. He dropped the crosshairs of his targeting system onto the 'Mech to enhance his view. The *Axman* started to turn, reacting to his appearance, just as Trahn's electronic noise came on-line and Kelly triggered both LongFire V LRM racks and his Blaze-Fire laser.

The ruby beam of the laser sliced nothing but air. Most of the missiles streaked past as well, though Kelly saw at least four of them slam home in a tight grouping on the *Axman*'s left shoulder assembly. Not particularly good shooting, but it got the *Axman*'s attention as proved by the two searing beams that passed over the *Lineholder*'s shoulder and shattered a centuries old pine.

The *Axman*'s pilot seemed to grasp the danger of his situation instantly. He turned his 'Mech and accelerated away on a course that made JJ's flanking maneuver an exercise in futility. That sent him nearer to Sam and Snell's *Commando*s, but it also put him on course for the nearest bend in the Red Elk River and the badlands that opened up on the other side of the river.

Kelly started after the fleeing *Axman*. JJ rushed forward too, turning his swing around into a charge at the *Axman*'s back. He closed near enough to launch a salvo of missiles at about the maximum range he could expect a hit. While that deadly flight was still in the air, the bandit, in a display of piloting virtuosity, swiveled his 'Mech's torso as the *Axman* charged forward. Blazing fire erupted from the *Axman*'s arm weapons and the Devastator cannon spoke.

JJ's *Javelin* was too far away to benefit from Trahn's electronic cover. Kelly expected the worst. But whether by luck or intent, the *Axman*'s fire fell short, cratering the ground and ripping great wounds in the soil. JJ, traveling at too great a speed, could not avoid the savaged earth. The *Javelin*'s feet slipped. The machine crashed to the ground.

The *Axman* absorbed the hits from JJ's salvo and ran on.

Kelly pounded after him, loosing more flights of LRMs. His fire wasn't accurate, not unexpected given the range and the fact that both 'Mechs were racing at top speed. Some missiles went home, but the damage they did was minimal. Yet, it wasn't damage he sought to do with those salvos.

The *Axman*'s pilot frustrated him by failing to turn and engage.

The *Commando*s cleared the trees they'd ducked behind and found themselves too close to the charging *Axman*. Swarms of SRMs burst from their launchers. The *Axman* replied with scything lasers and the deep, dangerous bellow of its Devastator.

When the smoke cleared, Sam's *Commando* was down, snarled in a tangle of tree trunks. The *Axman*, shedding armor plates, was terrifyingly close to Snell's *Commando*. The former gropo was trying hard to get his machine out of the heavy 'Mech's way, but his piloting wasn't up to it. The *Axman* slammed into the *Commando*, shouldering it aside as a man would a child. Snell's *Commando* went down and lay still.

The *Axman* stomped on, still heading for the river.

Three machines down. No, just two. JJ's *Javelin* was back on its feet. It seemed to be limping.

"Got a tear in my left leg's myomer bundle," JJ reported.

Sam was bitching and calling for help to get her machine untangled. Snell was silent.

The Vigilantes still had an advantage against the *Axman*. They could still catch him. But the bandit had shown himself an exceptional pilot and a dangerous opponent. Facing a stern chase against a modified machine that had better long-range firepower than Kelly anticipated was a very different game than his planned encirclement. And the Vigilantes would be two 'Mechs down if they pressed on now. Kelly decided he didn't like the odds; it was too likely he'd lose one or more of his light 'Mechs.

If he hadn't lost one already.

His eyes turned to Snell's fallen *Commando*. The new recruit still wasn't answering commo.

"Let the bugger go." The order tasted bitter in his mouth, but there were other concerns. He stopped his 'Mech beside Snell's.

"JJ, give Sam a hand," he ordered as he slipped out of his harness.

He put a voice lock on the controls and clambered to the ground. Once he got Snell's cockpit open, he found the man stunned, but apparently not seriously injured. The *Axman* was long gone by the time all the Vigilante 'Mechs were up and their pilots ready to move again.

"That was the bandit 'Mech that raided Severagol back before the war," said JJ.

"I agree," Kelly said. "He was headed for the sheeple ranch. And those people there seemed to be expecting a 'Mech."

"And we weren't who they wanted to see," Sam said.

"I don't think it was the ranchers the *Axman* was coming to visit," JJ said.

Kelly felt the same way. "DiMassi?"

"Who else?"

"So what business have the bandits got with the Word of Blake?"

"We could go ask the redoubtable Adept diMassi," JJ suggested.

Unfortunately, diMassi proved more redoubtable than they had anticipated and was gone. He had slipped his bonds and was now nowhere to be seen. A search of the ranch didn't turn him up either.

Kelly checked the crested accipiter's claws. The disk was gone, too.

On the way back to base, Kelly sent his 'Mech's computer to work on his copy of the disk's contents. It had no more luck than his portable.

He made his report and turned the data over to Veck. The base computer couldn't crack the encryption either, but it did reach a conclusion: the code was Capellan.

"Politics." Veck said the word like it was profanity. "This goes up the chain. You did good, Kelly. I'd bet that this data is worth every scratch and bruise the Vigilantes took, but don't expect anything good to come from this."

While they awaited the real fallout from Kelly's discovery, the war went on. Patrol by patrol, the Vigilantes gathered experience. Aldo Snell got his count's Honored Service award, which he seemed to think was good.

Proper, at least. Sam and JJ got over the indignities visited on them by the hot-shot bandit. Sally Trahn's voice, and manner, grew calmer. And Kelly got a little more used to being in charge.

The war seemed to settle into a steady state. Weeks passed. 'Mechs occasionally sparred with 'Mechs, but no serious engagements were fought. The serious fighting, and dying, was done by conventional forces, but even there stalemate seemed the way of the world.

Only in the propaganda war did anyone seem to be making a major push, and there it was the Duvic Palatine that was on the offensive.

And offensive was exactly how Kelly found their latest tack.

The Vigilantes, according to the Duvics, were war criminals, a bunch of hooligans led by a bitter, cynical killer by the name of Tybalt Kelly. They were guilty of all manner of war crimes, from murdering a defenseless mercenary before the war started to destroying civilian property from backyard gardens to entire sheeple ranches.

When the slandering broadcasts were aired in the rec hall, most of the MechWarriors laughed at them. Veck didn't. Though Veck's sober reaction offered pause for thought, Kelly dismissed the significance of the allegations. After all, he knew the truth of the situations that the Duvics were blowing out of all proportion.

"When the war is over," he commented to Veck, "the real truth will come out. People will see that Presider Price and her cronies were just power-hungry politicians, stirring up trouble to serve themselves."

"Let's hope so," said Veck. "When this is over, there will be wounds to heal. We have politicians, too. And politicians have little use for the truth."

"What are you getting at, sir?"

Veck shrugged. "Shouldn't worry too much about after. We have to survive first. Who knows? Maybe we'll get lucky and all the politicians will predecease us." He put a beer in Kelly's hand. "Drink to that?"

Kelly drank, though there was one who Veck might term a politician for whom he did not wish that fate.

35

Port Tsing
County Shu, Epsilon Eridani
Chaos March
3 May 3062

For a change, Gabriel Shu found himself listening as Major Ling-Marabie made yet another pitch for her Operation Bagration. Each day that the conflict dragged on, he found himself longing for a resolution more fervently. Neither side had resources for prolonged conflict.

Truth to tell, he didn't have the stomach for it either. He longed for a quick, clean decision, and in his weaker moments he came close to not caring which side came out the victor. His sense of duty kept him from stepping over *that* line, while the mounting costs of the past two months pushed him toward another.

Could the major be right? Could a hard, ruthless strike be the only answer? Was he being irresponsible in refusing to green light the operation? He found himself reconsidering Ling-Marabie's proposal and wondering if the road it offered, though hard, was the only one out of their problems.

"The situation is not quite as favorable as when you

first proposed this," Colonel Bua observed when the major finished.

"The operation is still feasible," insisted Ling-Marabie.

"In the past weeks, we have taken notable casualties," Ismael Shu-Larabie said. "And the cost of munitions is skyrocketing. We are not as strong as we once were."

"Neither is the enemy," Ling-Marabie stated. "They face the same problems that we do. We started stronger. We remain stronger."

"For the moment," said Colonel Bua. "Our casualty rates are higher than those of the Duvics."

"Propaganda," sneered Ling-Marabie.

"You seem to be questioning Colonel Bua's evaluation, Major," Gabriel said. "Perhaps you have information that the colonel and I have not heard. I, for one, would be grateful to hear it because I do not find it comforting to be losing soldiers faster than the Duvics."

The major harrumphed and waved away her objection. Bua nodded thanks to Gabriel and continued.

"Casualty rates aside, the balance of power may soon shift. I believe the information recovered by Commander Kelly to be reliable. We cannot afford to ignore it."

"Are you saying we need to do something and do it soon?" asked Whitehorse.

"Exactly," said Ling-Marabie.

The major started to pitch Operation Bagration all over again. Claudia Hall pointed out that she was out of order. The argument that erupted had less to do with procedure than personalities. While his counselors wrangled, Gabriel sullenly considered the operational plan still glowering down from the wall screen. Whether quickly or slowly, their chance to seize the initiative was slipping away.

Colonel Bua was right that the threat of the forces secretly landed to aid the Duvics was great. Possibly even greater to Epsilon Eridani as a whole than to County Shu. He ought to send the information to President Benton, but he feared that it would do little good. Benton would likely dismiss the computer disk as a ploy to smear Price, just as he seemed to dismiss anything Gabriel put before him. Without evidence of Price's perfidy, Benton would not move. Unfortunately, the evidence lay at Hinchuan, slowly being assembled into the weapon that would doom County Shu.

Gabriel stared at the map. Everything seemed so close together. Hinchuan looked a mere hop away from Lushon, but a hundred kilometers of badlands lay between the two locations. A hundred kilometers. Was that really so far? He traveled a hundred kilometers for an evening at the theater without a second thought. No, it wasn't far at all.

Of course, Hinchuan lay behind enemy lines, and that made it far away indeed. Or did it? Just how strong were the forces guarding the landing field? He passed the question to Colonel Bua through his computer screen as the others continued to argue.

MINIMAL, Bua responded. SECRECY MAIN DEFENSE.

Secrecy was indeed important to the Duvic plan. Clearly they feared to risk calling attention to the landing place of their illicit allies by garrisoning the place. His thoughts began to coalesce. Could it be that Commander Kelly's intelligence coup had given them the key to the door?

Gabriel tapped his console. "Gentlemen and ladies," he began, pausing while everyone settled down, "one thing we must agree on is that the situation will not get any better if we do nothing. Therefore, we must do something. Ultimately, as count, it is my responsibility to determine the course for the county. And so I will. Regretful though I am of the cost, I believe we must mount an offensive. Major, will you recall the stage one map for Operation Bagration?"

Ling-Marabie gave them all a triumphant grin as she entered the commands.

"We will use a variation on the Bagration plan. Instead of the Jenzo mining facility we will make our target the Huang-Lu Space Port. We stop the incoming reinforcements before they can debark. Best of all we ought to be able to keep civilian casualties and collateral damage down since the landing field at Hinchuan is isolated rather than being the heart of a populated settlement like the Lushon target."

"Laudable goal, but Hinchuan is over a hundred kilometers deeper into Duvic territory than Lushon." Ling-Marabie clearly disdained Gabriel's meddling in her perfect plan. "It throws all the timetables off. At best, it raises the butcher bill and at worst we'll be defeated in detail."

"I don't see why," Gabriel said. "The extra distance can't matter that much. We can form the strike force with our fastest BattleMechs. At their top speed, it will be no more than an hour travel time."

"Mechs do not travel at top speed in enemy territory."

Though Ling-Marabie's reply was made as to a child, Gabriel ignored the offense. "Then two hours. It will make little difference. The timetables can be revised accordingly."

"Our target will be obvious to them once our forces cross the Bechulla tributary. Hinchuan is sufficiently distant from that point that their BattleMechs will have ample time to react," stated Colonel Bua.

"Is that not what we want?"

"It could be a concern," the colonel said. "Our light forces could be destroyed, and their 'Mechs could then shift back to intercept our main force moving on the capital."

"But our forces will not move on the capital. We will engage their BattleMechs. We will have the decisive encounter at last. And we need not destroy civilians or their property to get it. We do not even need to destroy all of the Duvic forces. We need only bloody their noses and force them to retreat."

Justin Whitehorse put a voice to the confusion on the council's faces. "How so?"

"Isn't it obvious? Once we have captured Hinchuan and interned Price's Capellan support, we will surely recover more than enough documentation to expose Price's collusion. Public opinion will turn. Even our even-handed

President Benton will be forced to come down against Price. We will no longer stand alone. It is Price and her cabal who will be alone, and alone they cannot stand.

"We must be swift, gentlemen and ladies. We must be decisive." Gabriel stood and drew himself tall. "Let the word be sent out. Let us strike and end this war."

36

**Mirandagol District and Beyond
County Shu, Epsilon Eridani
Chaos March
6 May 3062**

In the next few days, the word on Operation Bagration was passed down from the count's council through Major Ling-Marabie to Captain Veck, who outlined it for the MechWarriors of the County Shu Volunteer Battalion.

"It's a chancy plan," Veck said at the briefing. "It stretches our forces, and relies on the enemy doing exactly what we expect of him. Now, before we get down to specifics, does anyone have any questions about the mission and goals of this operation?"

Instead of a question, Bayard Sten made a statement. "You don't sound like you approve of the plan, Captain."

"It's not my job to approve it, Subcommander. Neither is it yours. Execution is our responsibility. We are the ones who will take the brass's plan and make it happen."

"Or die drying," Kelly whispered to Sam.

Veck rounded on him. "You have a better plan, Commander Kelly?"

"No, sir," Kelly snapped back.

"Then what is your problem?"

"No problem, sir."

"Question, then? Desire? Wish? Need?"

"All I ask is that the Vigilantes be given a responsible part that we may acquit ourselves with honor."

"Asking for honor is a lot like volunteering, kid." Veck shook his head. "You just don't do it if you want to keep your skin intact. As it happens, your part is already chosen. All our parts have been."

Veck dismissed the ordinary pilots, retaining the lance leaders for a planning conference where he laid it all out for them. Kelly's lance had indeed been given an honorable role. Theirs was the strike mission against Hinchuan township and the capture of Huang-Lu Space Port. Militarily, it was a sideshow to the main event of the drive on the Duvic capital, but Kelly figured it for the real heart of the offensive. Success in Hinchuan would provide the evidence to expose Duvic-Capellan collusion and bring the weight of Epsilon E opinion—and probably military power as well—down on the Duvic Palatine and its renegade leaders. It was a mission whose success would aid the county whether or not the main objective of Operation Bagration was achieved.

Kelly's lancemates gathered around him when Veck finally released him. He had barely begun to explain their assignment when JJ interrupted.

"I'm glad you didn't get a chance to *ask* for this honor. They might have wanted each of us to weld one of our 'Mech's arms to its back. Just to increase the honor, you see."

"Wouldn't bother me," Sally Trahn said with mocking cheeriness. "My *Raven* doesn't have arms that'll reach behind its back."

"For you there'd have to be a special honor. Say, freezing your knee actuators so your *Raven* can stump its way there and back again."

"Enough," Kelly commanded. "You've got supplies to draw, and I want you all to make a thorough check of your machines. I'll have a tactical briefing for you then. If we're all lucky, we can catch a nap before we depart."

The military being the military and 'Mechs being

'Mechs, there were delays. The tactical briefing ate the remaining time, so nobody got their nap.

Nevertheless, the Vigilantes moved out on schedule, just after sunset, while the light was still making embers of the low clouds. Those clouds were part of the plan. They would hide the moons—Intel said they couldn't afford to wait until the next full dark—and shroud the land in a darkness suited to moving troops. The Vigilantes moved at a steady, but respectable pace, the sort that any chance observer might take as suitable for a unit traveling to a new camp. To aid that illusion, a convoy of trucks followed them.

And it was an illusion, for those trucks didn't carry techs and supplies, they carried footsoldiers. The soldiers were the follow-on force for the Vigilantes' mission.

When full dark fell, 'Mechs and trucks doubled back on the path. They moved more slowly, cautious in the dark. Sally Trahn was listening hard for any enemy transmissions, but she discerned no sign that the Vigilantes had been noticed. As Kelly was sure that all his lancemates were doing, he prayed that the Duvics remained ignorant. The Vigilantes' chances of success went up with each minute they remained undetected.

Two hours into the mission, they changed their course. From paralleling the "front lines," the column turned and headed directly for them. If Intel's maps were right, the force would be moving through a gap in the sentry posts. The 'Mechs crossed the line and entered enemy territory. The trucks followed for a short distance before going to ground to await the proper signal.

Somewhere behind them, other signals were being given. Searchlights would be blazing out to stab brilliant beams into the underbellies of the clouds. Comital infantry and armor would be moving by the light reflected off the clouds, leaving their jump-off points and approaching their assault positions. Soon they would engage Palatine forces and cut a hole for the CSVB to run through. Up north something similar was happening, as forces attacked in and around Severagol. Up north there were no 'Mechs to support or exploit the push since it was only a feint. Both attacks were expected to draw the Duvics' attention, the better for a lance of fast 'Mechs to slip through their territory.

Duvic radio traffic picked up. Some of it, thanks to panicky operators, was in the clear. The assault phase of Operation Bagration was indeed underway. Kelly was about to order an increase in speed when Sally Trahn dropped a commo laser on him.

"We've got an enemy tank formation headed our way," she announced.

"Are they deployed for action?"

"Negative. They're in column."

Kelly ordered an immediate halt. Better for the Duvic tanks to cross in front of them than behind, where they might note evidence of the 'Mechs' passage. Unfortunately, the Duvic tanks didn't know they were supposed to pass by. They altered course, not directly for the Vigilantes, but near, very near. Kelly saw at once that the track of the Duvic tanks would pass close enough that the risk of a sighting was high.

"Is General Murphy giving orders to those guys?"

"Say again, Commander," Trahn said.

"Never mind." He also saw that the local terrain offered the Vigilantes the chance of an ambush. "We'll try and take them. Dead tankers tell no tales."

He set Trahn's *Raven* and JJ's *Javelin* to crouch on the debris from a long abandoned quarry. He ordered Sam and Snell's *Commando*s into a stand of huge *shenko* conifers whose boles were massive enough to block the small 'Mechs from view. Kelly took up a fire support position to the left where he could command the tankers' line of retreat. If any survived the ambush, he could deal with them as they hightailed it home.

The tanks came on. There were four of them. The crews seemed unaware of the danger into which they roared. They had not even bothered to rotate their turrets for maximum surveillance. Kelly made them as *Scimitar*s, hover tanks armed with Armstrong autocannons and paired small SRM racks. They were seriously outclassed by the Vigilantes.

Time for their wake-up call.

"Sam, knock on their door."

She did, dropping all her missiles on the flank of the last in line. She raked her laser into the craters caused by her missiles and blew the tank to oblivion.

The *Commando*s advanced on the tanks using the "Double Weave" tactic Kelly and Sam had come up with back in training, and the tankers fell for it. Their fire was erratic and they shifted their positions badly, failing to anticipate which of the eccentrically moving 'Mechs would appear next.

One tank shifted to right where Sally needed it. She stood her *Raven* and launched a NARC beacon at it. The shell went home, attached itself to the *Scimitar*'s hull just forward of the engine compartment, and started crooning its siren song for Vigilante missiles.

Trahn blasted her paired lasers into the tank, lambent energy vaporizing significant chunks of the vehicle's Protec armor. The *Scimitar* survived the hit, but only for a moment. A combined salvo of sixteen SRMs from JJ and Sally, drawn by the NARC, devoured it.

The *Commando*s handled another one, convincing the last survivor to head for home. Kelly met it with a spread of LRMs and a quadruple spear of laser fire. Shattered, billowing smoke, the vehicle struggled on. A second missile flight ripped into it, blowing the air from its skirts and flipping it. The turret sailed in a different direction from the hull. Both components crumpled when they struck the ground.

"Transmissions?" Kelly asked Sally.

"None I netted."

That was good. His lance had done what needed to be done, functioning smoothly and as a team. He was proud of them. "Good show, people. Now we get back on track."

Hinchuan was nearly two hundred kilometers from the front lines. Kelly's *Lineholder*, the slowest of the Vigilante 'Mechs, could run that distance in less than three hours. Caution and secrecy dictated that they not move at top speed, so three hours later, they were barely more than halfway to the target. They moved in an extended vee formation with Kelly on left flank, JJ on the right and Sally on point where her *Raven*'s electronics could do their best sniffing for danger.

"I think we've got a shadow," Sally announced.

The vector she gave meant that Kelly's *Lineholder* was nearest. Kelly checked his own scanners. They showed a light 'Mech ahead of him and a little to his right. It couldn't be anything but a bandit. Chasing a skulking bandit wasn't the commander's job, but Kelly was the closest and this was a situation that had to be dealt with soonest. Besides, the bandit didn't seem to be aware of Kelly and was moving in on Snell's *Commando*, presumably for a better look.

"I'm on it."

On his screen, he could see that Sam was also responding, shifting over to close on Snell's position. She wasn't the only one reacting. Judging by the way the ghost was starting to cut back to the left, he had become aware of the approaching *Lineholder*.

Kelly accelerated and caught a glimpse of a long-legged shape with a horizontal torso and a low-slung cockpit that jutted forward. No mistaking that exotic silhouette. It was a *Jenner*. The 48th was operating two of them and as far as Kelly knew, the Kuritans had the only ones in the theater.

The *Lineholder*'s left arm came up and the BlazeFire lit the night. The beam grazed the *Jenner*, galvanizing it into a run. Ducking and weaving, the *Jenner* made no attempt to fire back. Its pilot clearly wanted no part of a fight with a 'Mech twice its mass, and his superb use of cover and speed made it impossible for Kelly to force the issue.

Sam and Snell charged past Kelly's position.

"Negative," he told them, calling off their pursuit. "No time to chase him, and we can't have him splitting us up." *Jenner*s were speed demons, easily capable of outdistancing any Vigilante 'Mech. Their high speed also meant they could run rings around the Vigilantes. "That pilot looks good enough to lead us on a snipe hunt."

"One of the Kuritans?" Sam asked.

"Be my guess," Kelly replied. "They're not our job tonight."

Kelly overrode Sam's protests. It was out of their hands. The *Jenner* would be reporting to someone, and they needed to get on about their business quickly before all surprise was lost. They could only hope that the *Jenner*'s bosses didn't figure out the Vigilantes' destination.

They returned to their formation and moved on. Two and a half hours later, having encountered no more stray Duvic forces, they were moving in a tighter formation and approaching their target along the Kennesaw Canal.

Like many of the settlements in the northern regions, Hinchuan was an oasis in the badlands built to exploit mineral resources. And like most of those settlements, it wasn't exactly a thriving metropolis. It was located in a broad valley punctuated by spires of weathered basaltic intrusion and buttes of the banded sandstone that made up so much of the continent's exposed geology. Processing buildings and machinery dominated the place, supported by warehouses and the occasional multistory housing complex, a tiny downtown section of offices and shops, and rambling tracts of private homes and small businesses. The whole place lay quiet and mostly dark under the lowering sky.

Near the edge of the settlement, hard by the canal-side loading yards was Huang-Lu Space Port. As it came into view, Sam asked sarcastically, "This is a space port?"

Huang-Lu was indeed a space port. Class Four, the references said. Kelly figured that rating only applied on a good day, with a congenial and properly bribed assessor, who also happened to be blind.

The ferroconcrete of the landing field was runneled with cracks and had spots that were pulverized into little more than a thick gravel bed. Kelly doubted they would support anything but the smallest of DropShips and them not much longer. But somewhere on the battered field there was a spot retaining sufficient strength to handle a medium-sized commercial DropShip, because there was one sitting in the lee of the biggest hangar.

Pumping up the magnification Kelly looked for Capellan markings on the DropShip. He didn't find any, and he wasn't surprised. Still, there was no reason to doubt that this was the ship that they needed to own.

At least it didn't look to be armed. He could not see any weapons blisters or gun ports on its hull. It could have concealed weapons or there might be 'Mechs aboard, positioned to fire out the airlocks, but such improvised defenses wouldn't be very effective. The ship's resistance would be weak. Kelly didn't want *any*.

Kelly positioned his people carefully, sitting them in a circle surrounding the target. He made sure that each was in the open and had a good line of fire that wouldn't cross the target and endanger a friendly. He also made sure they could move to cover quickly.

All remained quiet as they took up their positions. They had, it seemed, achieved the surprise they sought. They closed to ninety meters without sending up an alarm. At Kelly's signal, the Vigilantes turned on lights, swamping the DropShip in actinic glare. As Trahn started jamming the long range commo bands, Kelly keyed open his external speakers and made his broadcast on Duvic military frequencies, as well as open commercial channels.

"Attention, DropShip. You are under the guns of County Shu BattleMechs. We expect you to surrender. Fight and we destroy you."

For several moments nothing happened. Trahn reported a low level commo buzz aboard the ship. They'd gotten the message. The first question was, did they believe it? The second was, would they comply?

The answer to the second came as people burst from the DropShip and ran toward the hangar. Several of them were wearing cooling vests. MechWarriors. There would be 'Mechs in that hangar, possibly already warmed up. How capable of combat they might be, Kelly didn't know, but he saw no reason to give these MechWarriors a chance to demonstrate their 'Mechs' capabilities for him.

He used his BlazeFire laser in blatant overkill to gouge a furrow across their path.

"Any attempt to flee the ship will be dealt with. Take another step, gentlemen and ladies, and see how."

His demonstration proved sufficient. The MechWarriors retreated to the DropShip. Faced with ready opposition and stuck aboard a barely-armed and -armored commercial DropShip, the ship's commander soon surrendered.

JJ volunteered to be the one to dismount and enter the DropShip to ensure that its engines and any weapons were locked down and to do what he could to save the data that the hostiles were undoubtedly purging from their computers. His only real defense was his lancemates in their 'Mechs outside. And his only link to them was a short-range headset that fuzzed once he was inside the DropShip's hull. But the link held and so did the threat. JJ reported the hostiles sullen, but willing to let him do what he'd gone in to do once he'd made it clear that action against him would result in the Vigilantes opening fire on the DropShip and turning it into enough slag to patch up the space port.

As JJ tried to do his duty, Kelly prepared the coded transmission that would tell the brass he'd succeeded. He wanted to send it as soon as possible because, until he did, high command wouldn't dispatch the convoy of ground troops that Kelly needed to hold this place and control the prisoners. His 'Mechs were a big club, a wonderful threat, but too blunt and destructive for the rest of the job. Five Vigilantes were an insufficient force to ride herd on prisoners *and* make a proper search of the facility for the incriminating evidence Intel wanted *and* defend the space port against any attempt to retake it.

Still, he thought, it had been easy. Too easy? How could he tell? There hadn't been any opposition at the space port, but that was what he had been told to expect. The Duvics were supposed to be relying on secrecy and misdirection as their defense. Of course, they had the 'Mechs that were landing as a back-up, but they hadn't been able to deploy them because the Vigilantes, striking quickly and under their own veil of secrecy, had gotten here before the 'Mechs were ready. It was an operation that had worked according to plan, and didn't those always seem too easy?

Sally Trahn interrupted his thoughts, breaking in on the lance channel. "Remember when Captain Veck said the plan required that the enemy do exactly what the brass expected?"

He certainly did.

"Well, they're not," Trahn declared. "The enemy, I mean. I mean, they're the enemy all right, but they're not doing what the brass expects."

"Stop babbling, Trahn."

"Sorry, Commander. We've got BattleMechs on approach. A lance, maybe. Mixed tonnages, but there's a really big one."

"Hundred tonner?"

"How did—never mind, Commander. Yes, sir, a hundred tonner."

So much for too easy. "JJ?"

"I heard. Crawford's *Pillager*."

Kelly couldn't think what else it might be. They would be facing Kingston's Killers and playing well out of their weight category.

"JJ, you done in there?"

"I put an override code on their operating system, but it's not really—"

"It'll have to do. Get out here and saddle up."

"Acknowledged."

"Sam, Snell, once JJ's out, weld those hostiles into their ship. Trahn, try and get me IDs on the other hostiles."

He needed to know how bad it would be.

37

It was bad.

Besides the *Pillager*, Trahn identified the *Enforcer* and the *Clint*, which had been its companions before, and a *Catapult*. The bad guys were running with nearly twice the mass of the Vigilantes.

JJ cursed. "What are they doing here?"

"The *Jenner* that got away," Snell suggested.

"No, I mean, why aren't they down fighting off the big invasion?"

"It doesn't matter," Kelly said. "They're here, and we need to deal with them."

No one asked *how*, but Kelly knew they all had to be thinking it. Lord knew he was.

"At least we have superior electronics," said Trahn.

"And they have superior firepower," JJ pointed out.

"They're not surprising us like they did in Dori," observed Sam.

"And we did so well there. There were three of them then, there are four now. I seem to recall—"

"Enough," Kelly ordered. "However many there are, we can't sit and wait for them here. We need cover. And we have to assume they know we're here, but we don't have to make it easy for them. Trahn, start jamming their sensors."

He led them into Hinchuan. Leaving the objective behind bothered him, but he couldn't see a way to defend it on the spot. His mind raced, searching for a scheme to deal with the oncoming hostiles. A plan began to form.

"The *Catapult* gives them a long-range punch we can't match. So we don't try to. We'll move *near* the edge of the town, but not *to* it. Once they enter, we get buildings to screen us and they get their fields of fire cut. Trahn's jamming will make it hard for them to spot us and to coordinate their movements if they do."

Sam was the first to get it. "So they lose mutual support, and we get to gang up on them one at a time."

"Exactly."

Kelly moved his lance into an ore processing facility. The piles of tailings and bulky machinery offered a wealth of cover. Best of all, they had their back to a row of warehouses and factory sheds which would shield them as they pulled back.

Trahn edged forward to get a better scan. She informed them that Crawford's people were moving in, more slowly since Trahn's jamming went up. Even so, they were only a few hundred yards from the outskirts. The *Pillager* was in the lead, flanked by the *Enforcer* and the *Clint*. The two lighter 'Mechs were holding their speed down to that of the hundred tonner.

"The Cat's hanging back," she reported.

No surprise there. It was a long-range support vehicle, which primarily used its Arrow missile system to demolish ground troops. The Arrow wasn't designed for anti-Mech use, but a hit from one of the oversized missiles could end a 'Mech's—any 'Mech's—battleworthiness in a single shot.

"Don't let any of its mates force you into its line of fire," Kelly warned.

Kingston's Killers were wise in the ways of death. As they neared the built-up area, they spread out, each seeking his own path into the urban maze. They knew that to enter in line only offered the enemy a free target for any shots that failed to score on the lead 'Mech. It made sense. It also put the *Enforcer* quite near the Vigilantes' hiding place.

"We've got our first target," Kelly sent on commo laser.

They waited under the umbrella of Trahn's scanner fuzz and watched as the *Enforcer* came nearer. The 'Mech's head turned from side to side as he scanned for targets. Unfortunately for him, the biggest, fattest one around was him.

Kelly gave the word and the Vigilantes opened up. Lasers crisscrossed around the *Enforcer*, flashing a bloody red in the smoke of exploding missiles. Battered and hurting, the *Enforcer* toppled backwards. His fall was all that saved him from being tagged by Trahn's NARC. Her shot flew wide, planting itself on a gantry crane. Efficiently, she killed the transmitter before it lured their missiles to an unintended target.

Autocannon spewing shells, the *Enforcer* crawled toward cover of its own. Thunderous footfalls announced the charge of the *Pillager*, as it moved to aid its smaller partner. But Trahn had the monster on her scope and guided the Vigilantes away from its approach.

They pulled back, swinging wide around the gathering Killers then moving on the *Clint* as the pilot jumped the machine over obstacles in a rush to reach the scene of combat.

The high vantage must have let the pilot catch sight of at least some of the Vigilante 'Mechs. A second jump put the 'Mech near Sam and Snell's *Commando*s. The *Clint* fired as it came down. One of its lasers scored Snell's left leg armor. The *Commando*s scattered away from the *Clint*'s landing point. Dust and jet-blasted debris swirled around it and the myomer pseudomuscles flexed to absorb the mighty impact of landing. The *Clint* sprang out of its crouch, firing. Its targets were the dodging *Commando*s, but neither cannon shells nor lasers scored.

Kelly, too badly positioned to help, saw what the *Clint*'s pilot apparently didn't see.

Trahn's *Raven* strutted stealthily, moving from cover to cover behind the mercenary. The *Raven*'s torso twisted, turning to point at the oblivious Killer as the *Clint* stood its ground trying for a better shot at one of the fleeing *Commando*s. Trahn must have decided to concentrate and be sure of her aim for she only fired a single launcher. The NARC beacon didn't miss this time. It clamped itself squarely between the *Clint*'s jump jet exhausts. Trahn whooped on an open channel in celebration.

The *Clint* spun around.

So did the *Commando*s.

As the *Clint*'s weapons fire vainly sought the *Raven*, both *Commando*s launched. SRMs streamed in on the *Clint*, following the beacon's call. Kelly didn't know if it was from blast or damage, but the *Clint* went down.

Trahn warned that the *Enforcer* was moving in. Kelly vetoed an attempt to finish the *Clint*. They left the *Enforcer* to cover his fallen companion.

Prudence demanded it. So far they had been lucky and taken only the lightest of hits, but the element of surprise was fading. And the Vigilantes were now between the paired Killers and their master. It was not a position they could afford to stay in for long. To turn it to their advantage, Kelly ordered a running pass at the *Pillager* as they sought better cover beyond it.

They did their best shooting so far. Everybody tagged the beast at least once, but its thick armor meant that they didn't take out any vital systems. The *Pillager*'s return fire cost them more than both attacks against the lesser 'Mechs combined. Sam reported an armor breach in her *Commando*'s left leg and JJ said he was down to the last shreds of armor on most of his *Javelin*'s right side. The Kressily Stoneskin 30M armor of Kelly's own machine was badly cratered from multiple laser hits. It was only through the mercy of the gods, and Trahn's jamming, that no one had taken one of the *Pillager*'s nickel-iron gauss slugs.

Crawford shouted obscenities over an open channel and sent slug after deadly nickel-iron slug roaring at the retreating Vigilantes. The gauss rifle shells wrecked machinery and exploded buildings, but all that hit the comital 'Mechs was flying debris.

After the indignity that they had just handed Kingston's Killers, Kelly expected the hot-headed Crawford to order a full out pursuit, but it didn't happen. Trahn reported the *Enforcer* and *Clint* rejoining the *Pillager*, but instead of advancing, they held their ground.

"Waiting for us to come to them?" Snell asked.

"They'll have a long wait," replied Kelly.

"Commander." Trahn's voice was uncertain. "I think I just picked up a flash from the *Cat*."

"Commo laser?"

"Could be. The *Cat*'s outside my jam range, but she'd need a laser to get through to the others."

"So what are they talking over?" JJ wanted to know.

"They better not be calling in Arrow fire from the *Catapult*," said Snell.

"They'd be shooting blind," Trahn said.

"The *Catapult* could be passing on info from their headquarters," Kelly suggested. "He's outside Trahn's jamming."

"They already know we're here," Snell pointed out.

"But they're here, too," Kelly countered. "And they're not supposed to be. Maybe what they don't know about is what is happening elsewhere."

With timing that Kelly thought only came on holodramas, Kingston Crawford's voice boomed on an open channel.

"Rest of you go kick Ling-Marabie's butt. This bucket won't move fast enough, and Price's Protectors are gonna need all the guns they can get. Ain't nothing but Shoe trash here, and they ain't got the bullets, let alone the balls, to try to take me."

It was a challenge as much as a put-down.

"You hear me, Shoe trash?"

Kelly was too busy reviewing the scan that Trahn was providing. It looked like Crawford's broadcast orders weren't a fake. The *Enforcer* and *Clint* had turned around and were headed back the way they had come. The *Catapult* had backed down from its overwatch firing position. The only Killer 'Mech not pulling out was Crawford's own. The *Pillager* remained standing while he continued to broadcast his boasts.

The situation had taken a sudden change, and Kelly dared to hope that it was one for the better. The Vigilantes had the *Pillager* by more than half his tonnage, but the hundred-ton 'Mech carried weapons that could take down one of the lights with a single shot. In contrast, most of the Vigilante weapons were short-ranged and not particularly powerful. Still, they might be enough to use the old Warrior House strategy of Death by Many Stings. The *Pillager* would be vulnerable to it now that he was on his own. Once Trahn planted a NARC beacon on the big 'Mech, Vigilante missiles would swarm to it like bees to honey. It could work.

But Crawford was a good pilot. The *Pillager* wouldn't go down easy. There would be a price.

Who, Kelly wondered, would pay it?

38

But Kelly soon found out that Crawford wasn't going to cooperate in his plan to deal with the *Pillager*. Despite several runs at the big 'Mech, Crawford didn't take the bait and chase them through Hinchuan. Instead he pressed on, lumbering toward the space port. The Vigilantes speculated on his intent as they trailed him.

"He must want to keep us away from the DropShip," offered Sam.

"Then why is he leading us there?" asked Snell.

"He's not," Kelly said. "It's where *he* wants to be. He'll have good fire lanes from the field, the better to keep us away from the DropShip."

"He may have more in mind," suggested JJ. "Those MechWarriors that tried to leave the ship were headed to start up some partially assembled 'Mechs. I saw the reports while I was on board. The machines are unarmored but mobile, and some of them have functional weapons. They could give covering fire to Crawford."

"Without armor, they'll be easy meat if they engage us," Trahn said.

"Long as that *Pillager* is sitting where we want to be, we have to play the game *his* way. We do that, and it's us who may end up meat."

The *Pillager* reached the space port and stalked across the field to the DropShip. The Vigilantes couldn't actually see him do that, they didn't dare expose themselves for a direct sight, but watched a sensor-built map track Crawford's progress. For close to fifteen minutes, the *Pillager* stood on the field as if awaiting something. Then, expectations met or not, it moved closer to the ship. On the scanners, the images practically merged. The sound of tortured metal was soon audible through the Vigilantes' external mikes.

"Told you," JJ said. "He's trying to open up that can of a DropShip."

A 'Mech's lasers were adequate to melt armor and seal a hatch, but they weren't refined enough to cut open that same place, at least not safely. Crawford was likely using his *Pillager*'s hand spikes to pry up plates and open enough of a gap for him to get a grip for the fingers of his battlefists. With a good grip, the *Pillager* could wrench open an access to the DropShip.

"We can't let him," Kelly said. The odds were bad enough as it was.

Making sure that Trahn's *Raven* had him under its electronic screen, Kelly found himself a long fire lane through the streets of Hinchuan. He picked a spot that put his missiles at maximum effective range. He'd be in range for the *Pillager*'s intimidating gauss weapons, but the *Raven*'s Guardian suite ought to shift the odds in his favor. It wouldn't matter much, he told himself, he wasn't intending a duel. All he wanted to do was get out there long enough to send ten LRMs downrange. He just needed to distract Crawford.

He readied the shot, wishing that he was sending Inferno missiles. The sticky flaming gel could push up a 'Mech's heat debt, and they were probably the only way to get a 'Mech like the *Pillager* with its well-balanced weapon-to-heat-sink ratio into the danger zone. Kelly's *Lineholder* wasn't so well designed.

But since a duel wasn't his objective, just a fast shot followed by a duck and cover, he could afford to incur heat debt for this attack. Too bad that he didn't have the weapons for it. Still, he had his large BlazeFire laser. He did his best to align it onto the same target area as his missiles as he triggered the shot.

His missiles flew true, impacting on the *Pillager*'s upper back. The laser cored into the cratered area. A fierce plasma fire exploded briefly from the *Pillager*'s torso, telling Kelly that he'd caused critical damage to the target's jump jets. Too short to mean he'd canceled the *Pillager*'s ability to jump, though. At least he'd curtailed it.

He'd rather have hit the gyros, or far better still, the fusion plant.

Crawford turned his machine. Despite the penetrating hit, Crawford seemed unimpressed. "Thought that might flush you Shoe weasels."

The Killer sent gauss shells and lasers toward Kelly's position, calling, "Come and get it!"

Expecting the retaliation, Kelly wasn't there to receive it. And very glad of his absence he was, as significant chunks of Hinchuan real estate was demolished.

The extent of the destruction chilled him. The *Pillager*'s laser array was bad enough, punching out enough shattering power to match the beam armament of Kelly's *Lineholder* without the heat debt attached, but the twin Poland Main Model A gauss rifles were what made the machine a true demolisher. They were what the Vigilantes needed to fear the most.

But gauss rifles used ammunition and ammunition didn't last forever.

How many gauss shots had Crawford taken in this engagement? Kelly called up *Pillager* stats on his computer. He was dismayed to see just how much ammunition the machine carried. The only way Crawford would be approaching empty was if he started light, and Kelly doubted the mercenary had done so.

"Back shooting the best you can do?" Crawford taunted. "You Shoes are wimps with all the honor of a rim world slaver. Come out and fight!"

Sam and Snell obliged him, breaking cover and starting a double weave approach. Sam's first volley scored well and Snell even managed to get a few SRMs in, but Crawford didn't fall for the deception. Whipping the *Pillager's* right arm around, he potted Sam with his Defiance B3L laser. The shot stripped armor and tore at internal structure, but it wasn't a killer. Sam stumbled her *Commando* back under cover.

Kelly was grateful that the mercenary hadn't been sure enough of the target to use his twin Poland Main gauss rifles.

"Forget the fancy stuff," he told Sam and Snell.

"Already have," Sam replied. "What do we do instead, boss?"

Kelly was thinking as hard as he could. "We need to hit him from all sides. That way some of us will have shots from angles he can't reply to."

Nobody mentioned the obvious corollary that someone would have to be at an angle Crawford *could* reply to.

"Good as far as it goes," JJ said. "He's got the canal at his back."

That was true. The Kennesaw Canal was broad, an easy hundred meters, and there wasn't much cover within another hundred or so beyond it. The far shore would be little better than a practice firing range for the *Pillager*. Worse, any Vigilante 'Mech on the far bank would likely be outside the *Raven's* protective screen. If the *Raven* were over there, the reciprocal would apply to anyone remaining on the Hinchuan bank.

"If Trahn can cross somewhere down the canal, I could jump over anywhere," JJ suggested. "Her Guardian suite will give us the best cover we can get over there and we'll be in flanking position."

"The canal itself is better cover," Sam said.

"It isn't very deep," Kelly pointed out. It was three to four meters mostly, deep enough for the barges that traversed it, but barely more than waist deep to the light 'Mechs. "It's not enough for a submerged approach."

"We don't need it to be," Sam stated. "The banks give us another couple of meters. The *Commando*s can crouch, and moving along the near embankment, we won't be seen. Better still we might be able to stay within reach of Trahn's Guardian suite. Then, if the rest of you can get Crawford's fat behind away from the DropShip, we can pop up and give him a good kick in the pants. I, for one, would really like to do that."

Kelly approved the plan, but he had a caveat. "You can start your approach, but you don't show your heads till we get a NARC beacon fixed on that beast. We need maximum effective firepower on target the first time if we're going to make this work."

Tagging the *Pillager* with the beacon was its own problem.

Kelly found himself another long lane with a line on the space port. This time he didn't have the *Raven* to give him cover. Trahn had taken the *Raven* in close, as stealthily as she could. JJ had found himself a shorter line of fire. The idea was that Kelly and JJ would uncover and launch simultaneously, giving Crawford dual targets and distracting him enough for Trahn to uncover and get a good shot.

Kelly gave the word. Missiles arced down field. Explosions rocked the *Pillager* and the ground around it. Nickel-iron slugs cracked through the air, seeking a fast-dodging Kelly. Trahn emerged and launched. Kelly's screen lit with the call of the NARC. Success!

Unfortunately, their distractions proved insufficient as Crawford once again demonstrated his killer reflexes. The *Pillager*'s torso swiveled on the *Raven*. The twin gauss rifles spat their electro-magnetically propelled solid shot. The *Raven* caught a slug on its stubby right arm. Ferro-fibrous armor, weapons, actuators, and endosteel skeleton shredded as the light 'Mech's entire right shoulder assembly tore away. The shock of the hit cost Trahn her control. Spewing fluids, the *Raven* keeled over.

Fortunately for Trahn, it fell out of Crawford's line of fire. That didn't stop him from trying to drop a building on her by shelling the structure with his gauss rifles. Trahn pumped the legs of her 'Mech. Its stumpy "arms" made it hard for her to get it back on its feet in the best of circumstances. Recognizing that she wasn't making progress fast enough, she starting using the *Raven*'s powerful, kicking feet to shove the 'Mech along the ground away the impending collapse.

The rumbling crash of the structure sent vibrations that Kelly felt from a quarter kilometer away. Darting through the dust cloud, JJ's *Javelin* raced toward Trahn's position. The *Pillager*'s lasers lit the cloud, but they failed to hit the fleet light 'Mech. Kelly blasted at Crawford with missiles and lasers, even his Inteks that were out of range for doing any real damage, anything to distract him and give JJ covering fire.

JJ swooped down on the *Raven*. Using his *Javelin*'s hands, he helped the *Raven* back to its feet, and the two light 'Mechs sprinted for cover behind the warehouse line.

Kelly, finally catching Crawford's attention, managed to get behind a hangar with only minor armor damage from the *Pillager*'s large laser. Crawford chased none of them, which was good; they needed the breather.

"Sorry, boss. Lost my lasers," Trahn apologized.

"You did your job, and you're still with us. I've got no complaints."

But the real job had barely gotten started.

He confirmed that Sam and Snell had reached their positions. He let JJ pick his own spot and told Trahn to hang back. If it all went south, they'd need the cover of her electronics to get out. For himself, he picked a point where he thought Crawford would be waiting for a Vigilante 'Mech to show. He was on the edge of the *Raven*'s electronic umbrella. If he had to shift too far to his right, he'd leave it.

With everyone ready, there was nothing to do but give the word to strike.

At his command, the Vigilantes attacked. SRMs

swarmed in on the beacon. Lasers stabbed in at the *Pillager*'s back. More lasers, and a single more powerful one, sizzled from Kelly's *Lineholder*.

They hurt the *Pillager*, but it was, after all, a hundred-ton BattleMech. BattleMechs were designed to take a lot of punishment, and hundred-ton BattleMechs were the toughest of all. The *Pillager* withstood their assault.

Crawford howled his rage and returned fire.

JJ caught the Killer's attention first. The range was deadly for the gauss rifles, and the Guardian suite didn't help enough this time. Both slugs slammed home. Lasers clawed the *Javelin*, savaging it in a crimson frenzy. The battered light 'Mech cartwheeled out of sight in an explosion of metal. JJ's commo circuit went dead.

Kelly's grip tightened on his controls. He triggered everything he had at the *Pillager*. To hell with heat! Mr. Chill could feel no heat.

The fury of his attack staggered the *Pillager*. Lasers raked across the armored skin, devouring it. Detonating warheads gobbled chunks of it. A great slab of armor and its supporting understructure peeled away from the *Pillager*'s left thigh. In a sparking corona of electrical discharge, gauss shells tumbled out as one of the 'Mech's ammunition reserves was compromised.

Too late. Too damned late.

Despite the damage, Crawford's focus wasn't on Kelly. The Killer turned on the *Commando*s.

"Didn't get enough the first time we played, Liu?"

Sam sent eight SRMs along with her reply. "Eat this and die, dirt bag!"

Crawford's *Pillager* shrugged away the missile hits with almost contemptuous ease. His uplifted weapon arms swung away from Sam and he poured his fusillade onto Snell's *Commando*.

One nickel-iron slug ripped through the *Commando*'s right hip. The other snatched away the now detached limb. Lasers stabbed into the *Commando*'s guts, and its entire right side blew apart as ammo detonated. The *Commando* toppled backwards, disappearing under the water.

"So much for your little buddy." The massive 'Mech stepped forward and off the embankment. A brief flare of its jump jets eased it into the canal. Agitated water slapped at its thighs. Crawford waded his machine toward Sam. "I took you down once, little girl."

"No!" Kelly screamed as he charged his 'Mech forward. In his mind's eye he saw Sam's 'Mech disintegrating as Snell's had. It was a vision of horror that let him see through the armor that shielded the cockpit and though the visor of the neurohelmet to see Sam's face as she screamed in her death agony.

In reality, he could see none of it for Crawford's movement had taken him out of Kelly's sights.

"I'm going do it again today," he heard the Killer say. "And this time, I'm gonna make it stick."

Kelly heard missile launches. It had to be Sam, making her last defiant attack. Crawford howled in pain on the open channel. Sam had hurt him!

"You little bitch! You're history."

The *Lineholder* was at max, pounding forward as fast as myomer muscle could propel endosteel bone.

Kelly was close enough that his external mikes picked up the crackle of the gauss cannons reaching discharge capacity.

Slow. Too slow.

The *Lineholder* cleared the buildings that protected Crawford from Kelly's avenging fury. The death tableau wasn't quite where he thought it would be. Crawford had backed Sam downstream.

Kelly swiveled the *Lineholder*'s torso. He had to get enough weapons on target!

The shift brought howls from his gyros as mass fought momentum. Vertigo flooded through his neurohelmet's circuits. Instinctively, he fought to keep the *Lineholder* on its feet.

It cost him his chance to fire.

Sam was seconds from obliteration. Seconds he didn't have to save her.

His terrified, focused concentration was torn from the immanent destruction by motion behind the Killer.

A shattered hulk rose, dripping, from the depths of the canal.

It might have been a ghost of vengeance, leveling an accusing arm at the guilty. It was Snell's *Commando*. It stood on one leg, a feat of piloting skill worthy of the greatest House warriors, and the arm that it pointed at Crawford's *Pillager* carried a Defiance B3M medium laser.

The vengeful spirit image dissolved as Snell struggled to keep his machine upright. The 'Mech's arm drifted off target, compelled by the need to counterbalance the machine's sway. Snell fired anyway. His shot was off.

Still, the laser vaporized a channel in the water and struck the *Pillager*'s left knee. Actuators spasmed. The leg buckled just as Crawford cut loose. Only the edge of his deadly barrage caught Sam's *Commando*. The gauss rifles missed entirely, and the lasers, though they staggered the *Commando*, didn't cut through to its core.

Sam's *Commando* abruptly sat down.

The *Pillager* turned. Crawford, screaming vengeful oaths, unloaded on the near defenseless Snell. The ravaged *Commando* disintegrated under the assault.

First JJ. Now Snell. It was too much.

Much too much.

The scarred and ravaged *Pillager* began to turn on Kelly. It was not finished.

Neither was Kelly.

He blasted with his lasers, triggering them as fast as they cycled. His computer warned of heat rising and the chance of an ammo explosion. His response was to hit the override and to use as much of that ammo as he could. All he could see was Crawford's *Pillager*, and all he could do was send death at the Killer.

The LRMs were woefully ineffective at the close range. The lasers didn't care. They cut and sliced and melted and vaporized. Like a mountain toppling, the *Pillager* heeled to one side under the pounding and crashed down. Its fall sent up a wave that splashed high enough to wet the *Lineholder* standing on the embankment. The waters closed over Crawford's *Pillager*, leaving only bubbles to mark where it had stood.

His enemy gone, Kelly's thoughts were only for "Sam? Sam?"

"Okay," came her groggy voice. "I'm okay."

A weight he'd only just noticed lifted from Kelly's heart.

"Crawford?" she asked.

"He's down."

"Lots of incense for Buddha tonight."

Kelly jumped the *Lineholder* into the water. He had no jump jets to ease his landing, and he sank deeply into the mud that made up the canal's bottom. It took him a few moments to regain his balance and get the 'Mech under control. When he did, he started for Sam, eager to help her up.

To his left, something stirred. He turned, horrified to see the *Pillager*, shoving itself up by its arms, struggling to get to its feet.

"No," Kelly said. "Not today."

Kelly kicked the *Lineholder*'s leg out. The broad foot connected with the *Pillager*'s left arm. Armor crumpled. Kelly felt the shock of contact all the way up his spine. He yelped in pain as an actuator short sent a jolt through the neurohelmet's feedback system. But his kick was good. The *Pillager*'s arm slipped out from beneath it. The massive 'Mech slammed face first and disappeared again beneath the dark swirling water.

A burst of bubbles roiled the surface.

Bubbles?

Light exploded in Kelly's brain with all the energy of that escaping air. The *Pillager* was holed, its structural integrity gone! He remembered the damage he'd seen on the *Pillager*'s head. The cockpit had to be leaking air!

Switching his viewscreen to full infrared, Kelly could see the multi-chromatic shape of the *Pillager* struggling beneath the water. The motion was not the smooth coordination he was used to seeing from Crawford. There was a desperation in the mercenary's obvious attempts to get his cockpit clear of the water.

"Not today," he told the Killer.

Kelly hooked the *Pillager*'s damaged left arm with his *Lineholder*'s foot and pulled. The *Pillager*'s claws must have gouged furrows in the muddy bottom, but they did nothing to stop Kelly from sweeping the arm away from beneath the *Pillager*. The monstrous 'Mech slipped again beneath the surface of the canal. Kelly stomped down on the *Pillager*'s arm, forcing it into the muck. He leaned the full weight of his *Lineholder* down on it.

The strength inherent in the myomer pseudomuscles that empowered a hundred-ton BattleMech was enormous. But even its vast power had limits. The *Pillager* hit those limits as it struggled. Try as it might, it didn't have the myomer strength to displace fifty-five-tons of BattleMech.

Most of the *Pillager*'s weapons were torso-mounted. Face down in the mud, it could not use them. Its right arm-mounted Ceres Arms lasers flashed, boiling away water and blasting holes in the canal bank, but with the *Pillager* jammed into the mud of the canal bottom, Crawford couldn't bring them to bear against Kelly. All that was left for him was brute strength.

The *Pillager* heaved.

It bucked.

Kelly rode it out. This was not BattleMech combat as he had once dreamed of it. This was defeating the enemy the way it had to be. Brutal. Blunt. Ruthless.

This was war.

Kelly had no doubt that he was a true MechWarrior.

Eventually, the bubbles stopped rising.

The *Pillager* stopped moving, too.

Slowly, the waters stilled.

39

Hinchuan
Duvic Palatine, Epsilon Eridani
Chaos March
6 May 3062

Helping Sam get her *Commando* unmired was physically tough, but confirming that there was nothing to be done for Snell was hard in a way Kelly hated. Scraps of machine were all Kelly was able to dredge up. An empty, shredded pilot's couch was the final piece he bothered to examine.

Aldo Snell had died a hero. But he had died, and nothing would change that. Just like Stübel. Just like Slug. Just like JJ.

Kelly was glad to heave his 'Mech out of the canal and join the other two surviving 'Mechs on the landing field of Huang-Lu Spaceport. He looked over to the spoils of their victory. The DropShip sat there, squat and sullen. Crawford hadn't succeeded in prying open any of the DropShip's hatches; they stopped him in time. The Vigilantes had paid a steep price to do it.

Motion caught his eye. There were people moving in the deeper darkness beneath the ship. As he watched, another dropped from the belly of the ship, hit hard, and rolled.

The prisoners aboard the DropShip had obviously not been idle. Somehow they had worked out a route through the innards of the ship and found a way to an access port that they could open. Most of the escapees were making tracks away from the landing field, but Kelly spotted two skulking toward the hangar where the half-assembled 'Mechs lay.

He was in no mood to play games, and he had already warned those people. His BlazeFire laser lit the night. The would-be MechWarriors were no more.

Just to be sure, he wrenched open the hanger door. The darkness within was undisturbed.

He set Trahn on watch to stop any further escapes and took Sam to recover JJ's remains, if they could. Mauled BattleMechs rarely offered much of their unfortunate pilots for reclamation.

To his utter surprise and joy, they found JJ, broken but alive, in what was left of his *Javelin*'s cockpit. Given the condition of the wreck, it was a miracle. Kelly offered a prayer of thanks to every version of God that came to mind.

With his leg splinted and a couple of painkillers in him, JJ tried to sound like he was as good as new. "Hey, we won. Either that or the judge of the dead made a mistake and sent me to the wrong place."

"Don't worry, Jurewicz," Sam said. "You haven't accidentally been assigned to heaven."

"Didn't think I had been. *Mistakenly* assigned there, that is. So where are Trahn and Snell?"

"Trahn's back at the DropShip." Kelly couldn't bring himself to say the rest.

"Snell saved me from being toasted," Sam said somberly.

JJ nodded. He understood.

Sam carried him back to the landing field cradled in her *Commando*'s palm.

The town lay quiet. Trahn's long-range scans were empty of anything that could threaten them. Once she got off the *mission accomplished* signal, the order came back to stay put for the time being. They set up a makeshift camp at the spaceport and the weary Vigilantes rested from their labors.

Toward dawn, the citizens of Hinchuan emerged from whatever hidey holes they had wisely taken up during the night. A crowd slowly grew around the edges of the spaceport. Despite mangled and trampled boundary fences that couldn't offer the least barrier, no one ventured onto the field.

Kelly announced that the township was under Count Shu's control. There was muttering, but the citizens knew better than to challenge BattleMechs. He was glad of that. There had been enough death.

But neither did the crowd disperse. Not until two hours later when it began to melt with notable speed. Some people were actually running away.

"Not enough show for them, I guess," JJ said.

Kelly had suspicions. "Trahn!"

"I wasn't asleep," she replied. Her startled voice told the truth, that she had indeed been dozing.

"Check scanners."

"No," she wailed. "I'm picking up two light 'Mechs coming in fast. Got to be *Jenner*s. There's a third behind them, slower.

"The 48th," Kelly concluded. "That third 'Mech will be Namihito's *Panther*."

There wasn't a lot they could do to prepare to face the Kuritans, but they did what they could. Trahn kept monitoring the approach, providing updates to the others as they worked to get one of the partly assembled 'Mechs up and running for JJ to pilot. It wouldn't last long, but it had weapons they could use for the moment. Kelly didn't like the idea, but JJ insisted, saying, "I'm no gropo, and I'm not going out that way."

The work to get that skeletal machine going took too long. The Vigilantes were unable to get out and meet the incoming Kuritans as they had met Kingston's Killers. Firing positions from the town's edge would have been good to use against the incoming lights, but there were options nearly as good. The clear fields of fire from the DropShip berth would now serve the Vigilantes as they had served Crawford.

Kelly thought it a strange turnabout.

They waited, tense, while Trahn reported on the approaching 'Mechs. The *Jenner*s slowed at the outskirts, but only briefly before pressed on to move cautiously through the town. Kelly expected the *Jenner*s to charge straight onto the landing field, but they didn't. Instead they took up positions nearby, but out of sight.

"Waiting for their boss," JJ suggested.

The fact that they didn't move again until the *Panther* joined them confirmed it. The three machines started working their way closer. Kelly caught glimpses of them, but the Kuritans were moving with their characteristic stealth and fluidity. The chances of a good shot were nil.

"Something's up," Sam said. "Their launch tubes are shuttered."

Trahn agreed. "Yeah, and their energy weapons don't seem to be charged."

"They want to parley?" JJ asked incredulously.

"Looks like," said Kelly.

"The *Panther*'s moving up," Trahn reported.

In moments the 'Mech was in sight, making its way across the rubble Crawford had created when he tried to nail Trahn after she tagged him with the NARC beacon. The *Panther*'s right arm hung down, the muzzle of its PPC pointing at the ground. Kelly was impressed, but not surprised at the piloting skill it took to keep that weapon arm still while negotiating the tricky ground.

"Be our best chance to waste him, boss," Sam said.

"You really spoiling for another fight?" he asked.

"Got to do what you got to do."

"We don't need to lose anyone else. Time's on our side for this round. If they want to talk, I'm willing to listen. For a little while anyway." More for the morale benefit than because he believed it, he added, "Every minute our groundpounders are getting closer."

The *Panther* halted at the edge of the landing field, its foot assemblies toed up to the wire tangle. The pilot's hatch opened and a dark-skinned man emerged. Kelly used magnification to confirm that it was Namihito. The Kuritan dropped his access ladder and started to climb down.

"Gutsy snake," JJ commented.

"We already knew that," Sam said.

"I'm going to go meet him," Kelly told them.

"Is that bright, boss?" asked Sam.

Kelly heard the concern in her voice. "Who knows? But I think this one really is a 'got to do what you got to do.' "

He dismounted and met Namihito in the middle of the field. The Kuritan stood to attention and bowed in greeting. "Commander Kelly."

"Major Namihito." Kelly saluted.

"Your machines have been handled roughly."

"They'll still fight."

"Major Crawford?"

Kelly gestured over his shoulder toward the canal. "Impressing the bottom feeders."

"*So ka.* He was a fighter of notable skill, though even a poor warrior is dangerous in a large BattleMech." Namihito bowed respectfully. "You have done well."

"Thank you." Kelly made an awkward bow in return. He decided he didn't like standing out in the open and decided to cut to the chase. "So what are you doing here?"

"BattleMechs to fight BattleMechs, yes? Swift machines to cover ground and strike at secondary targets, political targets, while the heavy machines fight in the big battles. Such a disposition of forces is familiar to you, yes?"

The Kuritan had summarized the comital high command's plan. Of course, he shouldn't have been here to do it; the plan stated that *all* Duvic BattleMechs were to be drawn to the "big battles." Obviously, the plan wasn't being executed perfectly.

Namihito's recitation of the basic strategy was disturbing. How much did the Duvics know? And what, exactly did Namihito mean about political targets? Did he know what the Vigilantes had come here to prove?

"I was hoping you might be more specific about why you're here," Kelly said, trying to sound casual, to have the air of a man in command of the situation. "You didn't come in shooting, and that makes me curious."

"I bring you news. Unfortunate news for you, I am afraid. Your infantry column will not be arriving. They encountered a company of Duvic mechanized infantry. They fought bravely. The survivors have surrendered."

"Are you trying to tell me our position here is untenable?"

"You must decide for yourself the strength of your position. I merely report the situation."

But how honestly? If the main battle was going well enough for the Duvics that they could afford to detach the Kuritans, the situation couldn't be good for the committal position as a whole. Kelly *knew* the Vigilantes' situation wasn't good. With one man gone and another injured, they had only three and a half operational 'Mechs. The mercenary Kuritans were fresh, or nearly so. Fighting such expert warriors would be tough. And if the follow on force was really gone, the Vigilantes couldn't expect help. *Could the Kuritans expect reinforcements?*

The evidence that the Vigilantes had gained here in Hinchuan was important to the Shu cause, more so than ever if the military situation wasn't going their way. The brass needed and wanted what the Vigilantes had gained. There'd be a relief force. The Vigilantes wouldn't be abandoned.

"We're not pawns to be sacrificed carelessly," Kelly said.

"All men are pawns, if only to fate. Fate decrees that Count Shu's forces will not achieve their goals. But politics are not fate, and they need not have unconditional sway over a man's destiny."

Kelly got the sense that the Kuritan was trying to tell him something important, but he couldn't figure what. "I have only your word that the count's forces are losing."

"The battle continues. If they do not lose this one, they will lose the next. You have my word. It will happen."

"It's a trick," Kelly accused. He might as well have spoken to a stone. "You're bluffing," he tried again. "I know a bluff when I hear one."

"Then your ears are defective."

"Maybe it's because I'm not hearing anything worth listening to. If I want riddles, I can crack open fortune cookies."

"Some things may only be said in riddles. But some may be spoken plainly. You wish bluntness, yes? Consider this. I am permitted to take the surrender of your force, but it is not required. If you capitulate, you will all be interred. If you will not surrender, I am to eliminate your force. There is also a bounty upon your head."

A bounty? "Do Kuritans still take the heads of their slain enemies to lay before the feet of their lords and masters?"

"Very few follow the ancient customs."

"But you do."

"I try to hold to the ways of honor."

"Just how much honor can a mercenary have?"

"Enough to satisfy his soul, but every man's soul is different, yes? Some say that loyal and unquestioning service is the path to honor. Some say that the lord's honor is the samurai's honor. Some say a warrior must find his own path to honor. Where does your own honor lie, Commander Kelly? Do you know your own path?"

What was Namihito driving at? What did Kelly's honor have to do with anything? "We were talking about you. Didn't you tell me once that you were *ronin*?"

Namihito shrugged. "Even a *ronin* can have honor. Or do you not believe that?"

Kuritan concepts of honor were, as far as Kelly understood them, not very different from those espoused by the great Warrior Houses. But when *ronin* came up in the news, they sounded more like bandits. He found it hard to think of the man standing before him as a bandit or brigand of any sort. Namihito's quiet calm, assured manner, and demonstrated skill were attributes that

Kelly had admired among the greatest of the Warrior Houses. To have such virtues standing embodied before him unsettled him a little.

Thinking about having to go up against them in combat unsettled him a lot.

"It doesn't matter what a man is called," Kelly mumbled. "Either a man is honorable, or he is not."

"So you do not find being branded a war criminal diminishes your honor?"

"I don't like it. It doesn't change who I am."

"Exactly." Namihito bowed. "We have a basis for understanding."

The Kuritan's obtuseness was starting to make Kelly a little crazy. "Look. I didn't come here to philosophize about honor or the lack of it. I came here to take and hold this ship and the 'Mechs it carried. It's what I— what we are going to do. Those are our orders. That's something a samurai should understand."

"The burden of orders is something that I understand quite well, Commander. Did you find what you came here to find?"

"And if I say yes, you forget about the surrender stuff and wipe us out so we can't tell anyone about Presider Price's dirty little secret."

Namihito shrugged. "You have orders. I have orders."

"Then I guess we'll be fighting."

"We can fight. Many will die. You will lose."

"Maybe so. But you'll know you've been in a fight."

"Valiant MechWarriors will die. You will still lose."

Namihito's absolute conviction shook Kelly. He tried to put similar conviction in his own voice. "I'll take you with me."

"Perhaps." Namihito shrugged. "Death, as they say, is a feather."

"I'm not afraid to die."

"Someday you will believe that."

"It's true."

"Perhaps it is. Do you wish to continue boasting, or would you consent to listen to what I propose?"

The sudden shift caught Kelly off guard. "Propose?"

"Perhaps I put that too strongly. Let me say that there are matters about which we may speak." Namihito put a hand to the commo button in his ear. "Come. Matsumoto has finished preparing the room. It is quiet and private. We will drink tea."

One of Namihito's MechWarriors had dismounted in the middle of a confrontation and found a place to serve *tea*? "You're pretty sure of yourself."

"Of myself I am certain. It is with you that the question remains open." Namihito took in their surroundings with a wave. "Open spaces are rarely the best places for open discussions, yes?"

Kelly agreed with that. "Where is this room?"

"Midway between the positions of your lance and mine. One of my soldiers will be nearby, and you may bring one of yours. That is the etiquette, yes?"

"Near enough. I'll listen." He still wanted to believe that time was on their side and talking with Namihito was better than fighting him. But if it came to fighting, the Vigilantes couldn't afford to be down two warriors, especially if they were jumped while out of their 'Mechs. "But I'll come alone if that's all right. Call it a gesture of trust."

Namihito bowed acceptance.

He led Kelly to a building that, not surprisingly, had a tea shop at street level. Apparently not even traditional Kuritans carried tea ceremony gear with them in their 'Mechs. The shop had been cleared and a single table set. An exquisite ceramic cup sat at either place, and the scent of brewing tea drifted from behind the closed curtain to the back room. When they were settled, Namihito spoke.

"Let me begin by stating a fact. Any unsurrendered County Shu forces on palatine territory after a cease-fire is declared would be allowed free passage back to County Shu. The lone exceptions to this would be forces who violate the cease-fire and those who might attempt to transport 'state property' over the traditional borders. Such forces would be eliminated."

"You're saying we're only going home if we *don't* do what we came to do."

Namihito inclined his head. "Another fact is that, by the rules of war, a surrender still in negotiation at the time of a cease-fire is no surrender."

"You're talking in riddles again."

Namihito closed his eyes for a moment. "Consider. I might *guess* that you have evidence that the Duvic Palatine has undermined, if not completely betrayed, the common interests of the people of Epsilon Eridani. I *know* that I have orders to retake or destroy certain things that could conceivably be potential evidence of such activity should I find them in the hands of comital forces. If such theoretical evidence was in *my* possession, I would not need to destroy it. Thus, it would still exist and, by existing, it would *remain* a threat to the guilty."

"What are you saying?"

"I say what I say. Is it well known that guilty parties seek to hide all evidence of their guilt, yes? But who can say how successful they will be? Will they find it all? If copies of documents are made without their knowledge, will such things be found? Also, history tells us that the more people who are aware of the existence of a hidden thing, the less likely that thing is to stay hidden. It may be that what was sought and seized in war may only be possessed and used in a time when the guns are silent."

"Are you saying you want me to turn the evidence over to you so that you can preserve it, bringing it out later to use against Price and her cabal?"

"I could not say such words without violating my oaths."

Suddenly all the double-talk made sense. Namihito had begun by testing Kelly, trying to find out if he was the sort of man who would be amenable to the scheme. Then Namihito sought to bring Kelly around to understanding the proposal without saying such words as would compromise his own personal honor. Maybe some things *could* only be spoken in riddles.

Kelly studied the man who sat across from him. Namihito had demonstrated a mastery of the art of the MechWarrior and, for centuries, hadn't people said that the true master warrior was by nature a master strategist? Master strategist or not, Namihito had a subtle and devious mind. Kelly believed that the Kuritan could pull off this sleight of hand with the evidence if he wanted to. Certainly he'd do a better job than Kelly could. But did Namihito really want to?

Kelly looked the man in the eyes. He sought some hint of duplicity, but instead found calm, certitude, and, surprisingly, respect. There was also a sense of expectation.

"You're asking me to trust you, but Price pays your bills."

"I have no love for those without honor."

Kelly pondered. What was on the table could be called collusion with the enemy. It could also be called prudence. It might be the only way he could keep his people alive. And he'd learned the value of life in a way only death can teach. What would a Warrior House soldier do?

"A question, Major Namihito. What makes you think I believe you?"

The Kuritan sat silent for several moments. When he spoke, it was softly, in the voice of a man sharing a secret. "There are few men of honor in these latter days. Fewer still can tell the difference between a truth and a lie when they hear it. Far fewer yet when the speaker stands on the opposite side of a battlefield. You, Tybalt Kelly, wearing lies, know truth. Some fights are best saved for another day, yes?"

"The Warrior Houses used to say that a warrior does not fight a battle he cannot win."

"*So ka.* There is wisdom in that saying. Will you do as a House warrior would?"

Once Kelly would have answered that question instantly in the affirmative. But now?

What did it matter what a House warrior might do? There wasn't one here. Just Kelly. Just a man who was beginning to realize that there were some limits beyond which it was wise not to push. There were times when a man could not simply rely on himself and maybe a few close friends, times when you had to take a chance. And times to place your trust in another man, even if that man stood on the other side of a battlefield.

"Surrender," he said, "is often difficult to reconcile with honor."

"It can be, yes? But we may talk of it, yes?"

"While somewhere else a war grinds to a halt?"

"Yes."

"We can talk," said Kelly.

There was a discrete scratching at the back curtain.

"Ah, the tea is ready," said Namihito.

They sat and they drank. They talked. Namihito spoke of honor and how an honorable man would have no part in murder plots, and so Kelly came to understand at last why the *Panther* had fled from clearly inferior green MechWarriors in Dori. His last doubts about Namihito's honor faded away. The path they were about to embark on would not be easy, but if taken, it would mean that no more Vigilantes would die today. And today, that was enough for Kelly.

They talked some more. Then word came of the cease-fire.

The conflict between the Duvic Palatine and County Shu had come to an end. Empty-handed Vigilantes would be going home. Certain state property would be in sympathetic, honorable hands. The truth *would* come out.

Kelly savored the tea.

Some fights *were* best saved for another day.

About the Author

Robert N. Charrette was born, raised, and educated in the State of Rhode Island and Providence Plantations. Upon graduating from Brown University with a cross-departmental degree in biology and geology, (prepaleontology actually), he moved to the Washington, D.C. area and worked as a graphic artist. He has worked as a game designer, art director, and commercial sculptor before taking up the word processor to write novels. He has contributed novels to the BattleTech® universe and the Shadowrun® universe, the latter of which he had a hand in creating. He has developed other fictional settings, including tales set in another universe of revenant magic as chronicled in *A Prince Among Men, A King Beneath the Mountain,* and *A Knight Among Knaves*, and in a fantasy world as *The Chronicles of Aelwyn*.

Robert currently resides in Herndon, Virginia with his wife, Elizabeth, who must listen to his constant complaints of insufficient time while he continues to write as well as occasionally sculpt. He also has a strong interest in medieval living history, being a principal in *La Belle Compagnie*, a reenactment group portraying English life in the late fourteenth century. In between, he tries to keep current on a variety of eclectic interests including dinosaurian paleontology and pre-Tokugawa Japanese history.